AWAY WITH THE FAIRIES

It's the 1920s in Melbourne and Phryne is asked to investigate the puzzling death of a famous author and illustrator of fairy stories. To do so, Phryne takes a job within the women's magazine that employed the victim and finds herself enmeshed in her colleagues' deceptions. But while Phryne is learning the ins and outs of magazine publishing first hand, her personal life is thrown into chaos. Impatient for her lover Lin Chung's imminent return from a silk-buying expedition to China, she instead receives an unusual summons from Lin Chung's family followed by a series of mysterious assaults and warnings.

KERRY GREENWOOD

AWAY WITH THE FAIRIES

A Phryne Fisher Mystery

Complete and Unabridged

ULVERSCROFT
Leicester

First published in Great Britain in 2017 by
Constable
An imprint of Little, Brown Book Group
London

First Ulverscroft Edition
published 2018
by arrangement with
Little, Brown Book Group
An Hachette UK Company
London

A catalogue record for this book is available
from the British Library.

ISBN 978–1–4448–3842–8

Published by
F. A. Thorpe (Publishing)
Anstey, Leicestershire

Set by Words & Graphics Ltd.
Anstey, Leicestershire
Printed and bound in Great Britain by
T. J. International Ltd., Padstow, Cornwall

This book is printed on acid-free paper

This book is dedicated to my dearest twin, Jenny Pausacker.

With thanks as always to A.W.G., J.S.L.G., A.D.P., D.L.J.G., J.P. and S.T. They know who they are . . . And to Jenny Darling, proprietor of Wee Nooke.

The strong subject, nonwithstanding the efforts against him, survives and acquires fresh vigour. The people again cherish their sovereign, and the plotters have wrought their own over-throw.

Hexagram 23: Po
The I Ching Book of Changes

CHAPTER ONE

In concealment of illumination, it is beneficial to be upright in difficulty.

Hexagram 36: Ming I
The I Ching Book of Changes

'Drat,' said Mercy Porter, balancing the tray on a concrete cherub as she tugged at the latch on the Garden Apartment gate. 'Damn,' she said aloud as her fingernail snagged and broke. She nudged the gate open with her knee, marking her white apron – clean on that morning, and she had to do her own washing – with moss. As there were really no other expletives she could use aloud without imminent danger of the sack, she bit her lip and steadied the tray.

There had to be something else she could do for a living in this modern year of 1928, she thought, stepping carefully along the paved path through a forest of brightly painted stone figures. I hate all this useless rubbish. Why fill up a garden with statues instead of plants? That gnome with the fishing rod is always out to ladder my stockings.

She avoided the fishing gnome, ascended three stone steps and knocked at the pink door of the Garden Apartment. That Miss Lavender always went crook if her tea was cold, and the delay in the kitchen while the cook had been telling the

1

grocer's boy about her hay fever had made Mercy ten minutes late. The tea would be stewed if she didn't get it on the table quick smart, and then there'd be hell to pay.

The door remained shut. Mercy put the tray down on a convenient bird table and plied the fancy brass knocker in the shape of the Lincoln Imp hard enough to jar that demonic person's teeth out. The garden was silent and soggy on this wet, sullen morning. The blows of the knocker seemed to echo through the house.

The pink door swung open. Not like Miss Lavender not to lock her door. Mercy went in, tray first, kicking the door shut behind her, and turned sharp left into the sitting room of Wee Nooke. Miss Lavender had caused this name to be painted up over the door in letters of a pink which blushed for its presumption. The apartment, which had once been a gardener's shed before being extensively rebuilt, was overwhelmingly decorated and smelt, as always, of a potpourri of perfumes. Lavender, rose, almond blossom, talcum powder and a slight under-hint of gin. Mercy sneezed and wondered if hay fever was catching. Where was the old chook, anyway?

The tenant of the house was sitting at the table with her back to the maid.

'Miss Lavender?' asked Mercy. 'I've brought your breakfast. Nice hot tea,' she added encouragingly, pushing a music box with a fairy doll dressed in bright red gauze on top across the table and setting the tray down with a thump.

Miss Lavender did not move. She sat alarmingly still with her head bowed into her clasped hands as though she was praying. When Mercy, who had seven breakfasts still to distribute, touched Miss Lavender's shoulder, she slid sideways with a peculiarly boneless wriggle and fell to the floor. Her face was perfectly blue (which clashed dreadfully with her pink garments) and she was, Mercy was sure, extremely dead.

Mercy made it to the door and screamed for help before she fainted.

Phryne Fisher had dined the night before with Jane and Ruth, her thirteen-year-old adoptive daughters, a couple of wharfies called Bert and Cec, a policeman called Hugh Collins, her maid and companion Dorothy (Dot) Williams, a small humble dog called Molly because she looked like one, and the cat, Ember. This had constituted a reasonably merry party. A huge and delicious dinner had been cooked by Mrs Butler and served by Mr Butler. Much champagne had been consumed and the matter of the robbery from the Dean's safe thoroughly thrashed out. Other stories from her trip to Sydney had not been told except in a severely edited form. She had distributed the presents – a wristwatch each for Hugh, Bert and Cec, a crocodile handbag for Dot, a book on anatomy for Jane and, for the sensible Ruth, *Plats Nouveaux* by the celebrated chef M Paul Reboux, which might have the double benefit of tickling Ruth's palate and improving her French. Phryne hoped that she would not find his disrespectful comments on champagne too inflammatory. Phryne had never meant to acquire daughters. But, since the rescue of Jane from a nasty

3

destination and the removal of Ruth from domestic slavery, they had adorned her household. Though they had also introduced Molly. Her dependants and friends were all well and gratifyingly delighted that she had returned from Sydney and still loved them. And she did.

She loved them even more this morning because the girls were at school, Dot had gone for a bracing early walk, the animals were in the kitchen (the butcher's boy had just called) and Hugh, Bert and Cec had gone home to their several virtuous couches. Therefore Phryne was breakfasting alone, which was the way she felt breakfast ought to be taken. Phryne had never woken up wondering who or where she was, though in her Apache French phase she had been a little in the dark about who was reposing beside her. She felt that the day should not be bounced in on with rude energy, but carefully and delicately seduced into being, and children and animals were sadly impervious to reason on this matter.

She sipped another sip of aromatic coffee, forked in her last mouthful of perfectly prepared *omelette aux fines herbes,* and prepared for the exquisite pleasure of lighting the first gasper of the day.

She had just fixed the cigarette in its long ivory holder and raised the lighter to ignite it when the doorbell rang.

'Damn,' said Phryne. She lit the cigarette anyway. But at least she was now properly awake, and the day, though soggy, appeared to have been aired. Who could be at the door? Too early for the post. A delivery? They usually went to the kitchen

4

door. A visitor? No one knew that she was back as yet. An announcement would soon appear in social notes in *Table Talk*, of course, along the lines of 'The Hon. Miss Phryne Fisher has returned from her sojourn in Sydney to the delight of all her many admirers'. Then, no doubt, she would have callers.

Phryne avoided the undesirables by warning Mr Butler in advance that she was never at home to bores. He seemed to have a remarkable ability to weed them out at the door. When taxed with this, he replied magisterially that years of work at a gentleman's club had given him a certain facility. Phryne could only smile and approve.

Footsteps sounded in the hall. Mr Butler was admitting someone, taking their coat and umbrella and ushering them into the small parlour. Phryne blew a smoke ring and waited. Mr Butler appeared.

'Detective Inspector Robinson, Miss Fisher,' he announced, in tones more fitting to the breaking of news of the tragic death of a near relative.

'I wonder how he knew I was back? Please clear away, Mr B, and bring me some more coffee and some tea for the Detective Inspector. I'll ask him if he'd like some breakfast,' she added. 'You know how he likes Mrs B's cuisine.'

'Yes, Miss Fisher,' said Mr Butler, bowing a little at this appreciation of Mrs Butler's skill. He carried the detritus of the feast out to the kitchen while Phryne went to find her favourite policeman.

He was sitting on a cane chair, staring into the depths of a bowl of irises as though it might contain the answer to the question which was dragging his brows together. He was an un-memorable, subfusc man, with mid brown hair and mid brown eyes. Phryne had learned early in their acquaintance that if she looked away from Jack Robinson, she could not envisage his face. It was a very useful attribute for a policeman, and she supposed that his wife had some mnemonic which recalled him to mind. Or possibly he was tattooed with his name and address. Phryne tore her mind away from an indelicate speculation on where this information might be placed, and coughed to announce her presence. Robinson looked up from the irises. They had obviously not been informative. He looked stricken.

'Jack, dear, how very nice to see you!' she ex-claimed, putting out both hands to draw him to his feet. 'Do come in and have some tea. Or perhaps some breakfast?'

'Just tea, thank you,' he answered. Phryne was wearing a cherry red dressing gown and a Spanish shawl of far too many colours. Robinson had always admired her adamant refusal to wear pastels. The Spanish shawl, embroidered in red and blue and gold, dazzled his eye and provided a nice splotch of colour in the sea-green, sea-blue decor. Phryne herself looked well. Her holiday had agreed with her, it seemed. She looked even more like a Dutch doll than usual: pink cheeks, bright green eyes, shiny black hair cut in a cap.

'You're looking fine, Miss Fisher,' he said with an effort. 'Decided not to stay in the city by the bay, then?'

'Too fast,' said Phryne, fanning herself with a

corner of the shawl. 'Too busy and too, too hot. I have decided that I don't like the tropics. Come along,' she said, leading the detective out of the front room and into her own parlour, cool as the inside of a seashell. The table bore a fresh pot of coffee and a Chelsea teapot shaped like a thatched cottage with matching milk jug, sugar basin and cups and saucers. Phryne loved this set because the cups were big enough for a reasonable amount of coffee, and Mrs Butler doted on the design.

It seemed to affect Jack Robinson. He winced.

'Whatever is the matter, Jack, dear?' asked Phryne. 'Rheumatism or aesthetic twinges?'

'Probably the latter, Miss Fisher. Not that I'm saying anything against your teapot, though, if it's got tea in it. I'm parched.'

'It certainly has. But say the word and I'll have it transferred into my new Art Moderne silver pot – perfectly bare, just a shape.'

'No, no, please. It's real pretty and that sugar basin in the shape of a haystack is nice. It's just that I've been out to a suspicious death this morning and I'm a bit sensitive on ... er...'

'Porcelain which is just too, too cunning for words?' asked Phryne, pouring.

'Er...'

'Overdosed on what the Americans call "cute"?'

'Just that. You never saw such stuff. Thanks.' The room was silent except for the soft, soothing noise of a policeman absorbing tea. Phryne was intrigued. Jack Robinson had a habit of quoting Shakespeare, who he considered a good working poet with a word for every situation, but she had never suspected him of being at all precious. And that Chelsea set was worth a small fortune. It was one of the few things that Phryne had retained from her childhood. The only reason her father hadn't sold it in his indigent days had been that Phryne herself had hidden one of the cups, delighted by the country scene on the side and the fluted edging. Then her father had succeeded to the title, acquired a large fortune (his grandfather had married an American heiress) and had given the set to Phryne with a fine generous flourish. She had restored the missing cup, which tripled its value. Who was Jack Robinson to object to her Chelsea china?

The third draught seemed to have restored some life to the wasted frame of this unappreciative officer of the law. He set the empty cup down gently into its parent saucer. Phryne was slightly mollified.

'Now, if you'll not object to my pipe...' he hinted. Phryne waved a pink-tipped finger. Her cigarette holder described a perfect ellipse.

'Light up, and I'm warning you, Jack, dear, if you don't tell me what this is all about fairly soon, I'll self-combust.'

'Heard of an authoress called Marcella Lavender? Also known as Rosebud Peachblossom?'

Phryne stifled a giggle. 'No, never. I'm sure I'd remember the name if I'd ever heard it before,' she told Robinson. 'What does she write?'

'Books for kids,' said Robinson. 'Fairies. You know. Little naked flying creatures.'

'Usually seen over rather good botanical drawings. Yes, I know the kind of thing. I had a flower fairy alphabet when I was small, but I grew out of it rather quickly. A is for Apple-blossom, B is for Buttercup...' Jack Robinson was nodding his head gloomily. 'That was one of hers?'

'Yes. She did masses of them. And her cottage is crammed with pictures of fairies – no, you really have to see it, Phryne. You won't believe it.'

Phryne noted that Jack had relaxed enough to call her Phryne, which was all to the good.

'And...' she prompted.

'Well, the cook's assistant took her breakfast this morning and found the door unlocked and the authoress dead as a doornail. Just keeled over at the table.'

'Oh? And what makes this a suspicious death?'

'Nothing in the dying of it. Police surgeon says she died of respiratory failure consequent on possible thrombosis of the pulmonary artery. She was as blue as a cornflower,' added Jack Robinson, waxing unexpectedly poetic. 'With pink splotches.'

'Oh.'

'But he'll know more after the autopsy. Thing is, you see, she'd been to see us. Getting threatening letters. Someone threw a brick through her window. Felt she was being followed. Last week she was almost run down by a car. Just managed to jump out of the way in time. No damage except a fright and a pair of ruined stockings. No description of the car and no witnesses. Nothing much we could do.'

'So you thought she was a dotty old lady,' said Phryne gently.

'Yes, well, yes. We get a lot of complaints from people who have a few kangaroos loose in the top paddock.' Jack's stubby finger circled near his ear.

'Away, in fact,' said Phryne, 'with the fairies?'

Jack grimaced at the comment. 'Persecution complex, that's what they call it. Lots of people have it. And they're dead convincing.'

'Until you let them talk some more,' said Phryne, addressing the flower-filled grate. She did not want to look at Robinson, who would never forgive himself if he broke down in front of a woman. 'Then it comes out, whatever it is. I was on a train once with a perfectly charming old gentleman who was telling me all about the genealogy of the local gentry and I thought he was quite sane until he informed me that he was the illegitimate son of Queen Victoria and thus the rightful ruler of England. I had to call him 'Your Majesty' for five stations until I could manage to transfer into a Ladies Only carriage. Nice man, though. He conferred an earldom on my first-born son.'

'You're right,' said Robinson. 'And even though she was real irritating, she wasn't insane. I took her through the story several times. She showed me the notes. She might have written 'em herself, of course.'

'How did she come to see you, Jack? Poison pen letters aren't your usual fare.'

'No, well, she was a distant relative of the Chief, and he put her onto me. I did what I should have done,' said Robinson miserably. 'I sent a constable around to examine the house, I told the foot patrol to walk past and see that all was well twice a night, I told her to call me if she got any more notes, and I told her she wasn't in any real danger. I can hear

10

my own voice saying it. "These poison pen writers sound nasty but they never actually hurt anyone," I said.'

'But it's true,' said Phryne. 'They usually don't.'

'Not true this time,' said Jack Robinson, puffing at his pipe.

'But she died of a pulmonary thrombosis,' said Phryne.

'Maybe,' said Robinson. 'Maybe she was frightened to death. You should have seen her face.'

'No, I shouldn't, not so soon after breakfast. What do you want me to do, Jack?'

'Come with me and have a look at her apartment. I never saw a place so ... so ... feminine. I reckon you'd get a lot more out of it than I have.'

'Being female,' agreed Phryne.

'I'm not feeling too good about this,' said Robinson, in case Phryne hadn't noticed. 'I did all the required things, of course, but I really never took her seriously. I never believed her. Now she's dead...'

'You're feeling guilty,' diagnosed Phryne.

'I did what I could,' said Robinson stubbornly. 'I couldn't have done any more. Not with no witnesses. But I feel like I owe it to the old chook to at least take a close look at her death. Might be nothing in it. Probably isn't. But...'

Phryne decided that Robinson in his present mood could occupy the next couple of hours in going round and round in logical circles. Phryne had other things to do. Arrange some parties. Visit a dressmaker. Find out when her lover Lin Chung was expected home from his silk-buying trip to Shanghai. His last letter had mentioned the name of the ship SS *Gold Mountain*. Odd name for a ship. Phryne wondered if it had lost something in the translation. This would involve a visit to that alarming old woman, Lin Chung's grandmother. The matriarch of the Lin family lived in a house on Little Bourke Street and, although she accepted the relationship as inevitable, she approved of Phryne in the same way she approved of cholera morbis. Interviews with her were always testing.

Mrs Lin could wait. Phryne poured the detective another cup.

'I'll just get dressed,' she said, patting him lightly in passing. 'What sort of day is it?'

'Wet but not cold,' said Jack Robinson, already reviving under Phryne's influence. He watched, with affection, the red robe and Spanish shawl flick past him on their way up the stairs and he drank the tea.

CHAPTER TWO

Concealment of illumination in a basket is beneficial if correct.

Hexagram 36: Ming I
The I Ching Book of Changes

The landlady greeted Phryne at the wrought iron gate in a roughcast wall which would have kept out an invading army. She held out a distracted hand which had a small, pink feathered bundle in it, then almost dropped the dead bird in an attempt to transfer it to her other hand so that she could take Phryne's.

'The Hon. Miss Fisher, this is Mrs Needham,' said Jack Robinson. 'I'll take that, Mrs Needham. Miss Lavender's bird, was it?'

'Yes, poor little thing, as soon as his mistress went away he must have just piped a little song and then he died. He was on the floor with her. Well, they know, don't they?' said Mrs Needham, fixing Phryne with the meaningful look of the true believer. 'Animals always know, don't they?'

'Indeed,' murmured Phryne. Something was snuffling at her heel. Looking at Mrs Needham, Phryne was prepared to bet that it would be a small, spoiled, insanitary and probably neurotic dog, possibly a Pekingese. She was also prepared to discourage it privily if it showed signs of scrabbling at her silk stockings.

Mrs Needham wore a severe shade of mauve, the colour of Victorian half-mourning. She was about sixty. Her hair had not been shorn in the modern fashion but was secured in a bun which was showing signs of fraying at the edges. Her hands were cold and her nose red, signs of emotion or a defective liver – or possibly hay fever, as her cardigan pockets were bulging with handkerchiefs. She led the way through a small reception room redolent of beeswax furniture polish and into a corridor which opened into a square garden.

The old house had been divided into apartments quite recently. There were still traces of the builders' occupation: a few drops of paint on the

13

path, a lost stencil lurking in the agapanthus, and a faint but pursuing scent of wet stonework, or was that emanating from the cellar? It had been a big, solid, Victorian house with room for a family of eleven children and twenty servants. Impossible to keep up in these parlous times, when servants would rather work in the pickle factory and most women of high social class knew how to avoid having eleven offspring, or any at all.

'I inherited the big house when the old Mistress died,' said Mrs Needham. 'I was with her at the end.' She closed her eyes in the conventional gesture of pious devotion. 'Terribly old she was, no children of her own, and all the grandnephews were killed in the Great War, and her only nephew, too. Captain, he was. So she left it to me,' said Mrs Needham with an undercurrent of smugness. Probably against spirited opposition from the rest of the family, Phryne guessed, who hadn't bothered to visit their aged relative while she was alive but became remarkably gerontophilic when she was dead.

'There was a bit of money, so I had it divided into apartments. Serviced apartments,' she emphasised, taking out a wet hankie and sneezing. 'Of course they can do their own cooking, if they wish. But luckily Cook wanted to stay, and I only need a few girls part-time to clean and so on. The gardener left, retired to live with his daughter, so I made his accommodation into the Garden Apartment and Miss Lavender thought it was so beautiful! The first time she saw it she clasped her hands together and told me she'd never live anywhere else in the world.'

14

Phryne reflected that Miss Lavender had kept her promise, but said nothing. The big house was a respectable and probably expensive place to live. The apartments would be of a reasonable size, not like these modern hatboxes with no room to swing even a very cooperative mouse, and by the scent of lunch preparing, the food would be good. Miss Needham mentioned the rent and Phryne heard Jack Robinson gasp.

'How long had Miss Lavender been here?' she asked quickly, to cover the sound. Miss Needham, however, had heard it.

'I'm sure that it's a reasonable rate, Detective Inspector, considering the service. Miss Lavender never had any complaints. She lived here from the first. Almost a year I've been open. And now a thing like this has to happen. Poor Miss Lavender! She never told me that she had a weak heart.'

'This is a very nice sunken garden,' said Phryne appreciatively. It had been laid out by someone who had seen the Boboli Gardens in Florence, or at least pictures of them. There was a fountain made of a series of shallow dishes which tinkled into a pool where fat goldfish swam under the waterlilies at their approach. The concrete walls had been limewashed and set with Della Robbia plaques in blue and white. Marigolds grew all around the edges of a very neat square of lawn. White painted birdbaths and raised pedestals bore lobelia and nasturtiums. There were cane garden seats under awnings made of natural canvas. One cumquat tree rose from a terracotta pot and two bay trees flanked the entrance to the house. Very clean, very Tuscan. One looked for

15

the Medici crest. Someone had devoted a lot of time and care to it.

'Pretty,' approved Phryne.

'Yes. Bit bare, though, don't you find? Mr Bell in number six asked me if I'd mind if he "pottered about in it" – well, gentlemen have their fancies. I said I didn't mind. The other ladies and gentlemen seem to find it soothing. They have little picnics out here when the weather is suitable. But Miss Lavender was responsible for this,' she said proudly, taking them along a path which wound far more than necessary and was entirely lined with brightly painted stone gnomes in a variety of poses.

Something was still snuffling at Phryne's heel, and now she felt the warning nip of teeth. Without looking round, she gave a sharp shove with her foot, and was rewarded with a yelp.

'Oh dear, I seem to have trodden on your dog,' said Phryne, as Mrs Needham scooped up a snuffling, affronted, fat, mangy Pekingese which immediately bit her on the finger.

'He's upset, isn't he?' crooned Mrs Needham. 'Poor little Ping. Did the lady stand on you? Poor Ping!'

Phryne was suddenly very sorry for Mrs Needham, a sentiment which would have astounded the lady. She said to Ping, 'I apologise, Ping,' and got in a faster than light pat before the dog's reflexes had recovered enough from the insult to snap at her. Mrs Needham seemed mollified but carried the creature with her as she led the way up the stone gnome path to the open door of a cottage which called itself Wee Nooke.

16

Phryne closed her eyes briefly. No wonder Jack Robinson had winced at a Chelsea tea set. Here was 'cute' in unbearable profusion. The apartment was small. It had a table in the bow window, overlooking the sunken garden. There was a sitting area with furniture piled with magazines and what looked like proofs. Behind that was a small kitchen and a smaller bathroom. A flight of highly polished wooden stairs led, presumably, to a bedroom above.

And every surface, horizontal or vertical, was covered in fairies. Bits which could not have fairies painted, embroidered, embossed, stencilled, hung or depicted on carpet were painted a peculiarly penetrating shade of fuschia pink. Puppet fairies hung from the ceiling. Gauze wings brushed the wall in the breeze from the open door, sounding like moths. The air was heavy with the scents of rose, lavender, almond blossom, and was that gin, perhaps?

'Thanks very much, Mrs Needham,' said Jack Robinson. 'Now we'll be a while, so perhaps we could see you on the way out?'

'Very well, Detective Inspector.' She was still a little stiff with a policeman who had dared to comment on her perfectly reasonable charges. 'Oh, I'd forgotten – what about Bluebird?'

'I'll take care of him,' said Jack Robinson.

'Bluebird?' asked Phryne, when Ping had been carried regally away. 'I thought it was pink.'

'Probably named after Maeterlinck's book *The Blue Bird*,' commented Robinson. 'Very popular with sentimental people, I'm told. Well, Phryne? What do you think?'

17

'Why don't you go out and find a suitable spot to inter Bluebird, and leave me here?' suggested Phryne. The policeman's presence was offending the extreme femininity of the room. He couldn't have been more out of place if he'd been an eight foot prizefighter smoking a cigar. Phryne sat down at the table where the previous tenant had been found dead, and looked at the room.

Fairies everywhere, yes, admitted. More pink than the mind could comfortably cope with, yes. Idly, Phryne wound up the musical box on the desk. It was surmounted by a celluloid fairy doll dressed in bright red gauze. It tinkled a tune which Phryne suspected was called 'Fairy Bells' and the fairy twirled around on her perch. The machinery gave a gasping wrench and died, leaving the fairy in mid-pirouette. Even the musical box missed its mistress, apparently. Very, very ornamental, if you liked that kind of thing. But underneath the tinsel, there lay the real woman. Who had she been, this Miss Lavender? Someone who really enjoyed 'Fairy Bells'?

A woman with a good business, that was clear.

Phryne saw paintings in all stages, from preliminary sketch to varnished and ready to frame, and in all forms, each carefully labelled and piled into neat stacks. Underneath a wicker chair (pink) was a supply of brown paper, packing labels, cardboard and string. And, of course, pink tissue paper for the initial covering. A large pink-lidded basket disclosed water colours, brushes, paper and prepared stretchers. The desk drawers contained headed paper (pink) and a neat rose-coloured folder full of clipped bills, despatch notes, invoices and orders. Things were booming in the fairy business, it appeared. Phryne took a pink notepad and scribbled down some figures.

Good, but not good enough, not for Mrs Needham's charges. Miss Lavender must have had some other source of income. Bank statements revealed that she was paid quite a solid amount every month from 'Marshall and Co.'. Now what did Marshall and Co. do?

Further investigation revealed that Marshall and Co. had been paying Miss Lavender this sum every month for the whole length of her tenancy, and possibly before. The Commonwealth Bank, which the departed might have patronised because it had a women's banking room, reported that Miss Lavender drew cheques to Mrs Needham and to Cash for her own expenses, and had a balance of two hundred and seventy-five pounds eight shillings and threepence as at the end of the last calendar year.

A nice round sum, thought Phryne. Saving for her old age, possibly. She got up and inspected the kitchen. The bench was clean and dry and the sink looked unused. The rubbish bin contained several envelopes, an orange rind, some brown wrapping and string and a crumpled letter.

'"You bitch you bitch I'll finish you you bitch",' said Phryne aloud. 'Not very informative. Common typing paper and – of course – not considerate enough to include a return address or a name. And you can't get fingerprints off paper. I'll have to have a look at the one which the deceased gave to Jack.'

Phryne stuck the letter in her pocket and looked

into the bathroom. A small wash-place blushing with rosy tiles and even a pink WC. The bathroom cabinet contained aspirin, a prescription bottle of codeine marked 'For severe headaches' and the usual toiletries. Miss Lavender had had headaches. But a headache hadn't killed her. Phryne noted the name of the prescribing doctor and continued.

Upstairs was a surprise. It wasn't pink.

The bed was neatly made – had Miss Lavender not slept there, or did she make her own bed? It was covered with a spread of a quiet fawn shade. The brown and blue Persian carpet was patterned with small intricate lozenges. There were no decorations except for a few framed pictures of Highland scenes which had probably come with the apartment. Next to the bed was a polished mahogany box containing letters in various hands, all in slit envelopes with notes scribbled on them. A stenographer's notebook and pencil lay on the bedside table beside a pile of mystery novels, a work of devotion and a half-empty glass of water. Beside that was silver salver bearing an almost empty bottle of gin, a bottle in which tonic water had gone flat, a glass and a sliced lemon. That explained the faint under-scent of alcohol. Miss Lavender liked a private snootful, that was plain.

Phryne prowled. The relief to the eye of this quiet, respectable room, obviously inhabited by a woman of means and sober taste, was remarkable.

The wardrobe door was open. Phryne ran her hands through the respectable clothes, emptying pockets and handbags and wishing she had Dot with her. Dot was good at searching. Phryne piled all the crumpled handkerchiefs, bus tickets and chocolate wrappers into the mahogany box and carried it downstairs with her. There she was assaulted afresh by fairies, and swore that if one ever fluttered through her window one night she would swat it flat with considerable pleasure.

She stood at the door, watching Jack Robinson sitting at his ease on a cane chair, talking to a Latin lover sort of young man in flannel bags and a gardening apron. She turned back to look once more at Miss Lavender's room. There was something glaringly wrong, and it itched at her consciousness. Fairies, indeed, they were enough to confuse the senses, and she had explained the scents – gin upstairs and oil sleeves over every lightbulb downstairs. The desk with its musical box, the piles of paintings ready to despatch, a large pink fairy puppet hanging from the staircase…

No. She couldn't pin it down. Perhaps the letters would enlighten her.

As Phryne approached Jack Robinson rose and introduced the darkish, youngish man. 'The Hon. Phryne Fisher, Mr Bell. I was just telling him how much I like his garden.'

'Yes, it's splendid,' agreed Phryne warmly. 'Very Italian. Boboli Gardens, hmm?'

Mr Bell ducked his head modestly. 'I like pottering about,' he said, as if confessing to a dreadful sin. 'So peaceful, gardens.' He lifted his face to the light and Phryne saw a puckered scar from a burn which rose from under his collar and disfigured his olive-skinned jaw and cheek. 'After the war I went travelling. Just me. And when I came to Florence

I fell ill. When I started to recover they took me every day to the Boboli. When I saw this sunken garden here I couldn't resist it.'

'You were a flier,' said Phryne gently. She had seen such burns before.

'Once,' said Mr Bell. 'Now I do a little stock-broking and a little antique trading and mow the grass.'

'And that's enough?' murmured Phryne.

'It has to be.' He looked away from her and coughed. Then swallowed and went on in a louder, hasty voice, 'Now, you wanted to ask me some questions, eh, Miss Fisher? How did I get on with Miss Lavender? I fought ferociously to keep her rotten gnomes out of my garden, but otherwise I had nothing to do with her.'

'Did you quarrel with her recently?' asked Phryne.

'No, she gave up on the gnomes months ago. Mrs Needham told her that she could have the path up to Wee Nooke and I had the sunken garden and that was that. She seemed to accept it. You'd never know from looking at her that she had such rotten taste, you know. Quiet sort of woman, nicely dressed. But you never know with people.'

'No,' said Phryne curiously. 'You never do. Who else lives here?'

'There's nine apartments,' said Mr Bell, relaxing a little. 'I live in number six, over there. The building is a hollow square, you see. Main flats at the front, others down the sides. My door gives onto the garden. In five, right at the back behind me, is Mr Carroll. Something in the city, I believe. Goes out to boozy parties with his friends until all hours. Past me there's Mrs Needham's apartment. In front of her, in seven, there's Mr and Mrs Opie and their child. Quite a nice child. Doesn't hurt the flowers. He's old money; I believe. They quarrel a lot. Ask them about Miss Lavender!'

'Why?' asked Jack Robinson.

'They didn't like her,' said Mr Bell, suddenly becoming reticent. He was more nervous than seemed appropriate. 'On the other side, behind the Garden Apartment, there's Miss Gallagher and Miss Grigg in four. They're journalists. Work for a magazine called *Women's Choice*. Old-style suffragettes, that's them, though don't tell them I said that, please. Three is old Professor Keith and his niece. He's retired. Nice old stick. Knows a lot about plants. Two is Mrs Gould, a widow. She's just moved in so I don't know much about her. Brought a lot of rather good furniture with her and a small painting of Venice which made my mouth water. I'd swear it was a Canaletto. School of, at least. And one is Mr and Mrs Hewland. Keep themselves to themselves. Very religious. Anything else?' He gave Jack Robinson a cheeky grin.

'I'm sure you've got lots of mulching to do,' said Robinson gravely. 'Always a lot to do in the garden at this time of year, Mr Bell.'

'Right you are,' said Mr Bell, and moved away. He glanced back at the box which Phryne held under her arm. He seemed about to ask something, then bit his lip and turned away, ostentatiously busying himself with clipping back some importunate nasturtiums. He took with him his smell of fear.

'You've spoken to all the inhabitants, have you,

23

Jack, dear?' asked Phryne, sitting down cosily next to the policeman on his cane lounge chair and lighting a gasper. It had seemed like sacrilege to smoke in Miss Lavender's apartment.

'Constable's doing it now,' he said. 'I'll get the reports in due course. I don't for a moment suppose that anyone will have noticed anything.'

'I wonder how one gets to the tennis court?' asked Phryne.

'What?' Jack Robinson was drowsing in the shade. Now he opened his eyes wide. Miss Fisher had a talent for non-sequitur.

'Well, there's no gate in this garden, it ends in the wall and one wouldn't want to go out into the street in one's tennis clothes, not in a respectable place like this, with a church on the corner. Stiff letters would be written to the municipal council.'

'I didn't think about it,' murmured Jack Robinson.

'There's a couple of players coming back now,' said Phryne. 'Let's watch.'

Two slim, flannel-clad figures were strolling across the lawn towards the garden wall. Just when it seemed that they were intending to climb over, they vanished, to reappear some minutes later in the walkway beside the main house.

'There's a tunnel,' said Robinson.

'Which means that, assuming someone came in and killed Miss Lavender by some means, they could have just wandered in through the tennis court and wandered out the same way,' observed Phryne.

'So it does,' agreed Jack Robinson, dolefully. 'That neat wire fence around the court wouldn't keep out a determined cat. Just like I always say, Phryne. People put up a wall, a portcullis and a ferocious dog at their front door, and protect the back with a sign saying "Please do not burgle this house". I don't know. It's enough to make a policeman discouraged. You know what thieves say, don't you? When charged, they say, "He shouldn't have left the keys in", or "They shouldn't have left the door unlocked", and I have to agree. Well, I'd better give Mrs Needham the speech about "Securing your Home from Robbers" and she'll tell me that they are all nice people around here and would never think of doing such a thing.'

'Off you go,' said Phryne. 'And watch out for that Pekingese. It bites.'

'Of course it does,' said Robinson, gloomily.

He plodded away. Phryne breathed in the scent of new-mown grass and allowed her mind to stray. Peking. Ping. Where was Lin Chung? On the sea? Even now returning with a large supply of new silks and stories to tell? The newspapers had not been encouraging about the situation in China since the death of Sun Yat Sen, Father of his People. Generalissimo Chiang Kai Shek had managed to hold on to some cities, but the Japanese were in Manchuria, the Russians were threatening at several points, and the rest of China had reverted to the rule of the warlords, which it always did lacking a strong central government. Palaces had been sacked. Foreign delegations had been assailed, some besieged, and most were leaving, withdrawing into treaty harbours or across to Hong Kong, taking away the last independent witnesses of slaughter and tyranny. Nuns had been murdered. Hundreds of people had been killed and thousands were fleeing across the face of that huge continent, seeking safety and a small plot in which to grow some rice.

Not an unreasonable quest, but perhaps impossible. And somewhere in that slew of refuge-seekers, murderers, looters and soldiers was the irreplaceable Lin Chung. It was not a comforting thought. He was certainly Chinese by race, but he had been brought up in the West. How current was his slang? How reliable were his relatives? And where was SS *Gold Mountain?* Phryne had failed to find it in the shipping lists. It looked like she really was going to have to seek an audience with Madame Lin.

She might have decided that it was time Lin married a suitable girl and sent him to the Four Counties to contract for a nice unspoiled virgin cousin. Probably, Phryne thought vengefully, with bound feet. That would make sure she didn't develop any life independent of Madame Lin.

'Pretty lady!' announced a voice at Phryne's knee. She opened her eyes.

A small child in a sailor hat which had extinguished all its features like a candle-snuffer was presenting her with a paper bag. Phryne took it gingerly.

'Three toffees,' said the child. It might have been male or female. The eyes were very bright. A small hand lay on Phryne's skirt like a pink, sticky starfish.

'Yes,' Phryne agreed. 'There are three.'

'Two for me,' said the child. 'One for you.'

'How kind,' said Phryne, managing to break off a corner of a toffee and putting it in her mouth. The taste of brittle Eton toffee brought back her own youth with a rush.

'What's your name?' she asked.

'Wendy Opie,' said the sailor hat proudly. 'What's your name?'

'Miss Fisher,' said Phryne.

'Pretty lady,' commented Wendy dispassionately. 'Pretty hat.'

'You are wearing a very stylish one yourself,' Phryne returned the compliment.

'Goes with my sailor suit,' said Wendy. She turned around slowly so that Phryne could admire the full beauty of the costume.

Matters were developing nicely when a harassed woman ran round the corner and grabbed Wendy, sweeping the child clean off her feet. Wendy, startled out of her composure, began to cry.

'You bad girl, Mummy's been so worried!' said Mrs Opie into the wailing face. 'I told you to stay and play quietly and I'd take you for a walk myself!'

'But the garden door was open and I followed a bird and he came here and I met Miss Fisher,' Wendy pointed out. Her tears had been stemmed as soon as the initial shock was over. The child obviously felt that she had right on her side.

'I do beg your pardon,' said Mrs Opie, putting Wendy down and tucking a strand of pale hair back behind her ear, from which it instantly slid loose again. 'I'm Helen Opie. I was especially busy this morning and then when I looked around Wendy wasn't there and I've been searching all along the road for her. She usually goes out the house door. I didn't realise that the garden door was open. I hope she hasn't been bothering you.'

'Of course not,' soothed Phryne, who had caught a glitter of emotion from Wendy which told her that the door hadn't been open until Wendy had found a way to open it.

'Isn't it terrible about Miss Lavender?' said Mrs Opie, sagging down on the bench. 'You can go and look at the fishes, Wendy.'

The alacrity with which the child obeyed told Phryne that her reason, or one of her reasons, for escaping from her mother was to go and look at the fish. Mrs Opie swatted at her dusty apron. She was a thin woman with prominent grey eyes and hair which would never hold a bobby pin. She had shingled it out of desperation but it was still always falling into her face.

'So, have you decided to take the apartment?' asked Mrs Opie artlessly. 'It's a bit overdecorated but you can always have it done in something more stylish.'

'I haven't decided,' said Phryne. Mrs Opie was sitting right next to Miss Lavender's box of letters, which was open. One hand was trailing, dropping to the edge. Phryne made a suitable comment about the weather. Mrs Opie replied conventionally, never taking her eyes off Phryne.

Miss Fisher was endowed with excellent peripheral vision. She could see Wendy leaning over the lower basin, trailing her fingers in the water. She could also see Helen Opie's fingers as they savoured the chocolate papers and the envelopes, seeking the right one.

28

There was a splash behind her, but Helen Opie did not react. The moment poised on a knife's edge. Would retrieving a letter or saving the life of her daughter win?

It was rather a disappointment when Mr Bell shouted at Helen to get a move on before the child hurt his fish. The hand recoiled, empty, and Helen Opie jumped to her feet with appropriate exclamations of dismay and retrieved her offspring, dripping wet.

As Mrs Opie bore Wendy away from a watery grave, Phryne saw a smile of perfect satisfaction on the child's face, and nothing but blank despair on her mother's.

CHAPTER THREE

Kau shows a female who is bold and strong. It will not be good to marry such a female.

Hexagram 44: Kau
The I Ching Book of Changes

'Curiouser and curiouser!' exclaimed Phryne with Alice. There was a Wonderland feel to this house, cut off by its great wall, supplied with a secret passage, and populated by entirely too many gnomes. She left the lid of the box open and invited Mr Bell over to sit with her by an inclination of the head which stronger wills than his would not have been able to resist. Mr Bell did not try. He dropped a strand of couch grass into a trug and wiped his hands on his apron as he walked.

A good-looking young man, or he had been, before getting burned. Phryne wondered how extensive the burns had been, how they had happened, and how he had adjusted to the world after the war. He walked easily.

'Shall I ask for some tea, Miss Fisher?'

'Not for me, thanks. I've just breakfasted. They create a lovely effect in the sun, those blue and white Della Robbias.'

'I've arranged the brighter ones in the shade,' he answered. 'Hard to get anything to grow against that wall. The house overshadows it. But it isn't wet enough for ferns. What are you doing here, most decorative lady?'

'Pure curiosity,' said Phryne lightly.

'Killed the cat,' said Mr Bell.

'So they say,' said Phryne, never taking her eyes from his.

'Why should you care who killed the old chook?'

'Who says that anyone killed her?' asked Phryne in a low, flat tone.

'But ... I assumed ... with the police here...' stammered Mr Bell, looking away at last and blushing. His burn scar blushed differently from the rest of his skin and for that moment he looked seriously deformed – white scar tissue on olive skin.

'This is presently called a "suspicious death", Mr Bell,' Phryne informed him. 'Detective Inspector Robinson called me in to have a look at the apartment, because he's at length noticed that I'm female, and females notice things about other females which a man would never see.'

'And have you?'

'Ah, that would be telling,' teased Phryne. Mr Bell laughed unconvincingly.

'No, but really, did someone kill Miss Lavender?' he asked after a pause in which bees hummed in the marigolds and goldfish surfaced. The sun glinted off gold, white and blue in a scent of cut grass.

'I don't know,' said Phryne. 'We'll have more information after the autopsy.'

'And will you tell me about it?'

'Depends,' said Phryne. She wasn't flirting. She was wondering how far she could push Mr Bell before he lost his temper. Someone who lost their temper was always informative.

Phryne had not pushed him far enough. He got up, bowed slightly, and stamped back to the weeding. Phryne hid a smile. She must find out much more about this young man. And, of course, the terrified Mrs Opie. What was in this box that she needed so badly that she might almost have let her little daughter drown while she searched for it? How did she mean to identify it by feel? By size of envelope, by shape, by texture, by frank or embossing, by sealing wax? Or was she not looking for a letter at all, but something else which might be in the box?

Phryne felt that this would be an interesting investigation, even if Miss Lavender hadn't been murdered.

She was staring abstractedly across the sunken garden when she saw a serge-clad arm waving at

31

her. It was an urgent 'come here' gesture from the apartment behind Wee Nooke. Phryne took the box and carried it with her. The arm belonged to a short, stumpy woman wearing a version of a man's suit and the sort of frilly apron made for someone a lot slimmer and given to tripping onstage in red slippers exclaiming, 'Ooh, la la!'

'You're Miss Fisher, aren't you?' she demanded in a gruff voice. 'Seen you in *Table Talk*.'

'You have the advantage of me,' said Phryne, bowing slightly.

'Grigg,' said the woman, shaking Phryne's hand vigorously. 'Come in and have some coffee. I approve of most of Needham's cuisine but not her coffee, which is dishwater with a coffee bean dipped in.'

Phryne followed her through a small garden in which tomato plants towered in cages of wicker mesh and the air was heavy with the scent of foreign herbs – basil, oregano – and some familiar ones, like mint, summer savoury, lemon balm, borage and thyme. Bees hummed industriously through the blue borage flowers and the yellow tomato flowers.

'This smells like Italy,' said Phryne.

'Similar climate,' said Miss Grigg shortly. 'Lived there for years. Came back to this dull food, sausages, chops, steak, eggs, tomato sauce made of red lead. Only way to get real taste is to grow our own herbs. Good soil, too. Loam. A handful of this and that makes even Needham's solid unimaginative stuff taste alive. And we're making a red rather like chianti, too, in the Barossa Valley.' Her voice was approving. 'Could even be in Rome on a hot night with the tomatoes and herbs and a glass of red.'

'And without the fascisti, the crowds, the motor exhaust and the danger,' prompted Phryne. Miss Grigg snorted.

'That Mussolini ought to be horsewhipped. If I'd had a horsewhip I would have done it myself. Stupid, puffed-up oaf, oozing self-importance from every unshaven pore. Italy is not the Roman Empire, and it never will be again. Fools! They'll get themselves slaughtered if they start taking on someone like the Greeks or the Turks. They play for keeps, as the children say. Do sit down, Miss Fisher. Have you been to Italy?'

'Not recently, though I wandered around there for a year after the war. I agree with you. One can see the contrast if one comes from Greece; the beaky, craggy faces of the Greeks and the soft *bella figura* boys straight out of a pastoral romance.'

'Pretty boys,' said Miss Grigg, pouring boiling water into the top of the coffee pot, sealing it, and watching the machine tip over to begin percolating. 'Precisely. How do you take your coffee, Miss Fisher?'

'Black,' said Phryne. Miss Grigg was nervous, despite her abrupt manner and her telegraphic speech. The cups rattled as she placed them in saucers.

Phryne looked around. The decor was Italian. The floor was slate with rush matting. The walls were whitewashed and decorated with brightly painted plates. The table was plain wood, the cloth plain white and the crockery majolica, handmade in the grotesque style, all arabesques, trailing vines, and odd, wicked little faces on impossible animals. Miss Grigg had doffed her frilly apron and sat down. She had salt-and-pepper hair, cut neatly short, faded blue eyes and a brick-red gardener's complexion. Her hands were square and gnarled with labour. But there was a blue stain, ingrained to the bone, on her third finger, which elevated her from drudge to writer.

The coffee was superb and Phryne said so. Then, instead of asking questions, she sat silent and waited. Miss Grigg drank her coffee with pleasure, set down her cup, and said, 'I like a woman who isn't forever chattering. That's what's wrong with most women – they must be always talking, talk, talk, talk. And they never say anything worth hearing either.'

Phryne smiled and nodded.

'I need to ask you a question,' said Miss Grigg. 'Miss Lavender. Was she murdered?'

'I don't know. Enquiries, as Detective Inspector Robinson would say, are continuing.'

'That's not an answer.'

'Best I've got,' said Phryne. 'There seems to be something funny about the matter. She was perfectly healthy one day, apart from headaches, and the next, dead. That's a suspicious death. The police are required to investigate. Why do you ask?'

'I'm interested, naturally.'

'Of course,' murmured Phryne. She waited. Miss Grigg stared at her for a long moment. Phryne returned the stare, bland as cream.

'Work for a women's magazine,' said Miss Grigg. '*Women's Choice*. You might have seen it.'

34

'Yes, I take it,' said Phryne.

'Do you? Strike me as more of a *Table Talk* girl,' said Miss Grigg. 'Thing is,' she added, dropping her voice to a confidential bark, 'thing is, you see, I see that you took that box of letters, and Miss Lavender, she...'

'Grigg? You there?' called a musical, feminine voice. Miss Grigg cursed under her breath. Then she yelled, 'In here, Gally!'

'Such a fuss outside,' complained the voice, getting nearer. 'Policemen all over – oh!'

Phryne saw with considerable interest that Miss Grigg and Miss Gallagher, though housemates, were of the contrasting style of female friendship rather than the identical. Miss Gallagher wore a red cotton skirt with at least one petticoat, a ruffled, white embroidered blouse and a head-scarf. She tossed her black curly hair back over her rounded shoulders and pouted when she saw Phryne.

'Miss Gallagher,' said Phryne, rising and put-ting out a hand to be taken in a soft, childish grasp. 'I'm Phryne Fisher.'

'Oh!' gasped Miss Gallagher again. The white frilly apron, thought Phryne, was definitely hers. The headscarf turned towards the seated woman. 'What's she doing here, Grigg?'

'I asked her in for coffee. Do sit down, Gally. Would you like coffee?'

'Tea,' said Miss Gallagher vaguely. 'I'll make some.'

Phryne reflected that if one could not avoid confrontation directly, one could easily avoid it by drifting around a kitchen picking things up

35

and putting them down again. This Miss Gallagher did. Miss Grigg looked at her with amused tolerance. Phryne watched in silence. Eventually, she thought, Miss Gallagher would have to actually find the pot, the tea, the kettle, the cup and saucer and strainer and teaspoon, the sugar and the milk. For how long could she draw out the process? With tea, the making of which was already a complex ritual, it could be hours, and Phryne wanted to get back to Robinson.

'Are you going to take the garden apartment?' asked Miss Gallagher.

'I don't know,' said Phryne truthfully.

'It's very nice. You could get rid of all the fairies,' suggested Miss Gallagher, picking up an apostle spoon, examining it, and putting it down again.

'Possibly,' said Phryne. 'Do you work at *Women's Choice* also, Miss Gallagher?'

'Oh yes,' said Miss Gallagher, staring at a saucer as though trying to redesign the grotesques in her head.

'She's cookery and preserves,' said Miss Grigg. 'I'm vehicle maintenance, home repairs and trades. Mrs Opie in seven is Your Child. She has one to practise upon, of course, which does help. Pity. She was a medical student before her Giovanni left her and she married that louse Opie.'

'Grigg!' exclaimed Miss Gallagher. 'Not before ... our visitor.' She angled a look at Phryne under long eyelashes. Phryne did not react. The pert mouth drooped in disappointment. Miss Gallagher, thought Phryne, is a terrible flirt.

'Does anyone else from the magazine live here?' she asked.

'Mr Bell is gardening,' replied Miss Grigg.

'So he's Agricola?' said Phryne. 'Excellent article he did on irises last month. Too late to plant any now but I've clipped it out for next year.'

She was lying. It had been clipped, certainly, but only at the special request of Jack Robinson. Miss Gallagher was examining Phryne with frank interest.

'I reckon she'd do, don't you, Grigg?' she fluted.

'Do for what?' asked Miss Grigg warily.

'For the fashion notes.' Miss Gallagher sounded almost scornful. 'Miss Alston's been doing them but she's away at the moment, you remember? Her mother's ill. We've got no one to do the fashion notes. I'm no good,' she said complacently. 'I don't know the first thing about fashion.'

'Well, yes ... but, Gally, you can't just drag Miss Fisher into *Women's Choice* because we've got a staffing problem.'

'You won't be dragging me,' said Phryne, making up her mind suddenly. 'I've never seen how a magazine works. I'd be interested. Where shall I go and when?'

'Well, if you mean it...' Miss Grigg sounded warier. 'Little Bourke, corner of Hardware Lane, third floor, tomorrow at nine.'

'See you then,' said Phryne, setting down her cup. She hefted the box, smiled at both women and left through the Italian garden, scented with basil and tomatoes.

'Miss Fisher?' Miss Grigg caught up with her. 'I meant to ask you, since you came in with that cop. Miss Lavender was doing a fairy page for us. She said it was finished but she hadn't yet had time to deliver it. I know this sounds callous, but business is business and deadlines are deadlines.'

'I'm sure that we can manage that. What's it called?'

'"Hilda and the Flower Fairies",' said Miss Grigg, evincing signs of well-controlled nausea discernible to the trained eye. 'Revolting, I know, but the Ed thinks that children like it. Their mothers do, anyway. When she was on hols and I did one issue and ditched the fairy page, I got letters of complaint by the armload. However. "Not that one woman can, but that every woman can". Ours is not to reason why. It's a double page foolscap with sketches of fairies all around the edge. It should be in an envelope addressed to the mag. Be obliged if you could bring it along – if you really meant it about the fashion notes.'

'I really meant it,' said Phryne. Miss Grigg gave a shy smile, endearing on her weathered face.

'Don't worry about Gally,' she said gruffly. 'She don't mean no harm. It's just her way.'

'No harm, no harm,' said Phryne, with Shakespeare.

'No, faith, boys, no harm i' all th' world,' Miss Grigg completed the quote complacently, and grinned.

Phryne found Robinson almost asleep in the Tuscan garden, with his hat over his nose. The scents were cooler here, of worn stone and water.

'Come along, my dear,' she said, tweaking the hat away in time to catch him with his eyes closed. 'I must get along home. I've got to start work tomorrow.'

'Work?' asked Jack, rubbing his jaw to stop a

yawn. 'I really must dig myself a little pond. A few goldfish, some nenuphar. And a little fountain. That tinkle of water is so soothing. Did you say something about work, Miss Fisher?'

'As from now, I am fashion notes for *Women's Choice*,' said Phryne proudly.

Jack Robinson stared at her and found no reply.

Phryne reached home. Something whipped past her nose as she opened the gate. 'A woman might almost think she was being shot at,' Phryne said to herself. If it was a shot, it had come from the road and the shooter would be long gone. The bullet – if it had been a bullet – was lost in the garden. Probably a bee, thought Phryne, or a flying chip of road metal. I really must control this tendency to paranoia, she thought, and knocked on her own door just as Dot was beginning to wonder where she was.

'Mrs Butler says cold collation tonight, but the beetroot is in aspic so it won't leap out on you like you say it always does, Miss. The magazines you asked for are on your desk. Have we a new case, Miss?'

'Yes and no. Or perhaps no and yes. And beetroot definitely has a fatal attraction to my person. The only thing I own that isn't attractive to the pestilential vegetable is that red silk shirt, and that's because it's beetroot coloured,' said Phryne heatedly. 'After dinner, Dot, dear, we must go through those magazines and work out the philosophy. Do you read *Women's Choice?*'

'Only since I came to live with you, Miss. Before that, the doctor's wife used to take in *Australasian*

39

Home Journal. Boring, I thought. All sketches of bathrooms and new kitchens with lots of pipes. Never went to the trouble of getting me a new kitchen, or a new sink either. Or a gas stove. Mrs Butler says she won't never go back to the old way of cooking with a fuel stove. Gas is clean and in weather like this the kitchen isn't like a foretaste of hell – that's what she says, Miss.'

Dot believed absolutely in both God and the devil, which meant she never used the word or concept of hell lightly. But she was a just young woman and added, 'And she might have been right at that. Those poor sinners, having to spend eternity in that kind of temperature. Must have made them regret all their sins.'

'Yes, it must have. I remember fuel stoves. Things have certainly come a long way since then. Though I think that the greatest of all inventions is hot water. The difference it has made in the world is remarkable. I used to cat-wash, Dot, did you?'

'Yes, Miss,' said Dot. 'Standing on a little mat in the bedroom with ice forming on the windows and the kettle getting colder by the moment.'

'And one was always cold,' said Phryne, consideringly. Both she and Dot shivered at the same moment, remembering the grubby flannel, the fugitive soap, the pervasive sense of not-quite removed-grime and cold.

'Never mind, Dot, dear,' said Phryne bracingly. 'We never have to do that again.'

Dot, thinking of deep baths full of lathery hot water above which the only part of Dot which could be seen was her nose, laughed and agreed.

'A bath,' said Phryne. 'Then dress for dinner, and a little research before I launch myself on the world of magazines. It should be most interesting.'

Later, lying deep in foam, Phryne was greeted by Ember, the black cat, who had never entirely reconciled himself to the idea that humans voluntarily shucked their fur and immersed themselves in the embrace of such an unreliable element, which would not even bear the weight of a decent feline. He batted at the bubbles with one sable velvet paw.

Phryne shook one hand as dry as possible and caressed his ears.

'I have had such a strange day, Ember, dear,' she said. 'I have met some very strange people. And tomorrow is likely to be even odder.'

Ember tapped her nose with a playful paw. He stood with perfect balance on the curved edge of the claw-footed bath, tail hanging outside for balance, witch's-familiar-black with eyes like emeralds.

'I'll tell you all about it when I get home,' promised Phryne. Ember purred, satisfied, and leapt down.

Phryne sometimes wondered about Ember. But if he was a fiend, as Dot had occasionally called him (his habit of clawing out the contents of stocking drawers had earned him some criticism, especially when the stockings were silk), he was so far keeping quiet about it, which was decently reticent of him.

Phryne, drying herself, decided that she would only have one cocktail before dinner.

CHAPTER FOUR

The third line, divided, shows the subject distraught amid the startling movements going on.

Hexagram 51: Kan
The I Ching Book of Changes

Phryne paused at the top of the stairs. The building had one of those turn of the century lifts which induce a desire for exercise in all but the terminally indifferent or famously brave. The landing was painted in a tasteful shade of ivory with several flower prints: a bottlebrush, a grevillea, a branch of golden wattle. The lack of style was familiar. Miss Lavender was an excellent botanist. No one could fault her meticulous, relentless accuracy. Her meticulous, faultless, uninspired and perfectly dead accuracy.

Phryne shook herself. She had dressed with care in a forest-green knitted cardigan ensemble, with pockets, and a green and silver georgette scarf. Her skirt was of medium length, her oatmeal straw hat was small and decorated only with a rose. Her handbag had a strap and her portfolio was the only jarring note: bright pink. It was, of course, Miss Lavender's, and contained the adventures of Hilda among the flower fairies.

Hilda, the flower fairies and the lack of a second cocktail had given Phryne the most peculiar

42

dreams, in which she flew on gossamer wings over a ruined island and saw Lin Chung crucified below her. Flies fed at the corners of his mouth. She had not read the letters in Miss Lavender's box, but she had read eleven back issues of *Women's Choice*. It was a sober, respectable journal for the thinking woman of taste and sensibility, and she was mildly interested to learn which personalities went with the pseudonyms.

Only mildly. Underneath the calmly fashionable exterior, a considerable part of Phryne was concerned with Lin Chung. That had been a very nasty dream. She opened the door and went into a large office.

It was full of desks, flowers, clothes, people, typewriters and confusion. Phryne stood back as a girl rushed past her with an armload of pasted-up papers, hair flying out of its bun and pencil behind her ear. A young woman with ink on her face exclaimed, 'Blast! Who's taken my scissors? Who's bloody stolen my damned scissors?', and an old lady with white hair reproved, 'Language, dear. Here, take my scissors, but mind I want them back.' A tottering crash announced that a huge pile of boxes containing something breakable had succumbed to gravity.

A youngish woman with a pale, blank face threw her pencil to the ground and said, 'That's it, then,' and burst into tears. The rest of the women rose to comfort her and the door at the end of the room crashed open.

'Ladies, I must have some quiet!' cried a short, plump woman in grey. She cast one look around the room and said, 'Oh dear. "Confusion on our banners wait", again. Now let's see, what's wrong?'

Phryne saw her surge into the room, patting, pushing and instructing with a brisk and motherly high-handedness which no one seemed to resent. This must be Mrs Charlesworth, the editress.

'Mrs McAlpin, can you take Miss Phillips out for a short walk? Say, fifteen minutes. You might bring us back some of the baker's biscuits. Take the money out of petty cash, there's a dear.'

Miss Phillips accepted Mrs Charlesworth's handkerchief, mopped her face, and put on her hat. Mrs McAlpin rummaged in a cash tin, took out precisely eighteenpence, and preceded her to the door. Mrs Charlesworth addressed the others.

'What was in the boxes? The china she was reviewing? Oh dear. Can't be helped. We shall just have to confess to the manufacturer, and see if we can give them a good review if the stuff isn't altogether ghastly, eh? Now, what more? Here are your scissors, Miss Prout. Why not tie a tape on them and attach them to your belt? Where is Miss Grigg?'

'Gone to talk to the radio people about the loudspeaker system they're touting. She had her doubts about it. But it'll fit in with our series on how to build your own radio and she's a whizz on all those technical things,' said a slim girl at the nearest desk. 'Gally's in the kitchen and her fashion plate is supposed to be coming this morning. She'll be late. Those clotheshorses have no sense of time.'

Slowly all eyes in the room swivelled to look at Phryne, now sitting on one corner of a desk and looking amused. They took her in, from delicate

44

French heel to georgette scarf, and a blush ran around most of the room.

Mrs Charlesworth, without a quiver of a smile, said, 'And I am giving you the next meditation to write, Miss Herbert, on the theme "Think before you speak". Five hundred words on my desk in the morning. I'm sure it will be most illuminating. Good morning. Miss Fisher, is it not? Do try to forgive us. We're going to press in three days, and that always makes us crotchety. We shall have tea when Mrs McAlpin gets back with the biscuits. Perhaps you would like to come into my office? Now, ladies, if you please, less noise. Miss Fisher isn't used to us, and I have an editorial to write. And I have already written one on "The Value of Silence". Miss Herbert, if you have a list of questions and the photographs, perhaps you could prepare them. Half an hour of absolute stillness and we may end the day relatively sane. Clear?'

General murmurs of agreement. With considerable dignity, Mrs Charlesworth conducted Miss Fisher into her office and shut the door.

She sat down and fanned her face with her hand. 'I can't imagine why I do this,' she murmured. 'But then, why do any of us do anything? I don't suppose you would consent to be interviewed on being a private detective, Miss Fisher?'

'No,' said Phryne.

'Professional confidentiality?'

'Yes,' said Phryne.

'I suspected as much. Never mind. We are quite at a loss for the fashion page now that Miss Alston has gone to see to her mother. She left some notes, perhaps they will be of use. And I am told that you have been called in by the police in the matter of Miss Lavender?'

'Just for some – well, fashion advice. Here is her last commission, by the way. I checked with the investigating officer and he said it was all right to take it.'

'"Hilda and the Flower Fairies"?' The editress's face was alight with pleasure.

'Regrettably, yes.'

'I know they are banal beyond belief and un-worthy of a sensible magazine, but the mothers love them. I suppose it fits in with what they think their children ought to be like, instead of the grubby little beasts they really are. It's all Dr Stopes's fault. Radiant Motherhood, indeed. But we do what we can, Miss Fisher. That's our watchword. "Not that one woman can, but that every woman can".'

'Miss Grigg quoted it,' said Phryne. 'What does it mean?'

'In every generation there have been remark-able women. Marie Curie, for instance. Dr Eliza-beth Blackwell. Women who have sacrificed everything – marriage, motherhood, even their lives, like Nurse Cavell.' Mrs Charlesworth pushed over a tin of gaspers and held a light for Phryne. 'But they could be ignored, for the purpose of changing how women are seen by the world of men. They assume the same position as saints, like Joan of Arc. Her heroism and martyr-dom did not change the general view of women one whit. The saints and martyrs and remarkable ones are freaks, sports, something so out of the common that no notice need be taken of them.

46

Am I making myself clear?'

Mrs Charlesworth's eyes were bright with intelligence, hazel eyes full of passion. Phryne wanted to hear more, so she said, 'Not entirely. Do you mean that the ordinary man on the train will not look across at a shop girl and say, "She is of the same sex as Queen Elizabeth"?'

'Yes! One can look at a plumber, a labourer, and say without a great sense of irony, "He is a man, capable of the same heroism as Admiral Nelson or Saint Francis of Assissi". But no one looks at a woman and says, "She is a woman, she is capable of the same heroism as Lady Godiva or Anne Askew". Our heroines are separated from us. So instead of trying to make Man accept us as daughters of heroism, we must raise all women to the level of heroines. "Not that one woman can do it" – because a woman, like a man, can do anything provided she sacrifices everything, including her life, to that one idea – but that "Every woman can do it". Every woman can be educated, can have a career, can be the breadwinner for her family, can run a household and go into parliament or medicine or the law, and when there are enough of us as doctors and lawyers and parliamentarians, when there are many women in public life, then Man cannot ignore us. We will take our rightful place.'

'At the side of Man?' asked Phryne evenly.

'At the head,' said Mrs Charlesworth fervently. 'Look at the world, Miss Fisher. Does it seem well run to you? Women and children are hungry and ill-used all over the world. Men who played with toy soldiers as children grow up to play soldiers with real lives and create nothing but waste and devastation. But that war, for us, was good. It removed thousands of young men, broke thousands of hearts, and made women find out that they were strong. We could do many things which men had kept as their especial preserve. Fight fires. Drive trains. Mine coal. I remember driving a delivery truck. I only had to work nine hours a day. I got meal breaks and smokos. I had been looking after three children under five on my own on a soldier's wife's pension in a cold-water second-floor room in Richmond. On my male wages I could afford to hire two women to look after my children and still have enough left over to buy luxuries like butter. After a year I could afford to move into a house. Of course, after the war my husband came home, and I returned to the house. Such wild fancies as paying women a living wage only happen in wartime. But it was a very important experience, Miss Fisher. That's when I resolved to start a magazine which would inform women, encourage them, educate them.'

'But not go too far,' mused Phryne. 'To salt your magazine with enough fashion notes and "Hilda and the Fairies" so that you won't shock your readership and drive them away. But, in fact, you want to seduce them into taking over the world?'

Mrs Charlesworth beamed. It was the innocent, double-chinned beam of a happy baby, belied only by the shrewd eyes.

'Exactly,' she said.

'Ah,' said Phryne. 'I wish you every kind of luck,' she added. 'Now, perhaps I'd better be getting on? I must go out at noon, but I can come back this afternoon.'

'Good. Miss Herbert, who should have recovered from her gaffe by now, will show you all the notes Miss Alston left. Nine hundred to a thousand words, room for illustrations. See Mrs McAlpin when she comes back if you require any photographs.'

'Mrs McAlpin? The ... er ... elderly lady? She's your photographer?'

'Try not to accept the errors of the dominant mythology, Miss Fisher,' said Mrs Charlesworth tolerantly, showing Phryne out.

Phryne drew up a battered kitchen chair and sat down at Miss Herbert's desk.

'Yes, do try,' said Miss Herbert. 'Myself, I find the dominant mythology irresistible. I'm so sorry, Miss Fisher. Made a fool of myself.'

'Understandable reaction,' said Phryne. 'This seems to be a very closed little shop indeed, and you can't take to outsiders just because they're fashionable.'

'Oh, we can. I'd kill for your sweet little hat with the darling scarf. But I expect it cost ten quid at a boutique in the Paris end of Collins Street?'

'Guineas,' said Phryne. 'What are we writing about?'

'Summer clothes,' said Miss Herbert. 'Here are the broadsheets, a copy of *Mode, Table Talk,* and Miss Alston's notes. What do you think?'

'Pretty terrible.' Phryne skimmed the pencilled notes. 'I can't agree that those Fuji prints are smart. They're vulgar. And they run in the wash. Plain colours wear better and you can wear printed scarves and shawls with them. Those shoes will break more ankles than hearts. And look at this list of rules! Red hair can only wear pale green, never pink, never red, never navy. I have one red-headed friend who looks stunning in burgundy. A pox on all of them. Let's have a look at the broadsheets.'

'They aren't your style of thing,' said Miss Herbert hesitantly. 'Not your level of fashion.'

'"Honest labour wears a lovely face", Miss Herbert,' said Phryne.

'It's all right for you,' said Miss Herbert sulkily. 'You started out beautiful.'

'No, I started out plain,' said Phryne. 'Lanky and pale with two plaits which stuck out like a Dutch doll's. I just made the best of my points. And if you want some advice, ditch most of your powder – you've got lovely skin – display your dark eyes and chestnut hair by wearing copper, bronze, black or dark red, and I've got just the hat. I'll bring it in tomorrow.' She paused to allow Miss Herbert to take offence, but Miss Herbert just stared, so Phryne continued. 'Tell you what. Let's allot ourselves a budget of ten pounds and see what we can get in these ads. Summer frocks or costumes, shoes, bag and hat.'

Miss Herbert, now wholly Phryne's slave, burrowed with a will into the advertising broadsheets, scribbling totals as she went. At the end of an hour, much refreshed by tea, coconut biscuits and Miss Fisher's Balkan cigarettes, they compared their sheets.

'I got two cotton dresses and a Fuji one, a pair of cheap shoes and a cloche,' said Miss Herbert triumphantly. 'Sixteen shillings and sixpence for the dresses, the hat was a bit more expensive, but there's a special on shoes at Clark's. We can stretch that out all right. Didn't see any handbag worth having. She'll have to use last year's. What have you got?'

'I spent nearly all my money on a tailored suit from Craig's. Eight and a half guineas in a lightweight fabric – crepe de Chine, say, in a solid colour like leaf green, lobelia blue or Mediterranean blue. Oatmeal for the faint-hearted. Wine for those with dark hair. Tailored for me, not the average woman who almost fits into size XS.'

'Nice, but you've used up all your money.'

'Not yet. I will then catch a tram to Chapel Street and go to the grand sale at Colosseum-Treadways. Elbowing through the multitude, I will there purchase a pair of pumps for three shillings and elevenpence (one cannot wear sandals with a costume), and two tunics in pale or contrasting Indian cotton for three and eleven each. I can there also purchase my straw hat, four and eleven. Removing from it all decoration, I can use one of the scarves (elevenpence) to wind around it. I will place all my purchases in a straw basket which will take two remaining shillings and I will bestow the rest on the poor.'

'Gosh,' said Miss Herbert.

'What's more,' said Phryne, lighting another gasper, 'next summer all I need to do to cheer my suit up is buy or make more blouses, get some more scarves and new gloves and stockings. Hemlines aren't going to rise any higher. No couturière is going to actually expose the knee, the ugliest

51

joint we have. If hemlines drop dramatically, then I can always let mine down, or get a new skirt to match the coat or contrast with it. As long as I choose the suit carefully in a colour I can actually live with, I've got summer clothes for ten years, while your poor lady is going to have to demand more money from her long-suffering husband for new clothes next season.'

'Gosh,' said Miss Herbert again. 'That's amazing.'

'I learned it all from my companion, Dot. When I asked her what she wanted in a dress, as a present, telling her she could choose absolutely anything she liked, I was rather surprised when she selected a tailored suit rather than something astounding in evening wear. Madame Fleuri, the French seamstress who made it, thoroughly approved. "While you 'ave my suit, ma'moiselle, you can be married in it or buried in it, which God forbid, but you will always 'ave something respectable to wear".'

'I'll remember that. I say, Miss Fisher, what if we publish this? Put both of our shopping lists together. "Ladies! You can buy this list and get new frocks but they'll only last one summer, or your suit and new blouses each year." What do you think?'

'Sounds good. Why don't we do that? If Mrs Charlesworth approves?'

'Oh, she couldn't care less about fashion. That's why we don't have a fashion reporter, only Miss Alston part-time. And I don't know as much about it as I thought I did. What about evening clothes, Miss Fisher? What do you advise on the same lines as your tailored costume?'

'Get a black dress,' said Phryne, 'of the most expensive, durable fabric you can afford. Not cut in any wildly eccentric fashion, hand-tailored or take it to a local seamstress and get it altered to fit you. Then use it as a base. Fling a voluminous Indian shawl over it, or a bit of that gorgeous Chinese silk, brocade for winter, gauze for summer. This has advantages,' she added, heading for the door. 'It doesn't matter what colour your corsage is, you can wear it to a wedding or a funeral with equal propriety, and...'

'Yes?' gasped Miss Herbert as Phryne opened the door to the stairs.

'You can wear a lot of diamonds.' Miss Fisher grinned, blew her a kiss, and vanished.

The Lin family mansion was enclosed in its walls like a jewel in a lotus. Phryne did not try to enter the main building, but asked one of the blue-shirted men in the silk shop, 'Will you ask if Madame Lin can see me?'

She waited until the message had been translated and relayed, occupying her time looking through the rows of inferior silks on display. Faded and depressed washing silks lined the counter. No wonder Lin Chung had been sent on a silk-buying trip, if this was the best the Lin family could presently offer.

The little shop was hot. Phryne was counting her time. Ten minutes for a reply was the utmost that could be expected when everyone had to translate the message. Twenty minutes was verging on discourtesy. Half an hour in a stuffy little shop was over the edge and trotting along towards a calculated insult.

Outside, Little Bourke Street went on its way, noisy, prosperous, alien, strangely scented and fascinating. Inside it was tedious and getting hotter. Cantonese voices began to sound metallic in her ears as she strained after the sense of what they were saying. She knew that she would never be able to master the odd, inflected, tonal language.

Well, there was always shopping. Phryne indicated a bolt of reasonable-looking black corded silk and the shop man mounted a ladder and hefted it down, displaying it with a flick of the wrist. It was dull but good. Very good, in fact, thick and faintly lustrous. Phryne rubbed it between thumb and forefinger. At that moment the shop man caught sight of her silver ring, a big entwined dragon and phoenix. It might be true that to Asians all roundeyes look alike, but he had clearly seen the ring before.

He shouted something urgent to someone at the back of the shop, then respectfully withdrew the corded black silk and returned it to its place. Another blue-coated man walked from behind the counter with a half bolt of glossy, fine, sensuous red so liquid that it almost dripped from Phryne's grasp. He bowed. Both shop men smiled nervously.

Phryne bought seven yards, paying by cheque and leaving her card so that it could be delivered. Madame Fleuri would make nightclothes out of that silk which would be as comfortable to wear as warm air on naked skin. The shop men bowed and smiled again, offering the distinguished cus-

54

tomer a wooden chair. Before allowing her to sit, the taller of them dusted it with a fine flourish.

Phryne sat down and composed her features as though she was in church.

Precisely twenty minutes after she had first entered the shop the blue-shirted man received a sharp order in a female voice, lifted up the counter top and bowed. Phryne walked through. Behind the counter was an open door. Beyond was an oasis of coolness and shade.

There was a girl waiting for her under the arch, which was studded with potted azaleas, salmon pink, white and claret. Phryne wondered if the white ones were the azaleas named after her patron, Phryne, the courtesan of ancient Greece.

'Miss Fisher?' The girl was anxious. Why was Phryne making the Lin family so edgy? That silk was worth four times what she had paid for it and clearly it was kept for special customers. They had never shown any sign of wishing to mark her out for special favour before. Rather the opposite, in fact. Tolerance was the best she could expect.

The girl was about sixteen, conventionally dressed like a schoolgirl, with a long plait down her back and a clear, high-coloured complexion. She had the Lin family's delicacy of feature. There was nothing remarkable about her but her self-possession, unusual in so young a woman, and her damaged hands. Rather touched, Phryne noticed that she bit her nails. 'I am Jane Lin, Lin Chung's cousin. Do sit down. Can we offer you some tea?'

'Madame Lin?' asked Phryne, who had not really expected to see the old woman but was anxious to make the point. Jane Lin looked away.

'Our grandmother is very old. She is resting. She feels sure that you will forgive her,' she said.

Phryne was not at all sure, but accepted refreshment and talked about the weather for the requisite time. She sat down on a curved iron garden seat, much more comfortable than one might think from the shape. She ate petits fours. She drank strong golden tea, the Iron Goddess which Lin Chung favoured. The taste reminded her painfully of him. Lin Chung the magician. Lin Chung of the mocking, clever, sensuous mind, the smooth, muscular body, the hands which could make her catch her breath. The dark eyes which remained forever unreadable. Lin Chung who had left long ago and gone into the maelstrom in pursuit of more pretty fabric to drape around female frames.

The cool green scent of the garden was very pleasant, but Phryne was not to be seduced. Finally she asked her question.

'Have you heard from Lin Chung?'

'Not recently. He arrived in Macao and purchased the silk, though there have been troubles in China, as you may know.'

Phryne nodded. 'Troubles' was a serious euphemism for what was happening there.

'He was supposed to be taking ship on the *Gold Mountain*, South China Navigation Company, for the voyage to Hong Kong. We do not know if he is aboard. There is no reason to assume he is not. He drew a draft on our Hong Kong bank for the silk and other things. But there is no post from China at the moment,' said Jane Lin. 'We are sure that he is safe.'

'How can you be sure that he is safe?' asked Phryne, reminded of her dream.

'It is not a safe world,' said Jane Lin. 'But he has Li Pen with him.'

'That should preserve him against all ordinary perils,' agreed Phryne. She remembered Li Pen. A quiet, unassuming, respectable man from the Temple of Confucius in Peking. A dedicated Shao Lin priest, a terrible fighter with the heart of a tiger. Li Pen the hunter. He would level whole cities rather than allow Lin Chung to come to harm.

'That is the situation,' said Jane Lin. 'Grandmother wishes to ask a question in return.'

'And what does Madame Lin wish to know?'

'Have you heard from Chung?'

'Only a note from Hong Kong six weeks ago, before I went to Sydney.'

'Nothing since?'

'No, nothing. But I will make a deal with Madame,' said Phryne, rising.

'Miss Fisher?' Jane Lin was a little shocked. Ordinary mortals did not make deals with Madame Lin, matriarch of the Lin family and mistress of all she surveyed. But then, this was the Silver Lady, Lin Chung's rich woman. No concubine, this, though her hair was Chinese black and her skin Manchu white and her mouth the colour and shape of a rosebud, as the ancient authors required of a beautiful woman. But her eyes were green, disconcertingly, alarmingly green as green jade. Those eyes were now fixed on Jane with a considering stare which reminded the girl strongly of her grandmother.

'If I hear from Lin Chung, I will tell her. In return, if she hears from him, she will tell me.'

'I am sure that this will be acceptable,' said Jane Lin helplessly.

CHAPTER FIVE

Sung intimates that although there is sincerity in one's contention, yet he will meet with obstruction and opposition.

Hexagram 6: Sung
The I Ching Book of Changes

Phryne walked quickly back to the *Women's Choice* offices, her heels clicking in a precise 6/8 which would have been the joy of any listening jazzman.

Think about something else, she told herself. What about the death of Miss Lavender? I really don't know anything about her, but she was strange. That odd house – all fairies and tinsel downstairs, all business upstairs. Did that mean that the fairies were just a pose? In that case, what was she hiding? Who hated her enough to kill her?

She paused to buy and eat a fine Tasmanian Ladies in the Snow apple before facing the return to the office. The apple was crisp, clean, delicious and far removed from pain and trouble. She drew a deep breath on the corner of Hardware Lane, listening to the city. The bird shop was loud with canaries. Phryne wondered what they were saying. It might be a mistake to learn the language of birds. They might easily be shouting 'Go away!' or 'I'm the best,' or even 'Shut up, you blokes, I've got a splitting headache!' An old clothes merchant dragged past a barrow on which were bundled, shabby and ashamed, the fashions of yesteryear. He seemed rather well dressed for a humble puller of barrows. Few labourers wore watch chains.

'Miss Fisher, yes?' he grinned around his cigar. Phryne dropped her apple core.

'Good heavens, Mr Katz,' she exclaimed. Then she fumbled for some suitable expression of regret that the person she had last seen as a prosperous cabinet-maker was reduced to manual labour of this type. He held up a hand.

'No, no, no need for the "Good heavens, Mr Katz", Miss Fisher. I'm helping out my cousin. He's moving his stock, rent's gone up through the roof, poor Sol.'

'A *mitzvah*,' said Phryne, smiling. 'A good deed.' She had always liked Mr Katz.

'And the reward for the chance of a *mitzvah*? Another *mitzvah*. Nice to know that I can still haul a barrow, *nu?*'

'Strong as an ox,' agreed Phryne.

'Oy, don't tell my Minnie that you saw me, Miss Fisher! She'll *plotz*. Hey, you're going into there? *Women's Choice*, maybe?'

'I'm doing their fashion notes,' said Phryne. Mr Katz leaned on the handle of his barrow. She

59

suspected that however strong he was, he was glad of a chance to rest.

'Tell them to buy second hand,' he said. 'Lots of good *schmutter* around. Here, see...' He burrowed through his load. 'This, it's Worth, see, the label? Little work, sew on a few more sequins, good as new, better than new. Prewar fabric, you don't get satin like this any more. For you...' he grinned again, as his mercantile nature warred with his sense of obligation. 'For you, nothing at all.'

The Worth label was plain to see. The dress had been a full skirted, heavy Edwardian ball dress in a startling shade of plum, which had faded to an enchanting bluish purple under its torn muslin overlay. It definitely had possibilities. The material, as Mr Katz had said, was of superb quality.

'How much would you charge for it in the shop?' asked Phryne.

Mr Katz shrugged. 'Two pounds, maybe three if the customer was exigent. Solly believes in spoiling the Egyptians. Only the rich can really afford bad manners.'

'Here's three,' said Phryne. 'No, I insist. You've given me an excellent idea and the dress is worth it for the fabric alone. Give me the address of Sol's shop, too, if you please.'

Mr Katz extracted the dress, loaded it into Phryne's arms, and said, 'Solly's just along from you in Hardware Lane, Miss Fisher. Come in and have a look! No obligation to buy,' he concluded, as Phryne opened the street door and he took up the handles of the barrow again. 'Mind you don't tell my Minnie, Miss Fisher!'

The office was in its usual uproar when she climbed the stairs. Miss Grigg had returned and was slowly and grimly pecking away at a Smith Addison as though it was a bear trap which at any moment might snap shut and injure her. Miss Herbert was typing quickly, angling her head so that gasper smoke flowed past her eyes. Miss Phillips was surveying a lot of broken crockery, making notes in a small book with a sharp pencil. Mrs McAlpin was polishing lenses and placing them back in their padded boxes as placidly as a church committee worker polishing the communion plate. To add to the illusion, she was singing softly as she worked. 'Oh worship the King, all glorious above, we gratefully sing, his power and his love.'

Miss Prout was arguing with Mrs Charlesworth.

'It's the way magazines are going,' she said loudly. 'More gossip, more advertisements, more photographs, more games – cartoons, even. Look at this.' She flung down a volume with a bright cover emblazoned *New York True Confessions*. 'See? How many readers can we drag in – shop girls, clerks, factory girls – if we could run "The Mad Elopement" or "The Diary of a Lonesome Girl"? This is real life, Mrs Charlesworth. You can't expect those girls to read nothing but "The Lives of Noble Women"!'

'Can't I?' asked Mrs Charlesworth gently. Mrs McAlpin picked up another lens and sang a little louder. 'His chariots of wrath the deep thunder-clouds form...' Miss Phillips concluded her notes on the shattered china and started loading it back into its box. This she tied up with string. Then she stood up and headed for the door, dead-heating Miss Nelson, the office girl, who knew the signs as well as anyone and had discovered an urgent errand at the printer's. Phryne dumped her Worth dress, took her seat and watched, fascinated. Miss Prout, it appeared, had a minimal sense of self-preservation. Mrs Charlesworth might look cushiony and soft, but she ran a monthly magazine and had done so for some time, which meant she must have a whim of iron.

'Let's see what we could put into our Australian magazine to give it popular American appeal, shall we?' asked Mrs Charlesworth gently. "Her Morning After"? "Dope"? The news that – let me see – the notorious nightclub keeper Kate Meyrick has been jailed for six months? That the Comtesse de Janzé has been put on trial for attempted murder of Mr Raymond de Trafford at Nice? That the Reverend Francis Bacon has been tried for supplying poisonous drugs to women? Nice, very nice. Sin, suffering and sorrow, all with a neat little moral plaited into the end. Don't behave wildly. Toe the line. Be a good girl and you'll be happy. Is that what you want us to tell our readers? That old lie?'

'And dark is his path on the wings of the storm,' sang Mrs McAlpin.

'We could have the whole state reading us!' objected Miss Prout.

'Poisons are attractive,' said Mrs Charlesworth. 'This, this drivel is as attractive as the drug in that story and twice as addictive.'

'So you agree that I'm right. That readers would eat this stuff up,' insisted Miss Prout.

'Oh, yes, they would. And vomit it right back. Read without reflection and forgotten, except for the moral stain. Are we going to produce articles on the lives of flibbertigibbet film "stars" and make our respectable women envy them? Are we going to tell girls that sex is forbidden, and make it doubly attractive? These rags are designed not to inform, but to titillate, and thus to promote the very actions which they pretend to protest against. They are poisonous, evil, corrupt and for the last time, Miss Prout, I will not have it!'

'But the advertisers– '

'Oh, yes, I can just see how Ovaltine will react. We might be all right with Tangee lipstick, they're selling sexual attraction, after all, and perhaps some of the face creams. But Salus? They take at least two half pages every issue for their Nutrax Nerve Food. I can't see the godly, sober and righteous being impressed with "Her Morning After", can you?'

'We could get other advertisements – we could attract a different market,' said Miss Prout stubbornly.

'Of course,' Mrs Charlesworth's voice was kind. 'Brothels, gin palaces, movies, there's a plethora of grubby little industries which would leap at the chance. Why not make up a list of them, Miss Prout? I'm sure that the Board will be interested. The meeting is on Thursday. I'm not trying to crush your enterprising spirit. But the furthest I am willing to go with gossip in *Women's Choice* is the riveting news that little Princess Elizabeth has learned how to curtsey. No, Miss Prout. That is enough for today. I still have an editorial to write and someone has to check over "Hilda and the Flower Fairies" and then take it down to the printer. You strike me as needing a little innocent diversion. Get Miss Fisher to help you – she could do with some, too, and a cup of tea, by the look of her. Now, silence, ladies. Complete, utter silence.'

She went back into her office and closed the door with a final click.

'Phew!' whispered Miss Prout.

'Come out,' said Phryne. 'Let's get some tea, maybe some lunch. Before we tackle Hilda and the fairies.'

'Tea!' scoffed Miss Prout. 'I need a drink!'

'Very well,' said Phryne. 'Then we'll go to my club.'

'The Adventuresses Club was formed in 1919,' Phryne instructed Miss Prout as they walked quickly down Little Lonsdale Street and mounted the steps into a three-storey building, solid blue-stone with sea-green tiles on the floor. 'Women who had done all sorts of things in the war – driven ambulances, climbed mountains, flown planes, written novels – could not find life comfortable without a few like-minded friends to talk with. In fact, Miss Elspeth, who started it, was a quiet woman with a very respectable husband. She said she could stand the respectability all week but occasionally needed to remember, in suitable company, what being unrespectable felt like. She bought this building meaning to open a small hotel. When several of her exploring friends came to dinner here and had a wonderful time, Miss Elspeth converted it into the Adventuresses Club.

It was going through a decline when I came to Melbourne and I was able to put a bit of capital into it. There's a quiet room where silence is absolute. No talking at all. In a woman's life, silence is the rarest commodity there is. There's a large room for parties and lunches, there's a few small bedrooms for visitors and there's an End of Tether room.'

'What's that?' asked Miss Prout, agog.

'It's soundproofed. One can scream and not be heard. Space to scream is another thing that's severely limited in modern female life. We keep a fairly good table, which will improve when I can lay my hands on a good well-trained female cook. At the moment we have M'sieur Paul, and he is very temperamental. Hello, Kate. One guest for lunch, I'll sign her in. This is Kate, doorman and chucker-out. Who's in for lunch, Kate?'

Massive Kate rippled a few muscles complacently. She was dressed in a military style uniform with frogging.

'Not much company, Miss Phryne. Miss Alice said you won't forget the Directors' meeting on Friday?'

'I'll be there. Have we found a cook yet?'

'Miss Joan reckons she's got a good prospect.'

'Jolly good. Come along, Miss Prout.'

'Is everyone called by their first name?'

'Yes. Have you ever thought that by losing your own name in marriage you lose a good portion of your identity? That to become Mrs George Smith is to be entirely obliterated except as an adjunct to, or relict of, Mr George Smith? The one name left is the one you were christened with. Besides, no

65

one who is voted into the Adventuresses cares a straw about titles. We've got quite enough status to be going on with. So everyone is Miss Whoever.'

'My first name,' said Miss Prout shyly, 'is Laetitia.'

'And mine is Phryne. Long story.'

'You're a private detective, aren't you? I've heard of you.'

'Yes, but I prefer not to mention it. This way.'

Phryne led Miss Prout into a modern electric lift. She pressed the button marked 'three' and they were whisked skywards at alarming speed.

'We got a modern lift to cut down the expense of keeping an elevator operator and to make getting to lunch faster. Some of us don't have a lot of time.'

The doors hissed open on a pleasant roof garden. White iron tables and chairs were scattered around a central fountain under striped awnings. It looked European and summery. Phryne sat down and extended a hand without looking and a uniformed maid put a menu into her grasp.

'Vegetable soup, roast lamb, ugh, in this weather, cold collation, lemon meringue pie or Charlotte Russe. Very good. Just the salad, entirely omitting beetroot, and the pie, Jill. Miss Prout?'

'I'll have the same, if you please.'

'And a gin and tonic, rather stressing the gin and adding a mere touch of tonic, Jill, please. I'm having a rather complicated day. Miss Prout?'

'I'll have one too,' said Miss Prout.

Phryne waited until she had a drink, then surveyed Miss Prout. She was an enthusiastic young woman with bad skin, a mass of unruly hair bandolined to her scalp, an unwise hat and too much Tangee lipstick in a strange shade of orange. Not bad looking if she would eat more fruit and omit the rouge. Brown eyes, however, alight with a mission. In this she strangely resembled Mrs Charlesworth.

'I've never been in a place like this,' said Miss Prout.

'Do me the favour of not writing about us. We like to keep ourselves to ourselves. But I,' said Phryne, 'am fascinated with this magazine world. Tell me about it. Is it always like it was today?'

Miss Prout took a vengeful gulp of her drink. The fact that she did not gasp at the strength of it was interesting. 'Yes, it's always like that. Me trying to make the mag more popular, Mrs Charlesworth trying to drag us back into the Middle Ages. She wants to make us a suffragist tract, no fun, no gossip. She only lets fashion notes in because the readers like it. She doesn't approve of it.'

'The same could be said for Hilda and her flower fairies,' said Phryne.

'Oh, well, yes, no one can really like that stuff, but the readers do, and it's well known that readers have no taste.'

'But they'd like the gossip and the film news,' prompted Phryne carefully.

'Of course. Everyone likes gossip, it's a natural human desire. People in Mrs Charlesworth's Middle Ages were probably listening with their ear to the castle wall, trying to get the latest on Guinevere and Lancelot. There's nothing wrong with giving the readers what they want!'

'Provided they want what you have to provide,'

said Phryne, picking up her fork.

'Well, of course.' Miss Prout looked at her cold collation. Someone had gone to considerable trouble to make curls in the celery and roses out of radishes and even the tomatoes were cut into interesting shapes. The ham was made into little scrolls, decorated with salad cream and capers. 'This isn't lunch, Miss Fisher. It's a work of art.'

'They say the first bite is with the eye,' said Phryne.

'It seems like sacrilege to eat it.'

'Go ahead,' urged her friend. 'There'll be tears before bedtime if you appreciate it so much that it goes back untouched. Apropos of gossip, aren't there gossip magazines? And, come to think of it, film magazines, and American "True Confessions" magazines. Why do you want to import them into *Women's Choice?*'

'A lot of women can't bring themselves to buy a magazine that is just about gossip. A respectable lady can't be seen reading *The Hawklet* in the street. Husbands would object to their money being spent on *True Confessions*. But a magazine that gives them that vicarious thrill – all right, I'm admitting it's a thrill – and still has a nice cover and some recipes for baked trout would pass unnoticed.'

'Miss Prout, why not go and work for *Table Talk?* Why this crusade to change *Women's Choice?*'

'Because I want to save it. New magazines will spring up with just this combination of gossip and recipes, and then *Women's Choice* will go the way of the dodo. It's a worthy mag with a lot of things to say which ought to be said. It can keep its famous historical homes and its book reviews and its articles on companionate marriage. And on birth control and "Divorce: By a Woman Barrister". But unless we sweeten the message a little, the readers will go elsewhere and all our work will be wasted. Anyway, Mrs Charlesworth's lying when she says such stuff will not sully her pristine magazine.'

The stiff drink was having the effect of loosening Miss Prout's tongue, at least. Phryne ate capers and murmured encouragingly.

'She's allowed the "Is This Problem Yours?" page. There's not a lot of difference between that and *True Confessions*. We only print the relatively quiet ones but we've had letters which would curl your hair. Women have written to Artemis about rape and divorce and horrible happenings. I don't know how Miss L ... Artemis stood it. Stands it... It's like having a sewer emptied on the desk. Revolting. And Mrs Charlesworth talks about poison! It's already out there, people doing things to children and women dying of ... illegal operations, and...'

'Yes. But I rather think that Mrs Charlesworth's point is that it should stay out there, not come into her nice clean office.'

'But still,' said Miss Prout, who had cleared her plate, 'it's rather exciting. To think that there are people – women – who do such things.'

Phryne's sympathy for Miss Prout was evaporating rapidly. Her fascination with the wickedness of the world was jejune and she would undoubtedly be a leading light in any true confessions magazine, inciting the readers to commit more sins so that Miss Prout could vicariously (of course) enjoy them. And the readers, not Miss Prout, would endure the consequences and Miss Prout would point the moral and adorn the tale.

'Who is Artemis?' she asked abruptly. 'You started to say Miss L and then stopped.'

'I meant...' Miss Prout thought frantically, 'I meant Miss Herbert, of course, but that's a dead secret. I'll be fired if they find out that I told you. And you mustn't mention it to her,' added Miss Prout cunningly. 'No one's supposed to know.'

'Of course,' Phryne agreed. 'No one will know from me, I assure you. If you'll excuse me for a moment, Miss Prout, I see a friend of mind over there. Back in a tick,' said Phryne. 'This may amuse you in my absence.'

From the sideboard she collected a bundle of scandal sheets from London, dropped them on Miss Prout's table, and walked quickly away, behind the fountain.

'Bunji, old thing, how lovely to see you. The Tasmanian flight went well?'

Bunji Ross, dressed in a frock in honour of her visit to Melbourne instead of her usual flying leathers, grinned amicably around a spoonful of Charlotte Russe.

'Hello, old bean! Flight went like a dream. Bit of a tricky landing but we got them back. Nasty place to shipwreck, the south coast of Tassie. You look a bit frayed, Phryne. Have a drink?'

'Thanks, I can't. Got a job on a women's magazine for a bit. I'll explain later.' Phryne patted Bunji's shoulder and went back to collect Miss Prout. She detached her with some difficulty from the scandals of London, and went back to

Women's Choice in some confusion of mind.

Miss Herbert as the guide philosopher and friend of "Is This Problem Yours?"? Miss Herbert of the inappropriate make-up, devoted heart and soul to the pursuit of fashion? Phryne didn't think so.

'What's that great bundle of fabric?' asked Miss Herbert, kicking a little away as she sat down with Hilda and the flower fairies.

'My Worth dress. I'll hang it up,' said Phryne. 'I thought we might do a special feature on re-modelling old clothes. If, of course, we can per-suade Mrs McAlpin to do the photographs for us.'

'What do you have in mind?' asked the elderly woman, picking up a pencil and a layout pad.

'We start with this ball dress, circa 1908. It cost me three quid. It's a couture model. Put it on a stand for the first photograph.'

'Never makes much impact, clothes on stands. Why not dress someone like Miss Herbert in it to show how it ought to look on the person?' asked Mrs McAlpin. 'Then we can show it being remodelled and cut down, and then a big picture of Miss Herbert in the finished product.'

'Sounds good,' said Phryne. Miss Herbert was struck dumb. She blushed and faltered, 'But you can't... I mean, I'm not a model.'

'Even better. We can save money on a model and we can show a dress on a real woman, not a painted doll,' said Mrs McAlpin flatly. 'Don't argue, Miss Herbert. Miss Fisher's idea will do, yes, it will do. Who will handle the remodelling?'

'Madame Fleuri,' said Phryne. 'I'm sure she'd

be tickled pink. Nothing a French dressmaker likes more than the chance to save a little money by ingenuity. We'll have to get rid of all that torn net, but the beading is magnificent. Well, that's settled.'

'Indeed. We might even have the fashion feature ready for the next month before this month's is done, which is, let me tell you, Miss Fisher, unheard of in our profession. Well, I must be off. Miss Nelson? Can you take the tripod? And the slides? Good.'

'Where are you going?' asked Phryne.

'To try and get a good picture of the St Paul's stained glass. I'm hoping that with a reasonably empty church, a long exposure and a strong afternoon light, we might actually manage an impression of them. Miss Nelson is going with me as my assistant. Someone else will have to get afternoon tea. Well, goodbye for now. Nice idea, Miss Fisher. Really quite a nice idea indeed.'

Still looking like a Ladies' Auxiliary worker, Mrs McAlpin hefted her camera in its case and followed her tripod out of the room. They heard her reproving Miss Nelson for banging the tripod against the stairs in the calm, concerned tone used by a nursery governess to a fractious child.

'Have we got any of Mrs McAlpin's photographs?' asked Phryne.

'Over there,' said Miss Herbert, still pink with mingled joy and fear. Miss Alice Herbert! A model! In a national magazine! But what would her mother say?

Phryne saw three large photographs on the far wall. One was of a burning house. Dark shadows of people were running in front of the flames. A man was being held back by three others as he strove to run back into the fire. A small child clutched a struggling cat in its arms. Water from a fire hose arced across the leaping pattern of flames. It was fierce, immediate and tragic. But what sort of cool mind could adjust a tripod and consider lenses while that was happening in front of her?

The second was a study of the waterfront. The huge blurry side of a liner formed one boundary of the photograph. Against it was a moving tide of immigrants, some running to embrace their relatives, some collecting luggage, looking at watches, patting their hair and calling after scampering children, intoxicated with all that space after weeks of being onboard. Just at the forefront was a man. He had a European overcoat down to his heels and a carefully brushed hat which had seen better years. At his feet was a leather suitcase with polished brass locks and a handle mended with string. He seemed young. The curve of cheek and shiny-bare chin seen under the hat brim were taut, even hungry. He was looking down at a piece of paper in his gloved hand.

Phryne blinked. She had been approached by such men, fresh off Station Pier, with almost no English, who thrust forward a bit of paper with an address on it and said, 'Miss? Plis?' That address, usually in Canton, was their only link with someone who might help them in an entirely alien land. What a photograph. Achingly vulnerable, but proud and hopeful.

The third picture was taken from a hill. It

73

showed the broad, out-of-focus sweep of a bay, somewhere like Queenscliff or maybe Portsea. The arms of the bay embraced the beach on which children were playing. The light was soft, hazy, protective. The naked babies toddled down to the edge of the kindly sea with their buckets and spades, watched by doting mothers and fathers reclining on blankets. It told a whole story. They would play in the sea until the sun grew too hot. Then they would retreat into the shade of small, cement sheet houses and eat a salad lunch and drowse away the afternoon in the scent of ozone and eucalyptus. The evening would bring a sausage and chop grill cooked over an open fire, or fish if anyone had caught some, and a few beers until the night grew cool enough for a walk by the sea, and so to bed and sleep tight.

Oh, she was a good photographer, Mrs Mc-Alpin. She was a magician with a lens. What on earth was she doing working for *Women's Choice?*

Meanwhile, thought Phryne with vast reluctance, back to 'Hilda and the Flower Fairies'.

Hilda was walking in the garden one day when she heard a little voice crying, 'Oh my, what shall I do?'

Being a good little girl and always willing to help others, Hilda knelt down and said, 'What is the matter?'

'Oh my, what shall I do?' cried the little voice. 'My rabbit has his foot caught in a snare, and I will never get to the ball!'

'Show me,' said Hilda, brushing her golden curls out of her cornflower eyes. Under a rhubarb plant she saw the tiniest, sweetest little bunny with his foot caught in

74

a cruel horrid snare. He was panting with effort, but he could not remove the noose which had bitten deep into his poor little paw.

'Let me help,' said Hilda. She worked at the wire with her pink fat little fingers until it loosened and the bunny could pull his paw free.

'But he is lame and I'll never get to the ball!' cried the little voice passionately.

'Let me help,' said Hilda. She searched around the garden until she found some dock leaves, which she wrapped around the bunny's paw and healed him instantly.

'Now he is all better,' said Hilda. 'Show yourself please. Who are you?'

'I'm the fairy of the bottle brush,' said the little voice. Onto Hilda's hand floated the smallest fairy, dressed in a sparkling tutu of brightest red.

'You are the beautifullest thing I've ever seen,' said Hilda.

'Then you shall go to the ball, too,' said the fairy. She waved her wand. Hilda shrank to the fairy's size.

Then she waved the wand again, and Hilda was dressed in palest petals, pink and white.

'Almond blossom,' said the bottle brush fairy. 'And now we must go to the ball,' she said. She clapped her hands. Several fairies rushed to harness the bunny. Hilda climbed into the carriage made from a walnut shell and the bunny hopped away to the ball.

'Beautifullest,' murmured Phryne.

'Bunnies,' said Miss Prout.

'Oh, well.' Phryne summed up the dead woman's effort: 'I'm sure that she meant well.'

The subsequent hour was spent arguing with a

printer who could not see why he should have to use photogravure when plate would do just as well and in helping Miss Phillips transport her broken china to the carrier, with an apologetic note to the manufacturer and a draft of a rather fulsome review.

CHAPTER SIX

When one's resting is like that of the back and he loses all consciousness of self.

Hexagram 52: Khan
The I Ching Book of Changes

As Phryne was restoring herself after her encounters with whimsy and printers with a cup of strong tea and a ginger biscuit, Miss Grigg looked up from her rewiring of what seemed to be transformer, tucked her screwdriver behind her ear and growled, 'Mrs Charlesworth wants to see you, when you've finished, Miss Fisher.' Phryne nodded and knocked on Mrs Charlesworth's door. It swung open. The editress was almost buried under drawings of furniture. She fought her way to the surface with a vigorous arm movement reminiscent of breaststroke, sending a pile of them to the floor with a swooshing thud.

'Miss Fisher?' she said. 'What can I do for you?'

'Miss Grigg said that you wanted me,' said Phryne, gathering up an armload of paper, stacking it and placing it on the chair. Mrs Charlesworth picked up a pencil, looked at it as though she had never seen one before, then put it down.

'Now what did I want to see you about? Ah, yes. We've had a little emergency, and one of our features has rather fallen through. I have approved Miss Herbert's slant on the fashion notes – quite satisfactory.' Her tone implied that for a dirty, useless, unpleasant job, Phryne had done it really much better than Mrs Charlesworth had expected of such an intelligent woman. 'And it was nice of you to distract Miss Prout. She yearns for glamour, you know. Just as addictive as cocaine, and far more pervasive. Poor Miss Prout! Destined to disappointment.'

'Why?' asked Phryne, automatically scooping up another load of papers and ordering them.

'Because her aims are impossible. No real woman can ever be as beautiful as those film women. No real woman can afford to spend all her time on personal adornment, diet, massage, make-up, hairdressing, and of course, complaisant photographers. She is a purveyor of grinding, ingrown envy.'

Phryne hadn't thought of Miss Prout's philosophy in that manner.

'That is a point of view,' she said, cautiously.

'Hmm? Oh yes, Miss Fisher, can you ask that policeman at Miss Lavender's cottage to release a box of letters to us? Some of them concern this magazine.'

'A box of letters?' Phryne repeated.

'Yes. Or possibly a portfolio of them. We have a feature called "Is This Problem Yours?" and Miss

Lavender was kind enough to...'

'Answer them for you?'

'I really couldn't say,' said Mrs Charlesworth, looking Phryne straight in the eye without blushing.

'I can ask,' said Phryne.

'Thank you. I believe Miss Gallagher was looking for you,' said Mrs Charlesworth, returning to her papers.

Phryne went out. Barefaced fibbing of such a high order, she reflected, was only to be expected in such a complex profession as Mrs Charlesworth's.

'Do try one of these,' said Gally, thrusting a tray of savouries at Phryne. 'You're my taster. The others are all full.'

Phryne surveyed the treats on display. Miss Gallagher expounded on them.

'Aigrettes of cheese – bit mustardy, I fear – angels on horseback, cheese straws, anchovy croutes and prune surprises.'

'What's surprising about the prunes?' asked Phryne warily.

'Half a devilled walnut instead of the stone,' said Gally. 'Well, perhaps it's not a *big* surprise.'

Phryne took a cheese straw. It was sharp and crisp. She said so. Miss Gallagher wriggled with pleasure and clutched the bosom of her frilly starched apron.

'So many of our readers give little tea parties or small dinner parties,' she said. 'These don't take too long to make and they stimulate...' she looked up at Phryne through her lashes '...the appetite. Have another?'

'No, really, I've had a big lunch. Try Miss Grigg, she's working hard.'

Miss Gallagher pouted. Fortunately, at that moment a wailing voice was heard on the stairs.

'Want an ice. Want an ice! Want an ice cream!'

The voice was familiar. This must be Mrs Opie's little angel, Wendy.

'Want an ice cream *now*,' the voice elaborated as well as any trade unionist, making her demands perfectly clear and, by the sound of it, about to stage a sit-down strike if the management did not produce the required ice cream, and that right speedily.

Excellent, thought Phryne. I wonder what Mrs Opie will say when she sees me again?

Mrs Opie was too occupied with attempting to arbitrate her daughter's demands. By the sound of her weary, irritated tones the management was getting exasperated by this continual reiteration and was about to suggest no ice cream and a spanking if the delegate did not resume co-operation with the stated aims of the company. 'You can't hold me to ransom like this, Wendy,' said Mrs Opie, confirming Phryne's fantasy and forcing her to stifle a chuckle.

'Oh Lord, it's that rotten child again,' snarled Miss Prout.

'You don't like children?' asked Phryne, always an inflammatory comment to make to anyone of the female persuasion, and always to be answered in the negative. Phryne had friends who would dare dangerous mountains and perilous love affairs, but not one of them would dare to say, as Phryne did, that she didn't like children. It was one of the few things that Could Not Be Said by a Woman.

'Of course I like children, but not that child,' said Miss Prout.

Miss Grigg grunted. 'She's all right, if you remember that all children are solipsists. Little Wendy is as self-centred as a pendulum which, as you will remember, always passes under its point of origin. Stuff the little wretch with enough ice cream and she becomes positively civil. Deny her her ice cream and she carries on like a two-bob watch. She's all right away from her mother. At least she knows what she wants,' she added, with a sidelong glance at Miss Gallagher. 'Eh, Gally?'

'Nonsense, she's a perfectly adorable...'

At that moment Wendy erupted into the office, red-faced and screaming, hitting Miss Gallagher at about knee height and causing her to drop the tray, broadcasting savouries all over the surrounding area.

'...little monster!' shrieked Miss Gallagher.

'Wendy, please,' begged her distraught mother.

Wendy paid no attention but continued to ullulate like the cannibals in a pirate adventure book. Phryne had the beginnings of the headache she always got from drinking gin at lunch and was in no mood for trifling. She moved until she was looking Wendy full in the reddened, tearless eyes.

'Wendy,' said Phryne flatly. 'Come here, sit down, be silent and I will buy you an ice cream. Continue to scream and you'll get no ice cream from me.'

The uncontrollable scream was instantly controlled. The child eyed Phryne with equal coolness, still panting. Her blonde hair, so like her mother's, flopped over her forehead, which was wet with sweat. The child had worked herself into a passion and her control over herself was remarkable.

'When?'

'Fifteen minutes from now. You can watch the clock if you like. When the big hand is at the top and the small hand is on the four. Not before. Not after.'

'All right,' said Wendy. She sat down on a chair and composed herself into the very picture of a good girl, hands folded in lap, golden hair flowing from her Alice band, feet in her patent ankle strap shoes, not kicking. If she had not seen the dervish who had entered the office, Phryne would have believed that she was sitting for 'My First Sermon'.

Phryne picked up her cup and realised that the rest of the office was staring at her. Jaws had dropped. Pencils had fallen from nerveless hands.

'How did you do that?' asked Miss Prout, distracted even from the scandal sheet she was reading under the desk.

'Yes, how did you?' asked Miss Herbert, swallowing to regain her hearing. 'Usually she goes on like that for hours.'

'Beginner's luck?' hazarded Phryne.

'Of course, you didn't get to see the bit where she throws herself on the floor and turns blue,' said Miss Grigg, commiserating with Phryne that she had missed this special treat.

'Thank heaven,' said Mrs Opie. 'I don't know how you did this, Miss Fisher, but I'm very grateful, and what ... I mean, I didn't know you... Are you visiting?'

'Just helping out with the fashion,' said Phryne. Mrs Opie looked in need of a cup of tea and a sit-down. Actually she looked in need of a stiff drink, a good tonic and two weeks at some serviceable spa. Miss Prout provided the tea and the chair and Mrs Opie sat down, took off her hat, and shoved her hair back from her face.

'Printer's waiting for your piece, Mrs Opie,' said Miss Herbert. 'Mrs Charles was asking after it this morning.'

'Well, it's finished at last. "Your Child". That's funny, isn't it? Here I am giving advice to mothers who are probably twice as good as I am.'

Her voice was rising in pitch and Phryne began to suspect whence Wendy got her temperament. The other women were also reacting to the warning signals. Miss Prout supplied a handkerchief and Miss Grigg reached into her office drawer and produced a bottle of white tablets.

'Aspirin,' she told Phryne. 'Calms the nerves.'

'What about Nutrax Nerve Food?' asked Phryne. A poster on the wall informed her that it was sovereign for all afflictions, mood changes, insomnia and other nerve troubles.

'Tried it,' said Miss Grigg. 'Don't tell Salus, but aspirin works better. Here we are, Mrs Opie. Chug a lug,' encouraged Miss Grigg.

Mrs Opie swallowed the tablets and sat still for a moment. Then she rummaged in a large, shabby straw bag and produced three pages of tightly written script.

'Damnation, Helen, haven't you typed it?' exclaimed Miss Herbert. 'I hope you're not expecting me to do it for you.'

'Why not? Miss Fisher's just written your fashion notes,' put in Miss Phillips.

'And you've just finished your article on china decoration,' Miss Herbert shot back.

Miss Phillips bit her lip. 'Yes, but I haven't typed mine yet, while you've got yours all down pat,' she answered.

'You have so typed it. I packed the box with the draft in it,' chipped in Miss Prout. 'You really are so lazy, Phillips! I don't know why you bother to turn up.'

'And why you want to drag this magazine down into that slime you're always reading, I can't imagine...'

The action, Phryne thought, was about to become general. Everyone was tired and the nearness of the printer's deadline had exacerbated the ordinary tensions of the office. Miss Phillips was now shouting at Miss Prout. In about three minutes, it would be any woman's fight. She cast a quelling eye on young Wendy, in case she felt that this might be a good time to demonstrate the tantrum deluxe. The child was paying no attention at all to the argument. Her eyes were fixed on the clock. Grown-up disputes, Wendy clearly felt, were common, but ice cream was ice cream.

Phryne's headache had not improved.

'Ladies,' she began. Her tone was so authoritative that the combatants were distracted from their dissection of each other's character, aspirations, morals and family background.

'I know that you have a lot to do, with the deadline so close. I'm sure you don't want to disturb Mrs Charlesworth. She did say that she had an editorial to write.'

'Oh Lord, is she still writing that?' asked Miss Prout. 'She said she'd sack anyone who interrupted her.'

'And she looks like a lady of her word. Now can everyone just shut up and bung over that aspirin?' said Phryne.

'Right away,' said Miss Grigg, grinning.

'Toss for it?' said Miss Phillips to Miss Herbert.

Miss Herbert lost, but had the consolation that the person in a remodelled Worth in next month's fashion notes would not be Miss Phillips.

'I'll be back,' said Phryne, putting on her hat.

'Why, where are you going?' asked Mrs Opie.

'I am taking Wendy for her ice cream,' said Phryne, a little surprised. The clock ticked over onto four and Wendy got up, adjusted her socks, pushed back her hair and came to take Phryne's hand, the picture of childish innocence.

'Oh, but you needn't...' began Mrs Opie. The insight which that statement gave Phryne into Mrs Opie's child-rearing methods explained a lot about Wendy.

'I promised,' she replied. Wendy preceded her and Phryne closed the door on Mrs Opie deciphering her handwriting for a puzzled Miss Herbert.

'It's an m,' she was saying. 'M for maternal.'

Out in the crowded, sunny street, Wendy so far forgot her preoccupation as to skip a few paces.

'What sort of ice cream do you require?' asked Phryne.

'Chocolate,' replied the child. 'And chocolate over.'

'A child of decided tastes,' said Phryne. She led the way to a milk bar and purchased a double chocolate with chocolate on top. Wendy accepted it with royal condescension and applied herself to eating. She nibbled the chocolate coating off first, Phryne observed, then licked the cone from the sides so that it would not drip. To this the child gave all the attention due to a religious ritual, and Phryne did not interrupt her. Finally she had nibbled the cone right down to the bottom. She gave a satisfied sigh.

'Mummy said I'd have ice cream then she forgot,' said Wendy.

'I see,' said Phryne.

'Because Daddy got cross,' said Wendy.

'Did he?'

'Then Mummy cried.'

'Did she? Like you?'

'No. Not like me. Sad,' said Wendy, turning down the corners of her mouth. 'And talked about her Giovanni. She says she should have married him, not Daddy.'

'Whereas you're not sad, are you? You're cross. That's why you scream,' said Phryne, wishing to squash any further familial revelations.

'Mmm,' agreed Wendy, a little disconcerted.

'You'll get better results if you don't scream,' Phryne suggested. Wendy shook her head.

'Oh. Yes, of course. Unless you scream no one notices you, do they?'

Phryne had no idea of how much, if any, of this conversation Wendy understood. Possibly most of it. She was what Mrs Butler would call an uncanny child.

'Come along,' she said.

Wendy dug in her heels. 'Want to stay here with you,' she said mutinously.

'Sorry. You can't always get what you want by screaming. And if you wish to scream, go ahead. But I am going back, and so are you,' said Phryne quietly.

Blue eyes met green ones. Steely will met steely will. But Phryne had had twenty more years of being determined. The child took her hand. Not defeated. Momentarily outclassed.

Back at the office Wendy, her raging addiction satisfied for the time being, sat down with Miss Phillips's collection of waste paper and began to draw peacefully. Mrs Opie gave up trying to decipher her script and dictated her piece on 'Your Child' extempore. Phryne watched Miss Prout laying out pages for the printer.

It was most interesting. The typed text was cut into pieces and glued to the layout page, which was the size of the finished product.

'See, we use demi folio with a one-inch margin,' said Miss Prout, scissoring around a sketch and gluing it firmly in place. The printer uses this as his guide, so it has to be right. No wobbly edges, no unruled headings, and never – horror of horrors – any unused space. Just down here I'm going to put the Laurel kerosene ad. It makes a perfect margin. Useful stuff, kerosene. Australians employ it for everything from cleaning off oil stains to treating tonsillitis.'

'That would certainly cure one of ever wanting

to have tonsillitis again,' said Phryne. The page grew under Miss Prout's expert touch.

'And Laurel have been great supporters. We need the advertising fees to fund the day-to-day running of the magazine. The subscribers pay for the production and distribution and sometimes we even have a little over. Feel like taking an advert, Miss Fisher?'

'Not today, thank you,' said Phryne, trying to watch everyone in the office at once. How would they react to the revelation of Phryne's trade which was about to be made by the loquacious Miss Prout?

'Why would Miss Fisher want an advert?' asked Miss Phillips. 'That's really very good, Wendy. What is it?'

'A horse,' replied Wendy with deep scorn.

'Oh yes, so it is.'

'You're holding it upside down!' cried the child. Phryne looked at her. She subsided. This woman held ice cream or no ice cream in the palm of her powerful hand. Wendy had discovered religious awe and was silent in the presence of the goddess.

'Why, she's a private detective, she's the famous Phryne Fisher who retrieved the Spanish Ambassador's son's kitten, and broke the cocaine ring, and found the kidnapped child of that lottery winner,' said Miss Prout loudly.

'It was nothing, really,' murmured Phryne modestly.

Interesting. Miss Phillips looked mildly intrigued, Mrs Opie was staggered, Miss Grigg likewise and Miss Gallagher, who in any case, having gathered her scorned savouries, had retired to the kitchen to sulk. Miss Herbert was fascinated. But Mrs McAlpin, returning from the cathedral, looked amazed and Miss Nelson dropped the tripod she was carrying with a crash.

'You really are a clumsy creature,' observed Mrs McAlpin evenly. 'Pick it up, do, and lay it against the wall where no one can trip over it. You're a private detective, Miss Fisher? How on earth did you become so?'

'Largely chance,' Phryne told her. 'I found out I had a talent for solving puzzles. That kitten, for instance, had merely followed its nose into a fishmarket and had been locked in. I just had to find the nearest source of fish and there it was. Cold, of course, and covered in scales, but perfectly all right. Just a matter of understanding human nature – or feline nature, in that case. How did the photography go?'

'I shall know when I get to my darkroom. I've taken six plates, that should be enough. But it was an experiment. I varied the shutter speed. Such a luxury.'

'What's a luxury?' asked Phryne.

'There we are, Miss Nelson, you can take that down to the printer. Are you all right?' asked Miss Prout. Miss Nelson was flushed and shaking.

'Oh, I'm all right, just the stairs are a bit steep. Give me your layout, Miss Prout, I'll take it right away,' said the girl breathlessly. She grabbed the rolled sheet and vanished.

There goes a guilty conscience, thought Phryne. I wonder what she's guilty about? Nothing worse than nicking more than her share of coconut macaroons, perhaps? Or something more?

'The luxury is having as many plates as I need to get the photograph I envisage. They're very expensive. Not as many plates as I want, of course. No photographer ever has as many plates as she wants. But as many as I need.'

'Paid for by *Women's Choice?*' asked Phryne.

'Yes, dear, of course. I'm the photographer. If I've got the perfect shot for the mag's purposes, I can use the rest on what I want to take.'

'You're very good,' said Phryne. 'I've been looking at your work.'

'Thank you,' said Mrs McAlpin, as though she had been complimented on the brilliance of her Harvest Festival flower arrangement. She sat down and folded her hands in her lap.

'You are about to ask me how I became a photographer,' she said placidly. 'Fair enough, since I asked you a personal question first. Well, there were all these photographic magazines in the attic at my father's manse, you see, and because I was often a bad child I used to be shut in the attic and told not to come out until I was ready to be good.'

'Ah, the child-rearing practices of yesteryear,' said Mrs Opie. 'Two m's in commendable, Miss Herbert, if you please. Responsible for so many neuroses.'

'Possibly,' agreed Mrs McAlpin dryly. 'But in this case, I was so fascinated by the photography magazines that I often didn't come down at all and had to be fetched and forgiven. My father, God rest his soul, thought that I was truly penitent. I'm not sure that I didn't manufacture naughtinesses so as to be banished to the attic, either. Anyway, I read all I could, and then I needed a camera. Fortunately, my brother had bought one and most of the equipment but had lost interest when he found out how difficult it was. Those old cameras were so slow – the exposures were three and four seconds – which accounts for the strained look on the faces of most of the portraits. I scrimped and scrimped from my dress allowance and bought plates and chemicals.'

'Didn't your family disapprove?'

'Not really, dear, they weren't really interested. They thought it was just a fad and I'd get over it when I married, as gels were supposed to do in those days. Ladies, you know, used to paint in watercolours and do poker-work and make fire-screens with tapestry depictions of Landseer dogs on them – terrible, time-wasting, time-killing rubbish. All their descendants flung the stuff on the bonfire as soon as they were safely dead. I wasn't going to fritter away my time on making bobbin-lace which no one would wear. My mother was furious when she found out how the acids stain the hands, but Father just smiled and said that I had to have something to amuse myself with, so she made me wear gloves on all social occasions. My first real photograph was of an oak tree. I still recall the thrill as I saw it develop in the rocker.'

'Perhaps photography has more rewards than painting,' Phryne observed. 'More immediate.'

'As a medium it is instant,' said Mrs McAlpin.

90

'One can spend hours setting up the shot, fussing about the angle, messing about with the focus. Then just as one whips the shutter open, the light changes, or some idiot walks in front of the lens. Anything can go wrong, even a wobble in the tripod. And, of course, one doesn't know how it is going to look until it is developed, and then it is never what one has actually seen. This theory that the camera never lies is false. The picture is never what a human eye sees, what a human mind interprets. And, of course, if it is ruined, one cannot do it again. The moment has gone.'

'Frustrating,' commented Phryne.

'Yes, but fascinating,' Mrs McAlpin smiled. 'The very first magazine had an article which began, "Now we can paint pictures with light". The phrase took my fancy.'

'And do you find your art improves with experience?' asked Phryne.

'Oh yes, dear, the best photographers are old ones. The equipment is improving all the time, the shutter speeds are faster, the plates more reliable, the cameras themselves are smaller and lighter. But beginning on those old, heavy, slow cameras was a great apprenticeship,' said Mrs McAlpin. 'They taught patience.'

'And Mother must never forget that Baby does not understand how she is feeling,' dictated Mrs Opie. 'I said, "Mother must never forget", Miss Herbert, not "always forget". Can't you try to get it right?'

'And patience,' said Mrs McAlpin, 'is a virtue.'

The day moved on to its close. Typewriters were covered. Ashtrays were emptied. Miss Nel-

91

son returned, collected her bag, and left, creeping down the steps like a mouse. Miss Grigg completed her rewiring, attached the machine to a small electric construction, and grinned as the machine whirred into life. Miss Herbert abandoned Mrs Opie's piece when it appeared that she would have to find the last page, having brought along a sheet of instructions on how to prepare banana fool instead of 'Your Child'. Mrs Charlesworth emerged in a smart hat and bade the office go home and come back tomorrow bright and early.

'Really must go, ladies,' said Phryne. 'Until tomorrow.'

She breezed out. As soon as she emerged onto the street she was immediately placed in a 'come along o' me' grip by a worried policeman.

CHAPTER SEVEN

Wei Yi intimates progress and success. We see a young fox that has nearly crossed the stream when its tail gets immersed.

Hexagram 64: Wei Yi
The I Ching Book of Changes

'Hello, Jack, dear! Are you arresting me?' asked Phryne, casting a significant glance at the hand closed on her upper arm. Robinson removed it.

'Sorry. We've just got the results on that postmortem,' he said, his unexceptionable face lined with worry. 'It's murder, all right, though I can't imagine how it was done. Or rather, there are far too many ways it could have been done.'

'What sort of unnatural death got meted out to the fairy lady?' asked Phryne patiently.

'Poison,' said Robinson. 'Prussic acid.'

'Ah, yes, that would explain the blue face,' said Phryne. 'So it's a murder investigation, now?'

'Yes, and thanks to that blasted doctor being so low on the uptake, all the evidence has got mucked up and the scene of the crime's been trampled over by half the inhabitants of Melbourne.' Robinson pulled bitterly at his hat brim.

'Never mind, Jack, dear. When we find out how, we may well know who. Was the prussic acid ingested?'

'Or inhaled. It dissipates rapidly in the bloodstream. I wish old Keats hadn't retired. This new young bloke isn't half as clever as he thinks he is.'

'You've collected all the food, plates, glasses, toothpaste, gin and so on from Wee Nooke?' asked Phryne.

'Of course. They're still being tested.'

'That's a good start. Now, I've been talking all day with the main actors in this little domestic drama. So far I haven't managed to bring the conversation around to Miss Lavender. I'll try tomorrow. But the editress, Mrs Charlesworth, asked me to ask you if she can have a box of letters which might belong to the magazine.'

'I suppose so,' said Jack.

'No,' said Phryne. 'You suppose not. You turn all constabulary and Tribune of the People on me and tell me firmly that everything found at the scene of the crime is evidence and she can't have them. *Répétez, s'il vous plait.*'

'I'm afraid that everything at the scene of a crime is evidence and cannot be released,' said Jack Robinson obediently.

'*Bon!* And a determined lady editress of a women's magazine won't change your mind?' asked Phryne sweetly.

Jack quailed a little but said, 'Sorry, madam. It's the law.'

'Very good. Stick to that like a good 'un.'

'Why?' asked Robinson. 'What's in the letters?'

'I don't know,' said Phryne. 'But I mean to spend this evening finding out.'

'We've got statements from all the people in the house,' said Robinson. 'But they don't say much. Nice lady, kept to herself, pity about her mania for fairies but each to his own, etc. Now we'll have to find out all about Miss Lavender – who she knew, where she came from, where she went...'

'And who hated her enough to kill her. Well, there is a fine selection of suspects in *Women's Choice,* though, as I said, I haven't talked about Miss Lavender yet.'

'You've been there a whole day,' said Robinson. 'What've you been doing?'

'Teaching them about style,' said Miss Fisher.

'You'd know,' agreed Robinson. 'But see if you can get something out of them tomorrow. My chief's going crook. Reckons if we can't come up with something soon the press'll get hold of it and there'll be hell to pay. I've got a young con- stable finding out all the usual details, birth certificate, that sort of thing.'

'All right, Jack, dear, I'll see what I can do.'

Phryne refrained from patting the Detective Inspector on the cheek in deference to the *Public Order Act* 1912, and took herself home on the tram.

Which one of the people in the house or the magazine would make a good murderer?

Access to the house was easy. One could just walk along the tunnel from the tennis court and emerge into the garden. From there one could infiltrate the house and spike any strongly flavoured comestible with prussic acid, which dissolved readily. It tasted and smelt of bitter almonds, but in Miss Lavender's highly scented house an almond smell wouldn't make a dent. In fact, it would just intensify the general aroma, because she used sweet almond oil in those lamp sleeves.

Lin Chung had shown her how to produce an ambient scent with a lamp sleeve. Where was he? His family were clearly worried about him. If they hadn't been worried about him Phryne would never have been allowed alone into the Lin family mansion, much less sold extra fine quality silk for a pittance. He could have sent her a postcard of Stanley market or the Peak from Hong Kong, at least, where the mails worked with British regularity. Phryne was incubating a nasty suspicion that something might have happened to Lin Chung which even the presence of a Shao Lin monk could not prevent.

Still, nothing to be done for the present. The tram clacked busily past the barracks and she dragged her mind away from the picture of his face and on to a consideration of other faces. So. The murderer got to Miss Lavender before the maid came with her breakfast on the Sunday morning. But it would be no use finding out where everyone was on Saturday, because if the poison had been put in, say, the corner of the toothpowder tin or in some staple in the kitchen, it might linger there for weeks until Miss Lavender found a need for vanillan sugar, drank the last of the lemon cordial or ate the last piece of cake. Indeed, one could inject cyanide solution into a raisin in a jar of raisins and then settle back, secure in the knowledge that, sooner or later, Miss Lavender would write her last episode of 'Hilda and the Flower Fairies', eat a few raisins as a celebration, and suddenly die.

Drat. The field was wide open. It would have to be a matter of finding out why, and then possibly one might ascertain how.

What were the usual reasons for murder? Greed. Passion. And in the case of the severely afflicted, of course, fun. Poisoners were usually women. They might start off by killing for a reason, but then they seemed to acquire an addiction and kept on. Phryne recalled Mary Anne Cotton, who, a century before Dr Stopes, might never have been a murderer if she had been fitted with a diaphragm. But she killed her children because she could not feed them, then a few husbands for the insurance, then more children. 'They get a taste for it,' Jack had said about one of his captives; a nice old lady who had wiped out half of her family and quite a few visitors by putting arsenic in their tea. No one would have thought of suspecting her until Jack Robinson, suspicious by both nature and calling, had distracted her attention and slipped the cuppa which the charming old lady had made for him into a providential jam jar. It had contained enough poison to slaughter an elephant. Unable to provide any reason, she was judged unfit to plead and had been taken happily away to a quiet institution for the criminally insane, where she sang hymns, knitted booties for the warders' children, and was never, never, allowed near the kitchen.

Cyanide acts by blocking the oxygen-carrying capacity of the blood. Thus the victim dies of suffocation. How volatile was it, Phryne wondered. I must get out Glaister when I get home. Perhaps it had to be put into the house within a certain time. That would be helpful.

Clack, clack, the tram groaned around the bend and Phryne lit a gasper, blowing smoke out between the legs of a strap-hanging clerk and enjoying his horrified expression. He was going to go home to his mother, Phryne knew, and tell her what he had seen on the tram today. A woman *smoking*. In public! Phryne hoped that it would lead to a productive discussion on the changing status of women, but knew it wouldn't.

Who might make a nice murderer in Miss Lavender's circle?

Mrs McAlpin? She had that strange photographer's detachment and access to poisons. Phryne understood that photography would provide the practitioner with a reason to buy cyanide. Another thing to check. Miss Herbert? Not unless murder had suddenly become the stylish woman's most modish accessory. Miss Prout? She certainly had the fanatical eyes of someone who might kill for a cause, but dragging *Women's Choice* into the twentieth century didn't seem to require the removal of Miss Lavender, though that would have to be investigated. Miss Nelson, the office girl, was certainly guilty about something, though what she had managed to get up to in sixteen blameless years was unlikely to concern the constabulary.

Mrs Opie wanted that letter back, whatever it was, and mothers had been known to be entirely ruthless if they perceived that their children were threatened. Phryne remembered the Parisian woman who had stabbed her assailant through the eye with great force. The skewer had actually pierced his skull. She was a sparrow-boned slavey who had been willing to lie down under a rapist to save her children, but when he said that he would kill her first and then them, she had taken a skewer and – snick. Not to protect herself – she didn't think she was worth protecting – but to protect them she would dare anything. '*Le bon papa capable du tout*' also applied to the *bonne mama*. Had Miss Lavender threatened anyone's children? If so, how? She had lived quietly and, apart from an unwise indulgence in whimsy, appeared unexceptionable as a neighbour.

Who else? Mrs Charlesworth could rid herself of her unwanted staff by firing them. Killing them did appear to be taking the new vigorous policy in industrial relations a little too far. Miss Phillips was an unknown quantity, except for her tendency to burst into tears, which seemed to indicate insufficient firmness of mind for such a cool, clever murder. Miss Gallagher had a flirtatious manner and a grumpy friend. Had a flirtation gone too far? Miss Grigg was strong enough to keep back a bull from staling, and Miss Gallagher might easily have taunted and teased her into doing something which she might later regret. She showed no signs of it however.

Perhaps Mr Bell had decided that someone who inflicted that many garden gnomes on the world was an enemy of humanity; and had taken condign action.

Phryne chuckled, butted out the gasper, and alighted from the tram with due regard for her stockings. St Kilda was simmering quietly in the strong sunlight. She might go for a bathe when she got home.

Just as she stepped out from the tram stop, a black car sped through a red light and passed so close to Phryne that the wind of it whipped off her hat. She swayed, grabbed the rail, and hauled herself to safety again.

'The hooligans!' exclaimed a woman behind her. 'They nearly ran over you!'

'So they did,' said Phryne. 'Did anyone see the number?'

'J something,' said a young man. 'Here's your hat, Miss. JV, I think.'

'Chinks,' said an old man's voice.

'Come along, Dad.' A harassed, middle-aged woman was leading an old man by the elbow. 'It wasn't Chinks, Dad.'

'Chinks, I say!' declaimed the old gentleman. 'I saw their slanty eyes. You can't trust 'em,' he added, as his daughter tried to steer him away.

'Don't pay any attention, Miss,' said the woman, grabbing at the old man and a straying toddler and dropping her shopping bag. 'He's been out in the East, see, and he sees Chinks everywhere these days. It don't mean nothing. Oh, come here, Elsie, do! Come along, Dad. Nice cup of tea at home. Not far now. I wouldn't usually take him out with the child,' she explained, 'but we had to go and get his eyes tested and my girl only comes in in the morning.'

'Of course.' Phryne recovered the shopping bag and hung it on the woman's arm, reattached the small child and smiled at the old man. This woman had more than enough to occupy her attention without Phryne insisting on names and addresses. The ancient gentleman was undoubtedly dotty. Even now he was reminiscing about the old days in Sarawak with dear old Brooke– 'Fine women, the Dyaks! Fine breasts! Like mangos!' – in a voice too loud for the street. His daughter was wincing with embarrassment and the toddler was whining to be carried.

Phryne put on her hat, thanked her helpers, and crossed the road. She was definitely going for a swim in the nice cold water.

But the double negative resounded in her mind. 'It don't mean nothing.' Which meant, of course, that it did mean something. Chinese? What reason would a Chinese person have for wanting to kill Phryne Fisher? An inch closer, and she would have been featured in a lecture from the Police Minister on Careless Driving Costs Lives. And, come to think of it, perhaps that flying bit of road metal had been an actual bullet.

The closeness of the escape sent a thrill of pure adrenalin through her. She felt more alive than she had for weeks. Something was moving.

She arrived home, collected her costume, bathing cap, sandshoes, adoptive daughters and a robe and crossed the road to the sea. Dot did not swim unless the temperature was over a hundred and the tide on the ebb. Jane and Ruth raced across the sand and into the water, shedding robes and Jane's glasses on the way. Phryne flung off her covering and ran, wading into the embrace of the cool water with relish, diving like a dolphin, only coming up occasionally for air. She set her sights on the horizon and began to swim for it, allowing the water to scour fear and sweat from her body.

She was a long way out when she turned and began to duck dive back, surprising a passing seal. For a moment it back-paddled as neatly as a rower, head out of the swell, whiskers quivering, its soft brown eyes and appealing wet nose exactly like those of a Labrador dog who had got lost from Labrador and stayed in the sea for a few thousand years. Phryne in her black bathing cap had caught its attention.

'Hello,' said Phryne affably.

The seal thought about it. Hmm... Moves like a seal. Same colour as a seal. Wrong kind of voice. Not a seal after all but – a human! It gave a snort and dived. Phryne ducked under to watch it flipper quickly away, leaving a broad margin around the human in case Phryne should suddenly manifest harpoons.

She was briefly saddened that it should be afraid of her, but charmed by the encounter.

Then she swam decorously back to where the girls were lying under a palm tree, discussing mathematics. Phryne leaned on the other side of the tree and listened.

It soon appeared that Jane was discussing mathematics and Ruth was thinking about something else.

'The Fibonacci Sequence,' said Jane, 'is expressed in a wavering line – plus one and minus one.'

'Mmm,' agreed Ruth. 'Were you listening in history when Taggs was going on about the Opium Wars?'

'Er … not really,' confessed Jane. 'I was thinking of the elegance of– '

'The Fibothingy sequence, yes. It's just that when Mr Lin told us about the Boxer Rebellion, he didn't put it like that. I mean, I don't remember him saying that the Great Powers were invited in to loot China and steal everything they could lay their hands on.'

'I bet Taggs didn't say that!' said Jane, abandoning her educational attempt. Ruth, despite her manifold virtues, would probably never understand the true beauty of numbers. Devoid of politics, of emotion, thought Jane, just pure ways of expressing the symmetry of the universe, a numerical law in the spiral of seeds in the centre of the sunflower. 'She would have said, "The Chinese were causing trouble and such was the indignation of the country that the government was forced to take forceful action in order to protect trade, the lifeblood of the British Empire. And every girl in this class may hope that she may do something to advance the cause of this most successful and just colonising and conquering Empire, which combines Empire and Liberty".'

'Well, all right, that's what she *said*,' conceded Ruth, 'but that's what the soldiers did. And they burned everything else.'

'That's how armies behave,' said Jane matter-of-factly. 'They kill people and destroy cities. Mr Lin would naturally have another view. It was his country they were looting and pillaging. And from the papers it is happening again. The Japanese have invaded Manchuria and have a puppet Emperor. The small generals are all fighting each other. Sun Yat Sen is dead and Chiang Kai Shek hasn't got enough people on his side, and then there are the Communists. And, you know, Ruthie...'

'You have been paying attention after all!' exclaimed Ruth.

'Miss Howard lets me read the paper in maths, you know that. She calls it "Social Studies". She says I can read until the class catches up with me and they've been absolute duffers this week,' replied Jane.

'Of course,' said Ruth affectionately. No one caught up with Jane in mathematics. She was always over the horizon, chasing stars.

'I hope Mr Lin is all right.'

'Why shouldn't he be?' asked Ruth, standing up and brushing sand off her legs.

'Things are pretty bad there, and Miss Phryne's worried about him,' said Jane, fumbling for her glasses. They were new. Phryne had caught her holding a book up to her eyes and marched her to an oculist. They improved her vision and the squint line between her brows was vanishing but they did give Jane, whose possessions already had a tendency to stray, one more thing to lose.

Ruth had a spare pair in her school locker, in case Jane lost her own and had to go a whole day without reading. That, for Jane, would be unmitigated torture.

'Shall we return, ladies?' asked Phryne. 'You're right. I am worried about Lin Chung. But there is nothing we can do about it from here.'

'Taggs – I mean, Miss Taggart would send a gunboat,' said Jane.

'Oh, how I wish I could,' Phryne replied. 'Now, listen, girls. I don't want to alarm you but I had a rather unnerving encounter with a car this afternoon, and one of the witnesses said it was driven by a Chinese. Admittedly my informant was completely gaga, but just in case, I want you to go to a state of caution. Nothing to be really worried about, but make sure the windows are locked or the screens are up, let Mr Butler answer the door, and make sure someone knows where you are if you aren't here.'

'A Chinese? Is this something to do with Mr Lin?' asked Jane.

'I can't imagine why it should be,' said Phryne honestly. 'Now, a drink, and then some dinner. I've been working for a living and I'm starving.'

Phryne sat down in her cool parlour after a light salady dinner with egg and bacon pie, one of Mrs Butler's specialties. Mr Butler had mixed her a soothing cocktail, stressing orange juice and ice, with a little gin and perhaps a touch of Cointreau? She had a pile of texts before her and the box of letters on the floor. Her pencils were as sharp as daggers, a new notebook was open in front of her, the air temperature was warm but not hot, the girls were playing with their puppy in the garden, Dot was mending stockings and listening to the wireless in the front room, Mrs Butler had finished the washing up and retired to her own apartment to take off her corset, Mr Butler was reading the paper over his after-dinner port and all was right with her world.

Why, then, was Phryne unable to get comfortable? She wriggled on her chair, went and fetched another one, moved to the sofa, moved back, gulped some of her cocktail. Finally she lit a cigarette and admitted that she was worried about Lin Chung, really worried, and until she got him back safe and well, a good third of her mind was going to be occupied with him and his fate.

That being so, she allowed the other two-thirds to get on with it, picked up a pencil, and began work on cyanide and its derivatives.

Prussic acid was used in making coloured glass, Glaister informed her, in dyeing cloth and in colouring paint. As arsenic had once been used in making green dye and poisonous wallpaper, and white and red lead were used in house paint, cyanide was used to make a fast blue. Apparently they had the stuff lying around by the pounds at certain factories. The potassium cyanide crystals could be converted into cyanide gas by the addition of any weak acid. Chemically, it acted like litmus, turning blue things red in the presence of the gas. It had been used in the Great War and also as a method of executing criminals in the United States.

As potassium cyanide it was a stable white crystalline powder rather like Epsom salts. It was miscible and water soluble. The only clue to its presence was the bitter almond scent, which at least one in five people could not detect at all. Taken internally it killed within four seconds, and although mixing it with some things could slow the reaction, it was always complete within an hour. A cyanide victim, unlike an arsenic eater, did not manifest odd nervous and gastric symptoms and fade miserably away over agonising months (nursed faithfully, in some cases, by his poisoner). A cyanide victim found that perfectly reliable oxygen exchange systems which had served them faithfully for years simply didn't work any more, and died immediately. Death was from asphyxia. Postmortem, there might be small red patches called petichial haemorrhage, giving rise to a suspicion of carbon monoxide poisoning. The postmortem appearances, said Glaister, could be confused with cerebral haemorrhage or thrombosis by an inattentive physician. As indeed they had been, Phryne thought.

She closed Glaister with appropriate respect and took up the box of letters. Lying on top of the envelopes was a clipped set of what looked like standard printed replies. There was also a schedule of fees.

Phryne raised an eyebrow. If one's letter were printed in 'Is This Problem Yours?' the woeful damsel received a postal note for five shillings, which might have comforted her spirits. Otherwise the service was free, apart from the postage, if the magazine published the letter. However, this was not the end of Artemis's talents. To receive a short private letter, one paid a shilling and enclosed a self-addressed envelope. A long letter cost two shillings and sixpence and all replies were despatched within a week. The reader was assured that her own letter would be either destroyed or returned to her, whichever she required. She was also assured of Artemis's complete confidentiality.

Phryne assumed the letters currently in the box must represent only a week's post. She flipped through Artemis's replies. They all began, 'My dear child, I feel for you in your trouble' and continued with an anodyne collection of clichés so brazen that Phryne's eye slid over them: 'God never sends you more burdens than you can bear'; 'Man is born to trouble as the sparks fly upwards'; 'Envy and malice can only be met with mercy and forgiveness'; 'You must keep your home together – that is the primary duty of every woman'.

Slightly sickened, Phryne laid out the original letters on the table. There were twenty-eight of them, each opened in the same manner by slitting the top of the envelope. The enclosures had presumably been read. There were cryptic notes in thick blue pencil on the outside, each surmounted by a tick. Three had a large star drawn on the back. They must be the ones which Artemis was planning to feature for this month's *Women's Choice*.

Phryne opened the first one and flattened out

the paper. 'Dear Artemis', it began. 'I don't know what to do. My complexion is all spotty and I cannot clear it. I have tried everything. Please help. I want my mother to allow me to go to a doctor but she says that it is just my age and it will get better.'

Artemis had replied that it was a pity to bother a doctor with such a trivial thing but if it would make her feel better she should see one and, in the meantime, eschew all fatty foods and wash her face in elderflower water. That seemed sensible enough.

Phryne opened the next, daintily written on pale pink notepaper scented with roses. 'Dear Artemis, I've never written to anyone before and I'm not sure how to start. Lately my husband has been late home from his business and when he does come home he seems cross. He often shouts at me to get the children to bed and when I do, poor little mites, he doesn't seem to want to talk to me, he just sits there reading the paper. I've asked him if there's some trouble at work but he just says it's none of my business. He isn't drinking and I'm sure that he's faithful. I've got three children. What should I do?' It was signed 'Mother of Three'.

Artemis had begun her reply with her usual 'My dear child', and went on to advise the reader to choose a day, put the children to bed early, dress prettily in a suitable gown and make his favourite dinner. Then, after dinner, when he is relaxed, to pour him a glass of port and ask him what the matter was. If this did not work, the matter was too deep for womankind and doubtless he would tell her in time. But it didn't mean that he didn't love her. 'Man's love is a thing apart, but 'tis a woman's whole existence' she quoted.

Phryne sighed and picked up the next letter. It was going to be a long and sententious night.

CHAPTER EIGHT

Ki intimates progress and success in small things. There will be advantage in being firm and correct. There has been good fortune in the beginning; there may be disorder in the end.

Hexagram 63: Ki
The I Ching Book of Changes

An hour later, Phryne found her head drooping down towards the paper and the print blurring before her eyes. Surely no one would kill on the basis of these letters? They were trite, they were foolish, they were occasionally touching, but taking them all in all, they were banal beyond belief.

If someone had killed Artemis because of one of these replies, it would have been an English professor, outraged by the atrocities which Artemis had inflicted on his beloved language.

Phryne rang for coffee.

Another hour later, she had sorted the letters into three piles marked A, B and C. The largest, C, contained letters which could not possibly have given rise to anything, except possibly a meditation on the emptiness of nice middle-class lives. A woman complained that her friend always belittled her possessions, insisted that the friend's child was better behaved, that her new curtains could have been got better and cheaper somewhere else, that the friend's cook made better cakes and her husband came home earlier from the office. Artemis explained the friend's motivations as envy and counselled compassion. That ought to annoy the friend enough to take herself off, Phryne thought. Good advice.

Into the C pile went also the girl with pimples, the request for advice on house-training a puppy, and the shamefaced worry that there was 'something wrong down below'. Artemis had sent the latter smartly to a female doctor, which argued a certain enlightenment. Phryne added to the Cs the advice on perfume ('the merest touch is sufficient') on cosmetics ('no one should know that you are wearing them'), and on care of the hair. There were three on this last topic, including a worried lady who was losing her hair and wondered if it would be *comme il faut* to wear a wig. Artemis had given her permission, but also sent her to a doctor in case there was some serious cause for it.

Phryne scanned four letters on etiquette, noting that one should always start at the outside of the cutlery and work inwards, that snail tongs were to be had at Chinese shops, that the correct way to eat asparagus was with the fingers and that children, who should be dismissed from table 'should they grow rowdy', should be instructed to sit up straight and not to crumble bread or to slurp soup. That ought to get rid of the little blighters before the main course.

Phryne had endured punitive lessons in table manners at a girl's school in the soggier part of the Cotswolds and thought that this explained why she had spent two years in the Quartier Latin in Paris, eating sardines out of tins and bread and cheese out of paper bags. Among other reasons, of course.

She smiled slightly as she remembered the other reasons. Dark, passionate, quick, with fierce moustaches which added a sting to a kiss. Where were they now? Dead, perhaps, or in jail, the voices which had recited Villon in the hot darkness, scented with absinthe and lemon blossom. Or perhaps transformed in that peculiarly French way into the Bon Bourgeois Papa with seven children and a job as a bank clerk, seen walking by the Seine on Sundays feeding the ducks. *'Voici le canard! Bonjour, M'sieur canard!'*

These letters really weren't very interesting. Phryne shook herself and considered pile B. These were the intermediate ones, which might have given offence if addressed to an unusually touchy person. The lady who signed herself 'Miserable' might have objected to being told to cultivate Christian resignation in the face of her husband's frequent drinking bouts and long absences from home. 'Wanderer' might have taken against advice that told her it was highly unlikely that a visit to Cairo would afford her the opportunity of attracting the attention of a desert prince who would carry her away on his white

111

stallion. Although Artemis's waspish comment that the white slave trade was stocked by 'foolish Misses with romantic novels on the brain and too much time on their hands' might be true, it could have been expressed more kindly.

'Mother of Nine' had as many children as the Old Woman Who Lived in a Shoe, and many of the same problems, without the chance of applying the same solution, the *Crimes (Cruelty to Children) Act* 1910 being what it was. She was not advised to use contraception by means of one of Dr Stopes's snazzy devices, but was instead counselled to 'reason with her husband and make him understand that chastity was the only path to follow'. Phryne could imagine how valuable this advice was to a woman whose previous attempts at reasoning along these lines had most palpably failed. This reply would have cost the recipient two shillings and sixpence, which would have been better spent on a consultation with the Queen Victoria Hospital's Family Planning Clinic.

'Wit's End' complained that her four sons were out of control. They were noisy, destructive, impertinent and would not mind. If she spanked them, they were quiet for a short time then broke out worse than ever. Her husband was staying away because the children were so awful and the house was a mess and they had smashed a ceramic bowl which had belonged to her mother. Artemis responded by suggesting the employment of a nanny and a housemaid or, alternatively, the banishment of all of the children to a good public school as soon as they were old enough. 'Boys often do not recognise the authority of a woman, who can be seen to be subservient to their father', Artemis had instructed. 'As your husband has not been present to impose order on them, it will be necessary to purchase this service. At a good school their wild natures will be tamed and they will come home for the holidays quite altered. In their absence you can have the house cleaned. If you cannot afford regular help, there are agencies who will come by the day, bringing all their own materials. You can then apply yourself to repairing the rift between your husband and yourself by going to a hairdresser, buying some new clothes, and ordering a special dinner. Of course one wishes to keep one's children with one, but sometimes this is not advisable.'

Nice if one had the money, perhaps, but doesn't the husband have some part in this, Phryne thought. They are his children too. And what if 'Wit's End' had followed this advice and something happened to one of the little hellions? She might be quite cross with Artemis. On the other hand, this letter was in the B list because 'Wit's End' sounded far too distracted to make a plan to murder anyone. If she did she'd probably find that the boys had pinched the cyanide to poison the cook anyway.

Pile B also contained a rambling, vague letter from 'Manon', who was wavering between a worthy but dull husband and a grand passion with a French gentleman belonging to the embassy. Another potentially explosive situation on which Artemis had made her views clear: 'You have a good husband and a nice house and a position in society; all of which you will lose if you pursue the second course. It is not entirely your fault, perhaps, that your affections have strayed, but now that you have come to the point, which would you rather have? The regard of a worthy gentleman or the passing passion of an unreliable Frenchman who will probably prove to be already married? Enquire, my dear, and find out if he has a wife in Paris. I will be very surprised if he has not. And if he will be unfaithful to her, be assured that he will be unfaithful to you in your turn when someone younger and prettier comes along. Don't be a fool', concluded Artemis.

Good advice. Could have been put more kindly. Phryne considered 'Manon' again and returned her to the B list. There was a faint flavour of fantasy about the letter, something not quite convincing. 'Manon', Phryne diagnosed, was indulging in daydreaming. But dreamers sometimes reacted violently if their dreams were shattered, and a mind which could make up a French gentleman of 'Gascon temperament' could certainly plan a murder. 'Manon' was in the B pile because she would very likely be satisfied with the dream and not need the reality.

The A pile contained the dangerous letters. The first, on pale blue notepaper in an envelope embossed with rosebuds, was written in a childish, stumbling hand and merely said: 'Artemis, how could you have suggested that I should try what you said? I did and it was terrible and now he won't even speak to me. You should be ashamed of yourself.' The writer had signed herself Anne, unusually for Artemis's correspondents, who were requested to use pseudonyms. There was no

114

return address on the letter. What had Artemis advised? Why hadn't it worked? Who was Anne anyway?

Phryne called out to Dot to search through the last few copies of *Women's Choice* to find a letter from Anne. It might have been published. The trauma appeared to be recent. Whatever the cause, Anne was in distress and so was her husband. She needed to be found. The postmark on the envelope said GPO, which was not helpful.

The next was a sheet of plain bank paper on which was scrawled in easy, angry capitals 'YOU BITCH YOU STUPID BITCH YOU DISSERV TO DIƐ'. Phryne noted the Greek E and the inability to spell. This was Miss Lavender's constant correspondent. His vocabulary was small but he employed it well. Phryne pondered on 'disserv'. Was that the way a truly illiterate person would spell 'deserve'? The hand was of someone used to writing in capitals. A mail clerk, perhaps, someone who addressed parcels? A tradesman used to marking bricks, tiles or planks? Interesting. She put it aside for comparison with the others.

The third envelope contained a page of ramblings so incoherent that it was hard to guess what the writer was trying to convey, except that he or she was angry. In several places the nib had ripped the paper. It was written in red ink which had dried to an unpleasant brown reminiscent of blood. 'I did what you said and look what happened', declared the writer. 'I followed your instructions to the letter and now I am in worse trouble than before and you're to blame Artemis I'm lost now lost lost and it's all your fault I did like you said and it all went wrong and I don't know what to do now you did this I'll kill you like you killed me.'

There was no signature. It had been posted in Kew. Phryne read it again. It made sense, in a way, though there was no internal clue as to what Artemis had advised, so Phryne had no idea what had gone wrong. A dangerous trade, the giving of advice, thought Phryne, putting the letter aside. Even the best advice can be wrong and the mere asking for advice can precipitate unfortunate events. What sort of trouble? Did the writer mean the usual female problem – pregnancy? Had Artemis given her advice about an illegal operation? Out of the question. Artemis had maintained the sort of consistent, conventional righteousness which a Presbyterian might consider too strict. She had probably never heard of illegal operations and if she had, she would consider them contrary to the law of God. And she would have said so.

What had Miss Prout said about the letters to Artemis? Replete with scandal, divorce, molestation of children? Phryne had not found anything like that. Had someone weeded the letters before they got to Artemis, taking out the scandalous ones in case Artemis's virgin rectitude might be outraged?

Now that was an intriguing thought. The letters went to a box at the General Post Office. Phryne made a note to find out who collected the mail and sent it on to Miss Lavender. Or did she come into the city and collect it herself? On the other hand, perhaps this was just a slow week in the scandal line.

Phryne opened the next letter on the A pile: 'Artemis (I won't call you dear Artemis)', it began. 'I took your advice. I did as you said. I had the walls stripped and painted. I used up all my housekeeping money on it. And now I have pale green walls and no husband. He took one look at it, shouted at me that I had wasted his money and I was a flapper with no taste and I'd mutilated his house and he left that night, taking all his possessions. I hate you. I hope you die. Moderne.'

'Dot! See if you can find a letter from "Moderne",' shouted Phryne.

'Right you are,' Dot yelled back. 'No luck with Anne, Miss.'

'Keep trying. And can you find those interviews for me? The ones Jack Robinson left.'

'They're on the other side of the desk, on the tapestry chair,' Dot called.

'Oh yes, so they are. Thank you.'

Right at the bottom of the box was the usual detritus of a writer's life. A bus ticket, a few scraps of shopping list, the cork from an ink bottle and three leads and a spring which had fallen out of a propelling pencil which no longer propelled. There was also a sealed advice letter which had 'return to sender' on the front. Underneath the address was written in angry capitals 'addressee deceased'.

Unfortunately, the letter had originally been sent to a post office box in St Kilda, and to pseudonym, 'Desperate'. Since the readers were required to send a stamped, self-addressed envelope, the handwriting on the envelope could be assumed to be 'Desperate's'. The envelope should have contained Artemis's advice to 'Desperate', either a short letter for a shilling or a long letter for two and six. What it actually contained was a sheet of blank paper. Phryne held the envelope up to the light. Just along the edge she could see where the flap had been opened. Steaming melted glue into patches and when an envelope was resealed, a strong light would reveal whether the envelope had been tampered with.

But what an odd thing to do! If someone wanted to hide 'Desperate's' existence, all they had to do was pinch the letter and bung it into the stove. What was the point of stealing the letter, steaming it open, removing the enclosure, substituting a blank and putting the letter back in the box – with its revealing post office box number? It made no sense.

Except as a false trail, perhaps, a means of leading an investigator on a hunt for mares' nests. Well, Phryne could just put on her mares' nest hunting hat and follow along. Even a false trail leads somewhere in the end. Jack Robinson could find out who owned the post box tomorrow and pursue the matter. 'Desperate' wasn't going anywhere.

'Miss? Here's "Moderne",' said Dot, laying the magazine on the table. 'I've been back all year and I can't find Anne, though.'

'Didn't get published and the letter would have been returned or destroyed,' Phryne told her. 'Never mind. What was "Moderne's" problem?'

'"I live in a big house with Victorian furnishing, red plush wallpaper and heavy carpets",' Dot read. '"I want to make it look more modern and fresh. All that heavy material keeps out the light and collects dust. What do you advise?"'

'Sounds like a safe enough topic,' murmured Phryne. 'Go on, Dot. What did Artemis say?'

'"Consult your husband and decide on a decorating budget",' Dot read. '"Then you can have the wallpaper removed, the walls washed some light shade, the curtains rehung in a light jazz fabric and the carpets removed. The floorboards can be stained and varnished for a small sum and they make the house very cool and easy to clean." Sounds nice.'

'And look what a harvest poor "Moderne" reaped,' said Phryne. 'She probably did it to surprise her husband and threw out his cherished Oriental rugs and Chippendale with the rubbish.'

'They can't have been very comfortable together,' Dot considered, laying the letter back on the pile. 'If he just upped and went like that. Not what I'd expect in a husband,' she added. Dot was fairly sure that she was indeed going to marry Hugh, a blameless policeman on whose profile she doted, but she wouldn't put up with behaviour like that even in a man who looked like Douglas Fairbanks. 'But she does sound upset, Miss.'

'Yes, and we have to find her. What do you make of this one?'

Phryne handed over 'Lost's' letter. Dot read it with concern. 'Poor girl,' she said.

'And here is Anne, who sounds absolutely desperate, and "Desperate" herself, who is dead. Or so the envelope says.'

'And so is Miss Lavender,' said Dot. 'Do you want those interviews? Perhaps we could go through them together. You look tired, Miss.'

'Thank you, Dot, dear. I'm just not used to working for a living. Who's first?'

'The housemaid, Mercy Porter. "I am required to take around the breakfasts. This is part of my regular duties. At approximately ten past eight I arrived at the door of the Garden Apartment. I was a little late that clay. I knocked at the door and no one answered. I pushed the door and found it open. This was unusual. Miss Lavender always kept her door locked. I have never found the door open before. I went inside and put the tray down on the table. Miss Lavender was sitting at the table, sort of slumped over. I thought she was asleep. I have never found her asleep before. She was always awake and at her desk when I brought the breakfasts. I touched her and she fell sideways. Her face was blue. I ran to the door and screamed for help. Then I must have fainted. I have never fainted before. She was a nice lady. She was strict about her meal times but she gave me a tip when I brought her extra tea or something. I have never had any disagreement with her."'

'Straightforward enough,' said Phryne, lighting a cigarette, leaning back, and rubbing her eyes.

'Then we've got Mr Carroll. "I occupy apartment five. I barely knew the deceased. I do not have any social intercourse with the other apartments. I have my own friends. On that night I had been out rather late with some chaps from the city and accepted their invitation to continue the party at a private club. I do not gamble. We were drinking and having a jolly time with a few girls we'd met earlier at the Green Mill. I did not get home until nine and then I walked into all this fuss. I know nothing else about this matter."'

'Scrub the jolly Mr Carroll,' said Phryne. 'Jack will have checked to see he was out carousing with witnesses. He doesn't sound like Miss Lavender's ideal man anyway. And the next, please?'

'"My name is Amelia Gould. I am a widow. My husband arranged to rent the apartment when he knew he was ill, but he died before we moved in. I didn't know what else to do so I came here after he died. We had already sold the big house and put the furniture into store. I've only been here a week. I never met the deceased. I don't know if I will be staying here."'

'Considering that Mrs Gould is in possession of what Mr Bell thinks is a real Canaletto, she could go anywhere she liked,' Phryne observed.

'"My name is Mrs Robert Hewland. My Christian name is Alice. We live in apartment one. On Sunday my husband and I go to divine service at eight, and then again at two. We walk to the Presbyterian Church which is about half a mile from this apartment. Because I like to be early, we left at half past seven. When we returned we heard that Miss Lavender had passed on. I did not know her well, but she seemed to be respectable. It is a pity."'

'Damned with faint praise! And Mr Robert Hewland supports this story?'

'Yes, Miss. Here's one in different handwriting. "My name is John Keith. I am Emeritus Professor of Botany at Melbourne University. I am making this statement not of my own free will but because a damned fool policeman is inquiring into my

121

movements and won't go away unless I write it. So here goes. I loathed Miss Lavender. She was an interfering busybody, a nosy-parkering old maid with nothing else to occupy her time but to spy on her neighbours. Nevertheless, I didn't kill the pestilential old besom. I live in apartment three. On the morning in question I was preparing to breakfast with my niece, Margery. She had made the coffee and we were waiting for the maid to bring the tray when we heard a god-awful screeching. We went out to investigate and found the maid collapsed on the path, gasping that Miss Lavender was dead. I looked inside the cottage. I did not touch anything. I saw Miss Lavender on the floor, dead as a doornail. I sent my niece inside and informed Mrs Needham that she had a vacancy. I know nothing else about the matter." Dot giggled as she replaced the statement. Phryne laughed.

'Fine line in invective the old gentleman has! I wonder what Miss Lavender interfered in? What does the niece say?'

'Same thing,' said Dot. 'Heard the scream, saw the maid, was sent back by her uncle. Here's Mrs Needham. "I am the proprietor of a set of serviced apartments. On the morning in question I was in the kitchen as usual, overseeing the preparation of the breakfasts. I was called away for perhaps ten minutes. I was called away by Mrs Opie, who needed milk for her daughter Wendy. When I returned I heard a scream and saw the maid Mercy Porter lying on the path outside Wee Nooke..." then the same story. She saw Professor Keith there and Mr Bell, also Miss Gallagher and Miss Grigg. "I always ask for references when I

122

have a prospective tenant. Miss Lavender gave me the name of the editress of a respectable journal and the Commonwealth Bank. I enquired. Both were satisfactory. I allowed her to decorate the apartment as she fancied and also to take charge of one part of the garden. I am unaware of any quarrel with any of my other tenants, who are all very respectable ladies and gentlemen." Who would you like next?'

'Mr Opie,' said Phryne. 'A shadowy figure. All I know about him is that Wendy says he makes her mother cry and regret her lost Giovanni. They are reputed to quarrel.'

'"My name is Stephen Opie. I am an architect by profession. On the morning in question I was awakened at four-thirty by my daughter Wendy screaming. I heard my wife get up to go to her. I found that I could not get back to sleep. I never can if my first sleep is interrupted. I got up and put on a dressing gown and went out of the apartment into the garden. It was not entirely dark. There was a full moon. I sat down on the seat under the awning and smoked a cigarette. My wife does not allow me to smoke in our apartment because of Wendy. It was very quiet in the garden. I sat there for about an hour and didn't hear anything. About half past five it came on to rain so I went inside again. There didn't seem to be a lot of point in going back to bed so I shaved and dressed and worked on some drawings I am making for a housing company. Mercy Porter delivered breakfast at seven-thirty, the usual time. We were just finishing when we heard a scream and I went out to investigate. There I found..." we know what he found. Mrs Opie says much the same "My daughter Wendy woke me at about half past four. She had had a nightmare. I sat up with her until she fell asleep again. I fell asleep too, in the chair next to her bed. At about eight she woke and asked for milk. We didn't have any so I went to ask for some in the kitchen. I got some milk from Mrs Needham and we had breakfast..." then the usual story. Who would you like next?'

'What does Mr Bell say?'

'Hmm, the usual story– "My name is John Bell. I live in apartment six. I am a dealer in antiquities."'

'That's interesting, Dot, dear. He told me he sold antiques. Antiquities is an entirely different solid marble kettle of Roman statuary. Well, well. Do go on.'

'"I also tend the garden. I am not paid for this. I like gardening. On the morning in question I was unable to sleep. I caught malaria in Italy some time ago and I usually dose myself with quinine in time to catch the attack before it gets bad. But I took too much and my digestion was disturbed. I spent most of the night, off and on, being ill. Towards dawn I began to feel better. I went out at about six to sit in the garden near the fish pond. It was a cool morning but it had stopped raining. There was no one else there and I didn't hear anything except the birds waking up. At about seven I heard someone walking up the path to the Garden Apartment. I did not see the person. The wall is in the way. It could have been anyone. I heard a door open and close and a brief conversation. I could not hear what was said. I did not see the person leave. I went back to my apartment. I didn't want any breakfast but I drank a pot of tea. Then I heard a scream..." and he went out to see what was happening, saw Keith, Opie and Miss Gallagher and Grigg there and Mercy Porter on the ground.

'He goes on: "I had a difference of opinion with the deceased on the subject of her ideas about garden decoration. She liked garden gnomes. I don't. The argument did become heated and I appealed to Mrs Needham who had given me permission to make my garden in the Italian manner. I wasn't going to have it ruined by Miss Lavender's mania for gnomes. Mrs Needham gave Miss Lavender permission to infest her garden with as many of the little stone abominations as she wished but told her to stay off my patch, and she did. Since then I have had no contact with the deceased at all. She wasn't speaking to me. But she wasn't a bad old stick. I believe she was very kind to Miss Gallagher when she was upset recently, and Mrs Opie. I did not kill her and don't know why anyone should."'

'Miss Grigg, Dot, if you please? She'll be less tiring than Miss Gallagher.'

'If you say so, Miss. "My name is Immaculata Grigg and I live with my friend Miss Gallagher in apartment four, directly behind the Garden Apartment. I am employed by *Women's Choice* as a writer. That night I was worried about a personal matter so I couldn't sleep. I gave up trying at about four. By the time I decided to get up and sit in the garden, I found that Mr Opie was there before me. I saw the glow of his cigarette end and there was enough moonlight to see by. Also, Miss Lavender's cottage has fairy lights all round it. So I sat in my own garden under the vine. It started raining at five-thirty so I moved under the eaves. I like rain. I was smoking and thinking when I heard someone come up the path to Miss Lavender's door. She opened it and I heard her exclaim "For me?" I didn't hear a reply. The person went away down the path. I could not see who it was, there's our apartment in the way. Then I went in to make coffee. Miss Gallagher got up at eight. She was still in her dressing gown when we heard a scream..." and went out, etc. Miss Mary Gallagher says that she slept like a baby all night and never heard a thing. She also says, "Miss Lavender was a very nice lady. She was very kind to me about a worry I had recently and I can't imagine who'd want to kill her."'

'Recent worry, eh? I wonder if it was professional or marital? Miss Grigg wouldn't like that, Dot, dear, not one bit. What does Miss Grigg say about Miss Lavender?'

'"I knew the deceased only as a neighbour. I didn't like her taste in decoration but that was none of my business. She seemed all right."' Dot put down the last statement.

'Grudging praise,' said Phryne. 'Well, Miss Grigg supports Mr Opie. No one saw Mr Bell. There was a visitor who brought Miss Lavender a present, and one can only presume that it was a terminal one.'

'Where next?' asked Dot.

'More investigations tomorrow,' said Phryne. 'But for tonight, I'm having a stiff cocktail and

I'm going to bed. This journalism is a hard life. No wonder they drink so much.'

Dot fetched a brandy for Phryne and a small glass of port for herself and said, 'Miss, we still don't know anything about Miss Lavender.'

'Tomorrow,' said Phryne, and drained the glass.

CHAPTER NINE

I indicates that, with firm correctness, there will be good fortune. We must look at what we are seeking to nourish, and by the exercise of our thoughts seek for the proper aliment.

Hexagram 27: I
The I Ching Book of Changes

Morning found Phryne Fisher very willing to rise. She had dreamed again, a vivid, short dream, just a picture: Lin Chung with cockroaches crawling over his face. She showered vigorously in cold water and dressed in a bright red suit and a daring hat.

When she left for the city, she was carrying a paper bag containing a bronze milliner's creation which she had never really liked, and a determination to find out who killed Miss Lavender. Until then, she could not hire a plane and start for China. Something was really wrong. One Celtic ancestor had not given Phryne reliable second sight but had given her a nose for trouble, and she could smell it on the wind as strongly as the tuberoses in Ireland's Florist as she passed.

Jack Robinson had promised to deliver the dossier on Miss Lavender as soon as it was made up and the staff of *Women's Choice* were about to face an inquisition.

No one was in the office when she arrived. An old man with a mop let her in, grumbling his way up from step to step, informing Phryne that his rheumatics were something chronic and he'd been to the doc and he wasn't no good. Phryne, that morning, was not a receptive audience.

'Cheer up,' she said brightly to the mop. 'You can always die.'

She went into *Women's Choice* and slammed the door on his '...it's not as bad as that...'

Feeling that she had done her little bit to comfort the afflicted, Phryne surveyed the office. Covered typewriters lurked like sleeping beasts. Who cleared the post box? What was the answer to that steamed-open letter puzzle? What, indeed, was the drill when a letter came into *Women's Choice?*

Miss Nelson probably collected the post. That's what office girls did, along with making the tea, delivering proofs, answering the telephone and obeying instructions. It was unlikely she was acting on her own.

Now, a quick search. With one ear on alert, listening for steps on the stairs, Phryne began with Miss Herbert's desk drawers. What a lot of clutter women kept! Apart from the tools of the trade like pens, ink, pencils and paper, there was a pair of laddered stockings and a patent object for fixing them, some hairpins, a tube of lipstick, three crumpled handkerchiefs, some private correspondence and five pennies. Phryne leafed through the letters. A Valentine's Day card with red roses on it, a note from a woman called Gillian about a lunch date, Phryne's own card, some advertising flyers and one of Madame Weigall's paper patterns for underwear.

Miss Nelson's table had no drawers. It bore a lot of layout work, a pot of paste and a brush, a grubby paper bag containing toffee, and several ledgers.

Phryne prowled. Miss Prout's drawer was locked, which was interesting. She chewed her pencils. Miss Phillips hoarded charcoal sticks, matches, sevenpence ha'penny in change and a romance novel called *Night of the Sheik*. Miss Grigg had bits of wire and several cogwheels in her drawer, together with a small bottle of oil, a salami, a postcard of St Peter's, Rome, and an envelope full of stamps. She also had a table of postal charges and a lot of string. The drawer was pungent with oil and garlic. The bottle was wrapped in a wisp of torn blue muslin.

Miss Gallagher's desk contained, as might be expected, a full make-up kit, a flask of Nuit D'Amour, a comb in a case, and approximately three thousand recipe clippings. Mrs McAlpin's desk contained a mass of photographs, one nice clean hanky, a purse containing one and sixpence, a diary and a lot of advertising material about cameras. On inspection it proved to contain nothing but notes on light and exposures.

Did Phryne dare to search Mrs Charlesworth's

room? Of course she dared.

She had her hand on the latch when she heard someone coming up the stairs. She quickly occupied herself with taking off her hat and finding a task. When Mrs Charlesworth came in, Phryne was arranging the Worth gown over the back of a tall chair. She turned with a look of keen innocence which Mrs Charlesworth instantly distrusted.

'Good morning,' said Phryne. 'Mrs Charlesworth, I have grave news and perhaps you had better sit down.'

'Miss Lavender was murdered?' asked Mrs Charlesworth, sitting down in Miss Herbert's chair.

'Yes. Poisoned. By later today I should know more about her. But I've been allowed to ask your staff questions, on the grounds that I'm less likely to upset them.'

'I can't imagine why your policeman thought that,' said Mrs Charlesworth. 'You're much more likely, I suppose, to get at the truth. Well, Miss Fisher, what do you want to know?'

'Who was Artemis?'

'I can't tell you,' said Mrs Charlesworth. She took off her hat and jabbed a hatpin clean through it.

'Why not?'

'We promise our readers confidentiality.'

'Mrs Charlesworth, I can't believe that you are as naive as that.'

'Can't you?' asked the older woman. 'Try.'

'Not even someone who could believe six impossible things before breakfast could believe

130

that,' said Phryne firmly. Mrs Charlesworth surveyed the green eyes and the firm chin and gave up. Strong will recognised strong will. She shrugged.

'Oh, well. Artemis wasn't always one person. She used to be whoever had a spare moment, but Miss Lavender more or less took over because she had a lot of spare moments and needed a little extra income, poor soul. And when she was talking about anything other than fairies she was quite sensible. Did you ask about that box of letters?'

'Yes. They won't release them, I'm afraid. They're evidence.'

'Oh well, then we can use last month's.'

'Last month's? I thought they were returned or destroyed.'

'Most of them are, dear. We only keep the ones that don't have a return envelope or address. In case they write again, you know, and demand to know what has happened to their letter. Every now and again someone throws them all into the fire. They never leave the building once Miss Lavender sends them back.'

'Where are they?'

'In my office. Why?'

'Miss Lavender had five threatening letters. One of them came from someone called Anne. I also need to see "Desperate's" letter.'

'I don't know...'

Phryne decided to discard the velvet glove.

'Mrs Charlesworth, how do you think the directors would react to a big, stand-up, public scandal all over the front pages of every paper from the *Age* to the *Hawklet?*'

'Is that what we are facing?'

'Oh yes.' said Phryne. 'And, of course, Miss Lavender's untimely decease. Murder, you know.'

Mrs Charlesworth had been galvanised by the threat to her magazine. She rushed Phryne into her office and shut the door. Then she produced a large cardboard box-file half-full of letters.

'This is all that are left. What sort of scandal?'

'I suspect that at least one letter has been stolen, and that others may have been answered ... inappropriately. Who collects the post for Artemis?'

'Miss Nelson. She is meant to rewrap the parcel at the post office and send it on to Miss Lavender. At least...'

'At least?'

'I have been wondering about Miss Nelson. We usually take the brightest girls straight out of school, you know, and she was very bright. Cheerful little thing. But lately she's been a little down. I had been meaning to have a nice chat with her once we get this magazine to bed.'

'What's the procedure for recording what letters come in?'

'Oh, they're all in the letter book. Miss Nelson used to collect the Artemis letters, bring them back here, record them all, then parcel them up and walk back to the post office. But Miss Prout pointed out that she could save a trip by just taking parcel materials and the letter book to the post office and packing the parcel there.'

'There's your breach in security,' said Phryne. 'And how helpful of Miss Prout to think of saving

Miss Nelson's legs.'

'Yes, it was, wasn't it?' observed Mrs Charlesworth. She was unhealthily pale and passed a hand over her forehead. 'This is terrible,' she said flatly.

'Yes, it is, but we might be able to retrieve the situation without telling anyone, provided that the persons involved didn't kill Miss Lavender.'

'Might we?' asked Mrs Charlesworth, a middle-aged, stout ringer for Burne-Jones's 'Hope Awakening'.

'Possibly. But I need your cooperation.'

'Save my magazine, and you have it.'

'I'll do my best. Now, I want you to lead the office in a reminiscence of Miss Lavender. I need to know what everyone thought about her. There will be an item in the paper today about the murder – don't worry, it doesn't mention *Women's Choice*. That might provide an opportunity for a little speech about not speaking to the press. Don't talk to Miss Nelson yet. The poor girl's riddled with guilt. She might actually come and confess, which would be better for her and then you can forgive her.'

'Can I?' asked Mrs Charlesworth, smouldering a little around the edges.

'I don't think it was her idea,' said Phryne. 'You should be allowed a little stupidity at sixteen.'

'Fifteen. Perhaps. I was certainly foolish enough at that age. All right, Miss Fisher, amnesty for Miss Nelson if she confesses, but anyone else who has done this to me will be out on the street so fast they'll think their camiknickers were on fire.'

'An understandable reaction. Now, let's make

some tea and you can lead the congregation later.'

'When the kitchen page is finished. And when Mr Bell finally deigns to bless us with his presence and we can get the gardening layout done. Mrs McAlpin has the photograph all ready, we just need the text. And, of course, drat, the "Your Child" feature isn't finished. Miss Fisher, can I prevail on your good nature to take little Wendy out for an ice cream again when Mrs Opie comes in to complete the wretched thing? You seem to have a strange influence over that temperamental child. Then all we have to do is wait until the printer delivers the proofs.'

'What then?'

'Then we proofread, argue a lot, add bits that have been left out by mistake, take the galleys down again and have a quarrel with the printer because he has to reset some of his type and then – at last – we make ourselves the celebratory gin and tonic (or orangeade for Miss Nelson), eat ginger biscuits and begin again. I can't imagine why we do this to ourselves, but there you are. That pause after all of the pages are delivered is a perfect opportunity for your interrogation, Miss Fisher.'

'I think,' said Phryne, suddenly liking Mrs Charlesworth, 'that you had better call me Phryne.'

'Georgina,' said Mrs Charlesworth, holding out a hand. Phryne took it.

Mr Bell arrived, looking apologetic. He was sorry but the gardening piece wasn't quite finished, could Mrs Charlesworth wait until tomorrow? He had a delivery of antiques coming in and they needed immediate attention. He was sure that one of the girls wouldn't mind typing it for him when he delivered it tomorrow, perhaps rather late tomorrow, maybe Thursday would be better?

Mrs Charlesworth drew a deep breath and began to speak. Before Mr Bell knew it, his straw boater had been hung on a peg, he was seated at a typewriter, the cover had been whipped off, a pencil had been sharpened for him and paper rolled into the machine, and he was advised that if the gardening article was not forthcoming within the hour, Mrs Charlesworth would be looking for a new incarnation of Agricola.

Raising one finger, he began to type.

The slow, hunt-and-peck clack of the Smith Addison punctuated the morning. Miss Nelson came in and was immediately despatched, to her evident relief, to the post office to bring back any of Artemis's letters and record them in the letter book. Mrs Charlesworth retired to her office to put the last touches to her editorial. Miss Prout finished the layout of 'Victoria's Stately Homes: Mount Macedon' after a brief but acrimonious argument with Mrs McAlpin on the reduction of her photographs.

'The trouble with photographers is that they believe that guff about every picture being worth a thousand words,' she snarled.

'The trouble with writers is that they don't,' replied Mrs McAlpin. 'Well, Miss Fisher, we may as well begin the new issue with the first pictures of your gown. Miss Herbert?'

'You can't have Miss Herbert,' said Miss Phillips. 'Not yet. I have to clean up all these errors and I need her. After lunch,' she pleaded.

'Very well,' said Mrs McAlpin. She looked around for someone else to help and decided to go and fetch some biscuits for morning tea. Phryne went with her.

After a brief and enjoyable debate about the merits of coconut macaroons– 'To me they always taste like Koko for the Hair' was Mrs McAlpin's opinion – walnut whirls, petits fours, melting moments and gingernuts, they settled on plain iced shortbread and were walking back along Hardware Lane when Phryne was suddenly shoved violently from behind.

She was not entirely unprepared. Since the incident of the night before, she had been keyed up, physically alert. So instead of flying under the wheels of a labouring dray, she managed an airborne twist and grabbed for her attacker. She had him by the shirtfront. For a moment she stared straight into his face. Then he lunged away out of her grip, and she was left with a handful of torn fabric and the view of a retreating back.

A Chinese man wearing a blue Chinese shirt. Was the Lin family out to remove her for asking about Lin Chung? If so, she would have their hides. Nailed, as Bert would have said, to a haybarn door. What impertinence!

Mrs McAlpin said nothing but, 'What a disagreeable incident. Really, the city has become most uncomfortable. Are you hurt, dear?'

'No, but all this adventuring is hard on the stockings and I think I've burst a button.'

'No, it's just come undone. There we are.' Mrs McAlpin buttoned Phryne's jacket as though she was six. 'Ah, here's Mrs Opie and Wendy.'

'I promised to take her out for ice cream. I might go down to the ice cream parlour at the Regent. Hello, Mrs Opie. Hello, Wendy.'

Wendy came forward and took Phryne's hand, looking imploringly up into her face.

'Ice cream?' she whispered.

'Ice cream,' Phryne agreed. 'Mrs Charlesworth's waiting for that missing page, Mrs Opie, I'm sure you're anxious to get on. Suppose I take Wendy for a little walk and bring her back in about an hour?'

'That would be wonderful,' said Mrs Opie. 'Now you be good, Wendy.'

She took out a handkerchief and seemed about to spit on it and scrub the child, but was dissuaded by a dangerous glint in Wendy's eye. Mrs Opie sighed, shoved back her hair and went up the stairs with Mrs McAlpin.

Phryne walked down Little Bourke Street and into Swanston, turned the corner and strode on. Wendy did her best to keep up but after three blocks was dragging on Phryne's hand.

'Oh, sorry,' said Phryne, looking down and seeing a red face screwed up in a determination not to cry. 'I do beg your pardon. I've got longer legs than you have, eh, Wendy? Let's slow down. Would you like to look at the shops?'

'Ice cream first,' Wendy gasped. 'Then shops.'

'Very well.' Phryne slowed down to a stroll. The city was looking prosperous, well dressed and harmless. But someone had tried to kill her,

137

twice or possibly three times in two days. She had better make a contingency plan in case they succeeded while she had Wendy with her.

'What has your mother told you about getting lost?' asked Phryne.

'Find a policeman,' said Wendy promptly. 'And tell him my name and address.' She recited it in a fast singsong. 'And then he'll take me home.'

'What does a policeman look like? Can you see one?'

Wendy scanned the street.

'There.' Her finger shot out. A policeman was directing traffic in the centre of the Bourke Street intersection. That would not be too far to run, even on short legs. They continued to the only ice cream parlour in Melbourne, where Wendy absorbed an ice cream sundae with not only chocolate sauce but also sprinkles, wafers and nuts. She was not greedy. She did not gobble. She savoured every mouthful as though it was her last. Phryne watched her with pleasure as she ate a fruit cocktail.

With ritual obeisances and a sacramental payment, they left the temple of ice cream and idled back through the city. Wendy was much taken with the toy train in the window of Foy and Gibsons', but came away when requested and climbed the steep street without complaint, though she must have been tired by then.

Phryne carried her up the last set of stairs, fast asleep. She put the child down on the only padded chair without waking her and flexed a few muscles. Sleeping children gained weight according to the depth of their sleep.

Order appeared to have been restored in the office. Mr Bell typed his last word with a clack. The sheet was ripped out of the typewriter, the text and picture glued onto the layout block. It was added to the completed article on stately homes and the final version of 'Your Child', which Miss Herbert had typed. The editorial was complete, the contents page with its decorative border pasted up, the whole was enclosed in a large folder and Miss Nelson was sent out, rejoicing, to deliver it to the printer.

There was a general air of relaxation. The magazine had been delivered and mother and child were doing well. Miss Grigg put her feet on the desk and lit a small cigar. Miss Phillips stared blankly into space. Miss Prout and Miss Gallagher vanished into the kitchen to make tea. Mrs Opie dabbed at her face with a wet handkerchief, exhausted, looking as though she would like to have joined her daughter in a little nap. Miss Herbert exclaimed over her new hat.

'It's beautiful,' she said, turning the bronze creation around. 'But it must have cost pounds and pounds, Miss Fisher. You can't just give it away.'

'It's no use to me,' said Phryne. 'I misjudged the colour in the shop lighting. It simply can't be worn on black hair. Try it on.'

Miss Herbert obeyed. The hat was perfect. The bronze matched her hair and the bunch of cock's feathers threw a green light onto her high complexion, subduing it. On Phryne it had been just a hat. On Miss Herbert it was an accolade.

'Oh, how can I thank you?' she asked, kissing

Phryne on the cheek.

'It was nothing,' said Phryne.

Mrs Charlesworth came in, bringing her chair, and sat down in the midst of the desks. She looked pale and grave. Miss Grigg took her feet off the desk.

'I have a terrible thing to tell you all,' she said. 'The police have told me that Miss Lavender was murdered. There will be an investigation. And I want to warn you that I will take a very dim view of anyone who talks to the press before this is sorted out. I'm sure that it had nothing to do with this magazine, but adverse publicity would ruin us. I'm certain that you understand.'

Nods all round.

'And it might be proper,' she said slowly, 'if we all talked about Miss Lavender. Who knew her well?'

'Not me,' said Miss Herbert. 'I think I only met her once.'

'Nor me,' said Miss Nelson nervously.

'Mania for gnomes,' said Mr Bell. 'Mania for knowing things, too.'

'Really?' asked Phryne very gently.

'Oh yes. We live in the same set of apartments, you know. She got into a hell of a row with old Professor Keith. He said she'd been snooping into his affairs – though I fancy that it was only one *affaire*, you know,' said Mr Bell, warming to his topic. Who says men don't gossip? Phryne thought. Men say men don't gossip. 'If that pretty piece Margery is his niece I'll eat my boater.'

'And Miss Lavender knew about this?'

'I don't think she wanted to do anything with

140

the knowledge,' said Miss Grigg. 'She just liked to know. Gave her a sense of power, perhaps. I never knew that she had any friends. Never any visitors. No relatives, as far as I know.'

'No,' said Mrs McAlpin. 'She had no relatives. And her manias, as you call them, Mr Bell – in my day young men were more respectful to older women – were perfectly explicable.'

'Explicate,' urged Miss Prout, scenting scandal.

'She was raised in an entirely rationalist household,' said Mrs McAlpin with strong disapproval. 'No fancies, no stories.'

'No God, no angels?' murmured Phryne. Mrs McAlpin bestowed a smile on her.

'Precisely. No religion, which is appalling. She was an only child and she was educated at home on strict rationalist lines. Facts, nothing but facts. I believe that Dickens used this in one of his novels.'

'*Hard Times,*' said Miss Herbert.

'As it might be,' said Mrs McAlpin. 'Then the parents died and went, I trust, to their reward. I hope it was a hot one. What does a young woman with that kind of background and training do as soon as she has no guardians?'

'Gets into trouble,' said Phryne, and received another smile.

'And so she did. She made an unwise marriage, bore a child which died and turned for consolation to various spiritualist organisations. Then her husband died and left her a reasonable competence and she came to the Presbyterian Church for instruction. She has been a member of my church for twenty years now. Never married again. Never showed any signs of wanting to marry after her unhappy experience. And is it any wonder that the poor woman broke out into fairies when she had been deprived of any fiction in her youth? The world is too harsh a place to contemplate directly, without a cushion of fancy and belief.'

'Underneath are the everlasting arms,' quoted Mrs Charlesworth.

'But she was a terrible snoop,' said Mr Bell.

'She was very kind to me,' objected Mrs Opie with a sniff. 'I was walking in the garden late one night when Wendy wouldn't sleep and she invited me in and gave me a drink and asked me what was wrong.'

'Because she wanted to know all about you,' said Miss Grigg unexpectedly. 'She wanted to know all about everyone. She knew about Mr Carroll's drinking and your domestic problems, she knew about Keith and his flapper and pried into the Hewlands's religious beliefs. She was starting on Mrs Gould, she knew all about Mrs Needham and she tried very hard to find out something about Gally and me.'

'And me,' said Mr Bell. 'How was I burned? How did it feel when the plane went down? I can't answer questions like that, anyway, at the best of times. I didn't like her and I don't care who knows it. But I understand her better,' he said, smoothing the side of his face. 'I always thought there was a false note in all those gnomes. She was like those Melanesian tribes which have never been exposed to measles. They die when the traders arrive because they have no immunity. Miss Lavender had no immunity to fantasy and so it proliferated.

Now, if you ladies will excuse me, I really have to get down to my warehouse and unpack these new goods.'

'Where's your warehouse?' asked Phryne idly, lighting a gasper. 'I might drop in with a cheque book and have a look. I need a new table.'

'Sorry, Miss Fisher, I only sell to trade – I'm sure you understand.'

Phryne thought that she might be beginning to understand, indeed.

The meeting on Miss Lavender continued desultorily.

'She was nice,' Miss Gallagher insisted. 'I had a bit of a difference of opinion with my dear Grigg here one night and she was very kind. Told me that friends mustn't fall out and friendship was worth more than gold.'

Miss Gallagher seemed to be in earnest. Miss Grigg was watching her narrowly, probably wondering what the gushing Gally might have told the retentive Miss Lavender about their private affairs.

'Just the sort of thing she would say. She was dreadfully old-fashioned,' said Miss Prout. 'I mean, her advice was so ... staid.'

'We are a staid magazine, Miss Prout,' Miss Charlesworth reminded her.

'Yes, but all that stuff about Christian resignation, keep the home together, put up with the beatings and the drunkenness.'

'And what would you have advised?' asked Mrs Charlesworth.

'Leave the b – beggar,' said Miss Prout.

'Easy to say,' said Mrs McAlpin. 'Divorce is

143

difficult and expensive and at the end of it one may have an allowance sufficient to feed the children but one will probably be faced with trying to work and trying to care for children without help. Ask Mrs Opie how easy that is.'

'Oh yes, it's very difficult. But I don't want to stop working. When I had Wendy I read *Radiant Motherhood* and I tried, I really tried, to adore the child as she suggests, but babies are not really very adorable. I felt stupid and clumsy and cow-like and my husband ... doesn't understand. Well, he's a man,' said Mrs Opie tolerantly. 'I wasn't prepared for how tired I'd be, crying for lack of sleep, and Wendy, I swear, never slept a wink until she was eight months old. But it's getting better. And I don't care what Mr Bell says, Miss Lavender was kind. She did like knowing things, I admit.'

'And clearly someone objected to her,' said Miss Phillips, 'or they wouldn't have killed her.'

There was a gasp. Mrs Charlesworth folded her hands.

'We will now say a short prayer,' she announced. 'Almighty and merciful God, we commend our sister Marcella Lavender to thy tender care, knowing that whosoever believeth in thee shall not perish, but have everlasting life.'

'Amen,' said *Women's Choice*.

CHAPTER TEN

In the third line, undivided, we see the superior man active and vigilant all the day and in the evening still careful and apprehensive. The position is dangerous, but there will be no mistake.

Hexagram 1: Khien
The I Ching Book of Changes

Phryne got home without anyone else trying to murder her and arrived at her own front door with a sense of accomplishment and a box binder under her arm. Dot opened the door and smiled. Phryne gave her the box.

'Good evening, Dot. How has your day been? Hang on to that for me, it's pure trinitrotoluol and ought to give us some valuable clues. Hello! There can't have been another postal delivery today. Where did that letter come from?'

'Hand delivered, Miss. Just a few moments after you left.'

Phryne turned the letter over. It was much thumbprinted, shabby and closed with a red wafer. Although she could not read Chinese, she recognised the characters for Lin, written in an ancient decorative script. She knew that seal.

Something made her examine the letter carefully before opening it. 'Who delivered it?' she asked, walking to her desk and turning on a

145

powerful lamp. The front of the envelope had an inscription in Chinese on one side and on the other her own name and address written in precise, well-formed characters. Lin Chung's writing without a doubt.

'A man, Miss. Not a young man. A sailor, maybe. I gave him five shillings like it says on the back.'

Phryne read the note on the back. 'Please give the bearer of this letter five shillings on receipt.'

'Did you ask him where it came from?'

'Yes, Miss, but all he said was "Five North. I found it, see? So the five bob's mine." I thought you'd want the letter so I gave him the money and he went away.'

'I see,' said Phryne. She was fighting a superstitious urge to hide the letter. She really didn't want to open it.

'Did I do wrong, Miss?' asked Dot, alarmed by Phryne's stillness.

'Eh? No, no perfectly correct, Dot. Now do go away, there's a dear.'

Dot went. Phryne drew a deep breath, held it, let it out, grabbed her paperknife and slit the envelope.

It had seemed rather misshapen. This was explained when she saw the enclosure. Laid out on the pale blue blotter was a folded letter and a scrap of something like oilskin. It smelt disgusting, like partially cured meat, like the breath of Pennell's Boiling Down Works which blanketed Richmond with a charnel house reek whenever there was a hot north wind. Phryne turned it over with a pencil.

Then she saw the scrolls and foliations of a human ear, lobe and channel complete. It had been severed with a sharp knife and dipped in some chemical solution and somewhat flattened by its journey in the envelope from – wherever the envelope had come from.

Phryne turned away from the smell for a moment and fought down horror with a will of adamant. If this was what she thought it was – Lin Chung's ear – then someone was going to suffer, someone was going to be really, really sorry for doing this, before Phryne let them die.

Horror and weakness vanished. No one in her immediate circle had ever seen Phryne really angry and ordinarily she kept this killing rage, a legacy from her Celtic ancestors, a close secret. In this state, she knew, she was literally capable of anything, and not since she had interrupted a couple of her schoolmates torturing a dog had she lost it. Then it had taken the combined efforts of three teachers to hold her and prize the remains of the stable rake from her grasp. She had never regretted learning in that way what a really good rage can do, although – as usual – she had been expelled. She had taken the dog with her, and was willing to bet that those two girls would be very chary of even looking unkindly at a dog ever again. After they got out of the infirmary, of course.

But such a rage was not to be loosed, in case she found herself coming out of it with a mangled corpse at her feet and nothing much to say to the arresting officer but 'Oops'. Therefore she had kept it under rigid control ever since.

Now, however, she was willing to make an exception.

She unfolded the letter. The ink had run where the grisly enclosure had seeped fluid into the paper. She pinned it flat under a paperweight and sat down with a magnifying glass to construe.

'Silver Lady', it began. Lin Chung's writing and one of his names for her. 'I do not expect to see you again. She of Bias Island has plans for me. My family must comply with her request and I fear that they will not find it expedient. Take this relic to Grandmother with my respectful regards. Farewell. Remember when you see the moon that I will be there, and death cannot destroy love. Lin Chung.'

Phryne read it again, then copied it in her fast, clear script onto plain bank paper. She sat still for a while. Twilight grew in the cooling parlour. Phryne stared at the rising moon through the uncurtained bow window. 'Remember when you see the moon that I will be there.'

But he was not there. He was on Bias Island, wherever that might be, and someone called She of Bias Island had plans for him which his family might not comply with – might not find expedient? Death cannot destroy love? Possibly not, but it could certainly delay it adequately. Moonlight silvered the dreadful object on the blotting paper.

'No,' said Phryne very softly. 'No, I will not accept this.'

She picked up the heavy blue glass paperweight, hefted it consideringly in both hands and then threw it with all her force into the black-leaded grate.

It exploded with the noise of a four-inch shell in that silent parlour.

Five seconds later the entire complement of the household was in the room. Phryne was standing amid a litter of blue glass shards. Her face was white, her eyes blazed like emeralds, and no one who saw her had any intention of saying anything but 'Immediately' to anything she ordered.

'Mr Butler, telephone the Lin residence. Say that Miss Fisher has received a communication from Lin Chung and requires – not requests, Mr Butler, requires – an audience with Madame Lin at noon tomorrow. Mrs B, fetch me a small jar from the kitchen and fill it with coarse salt. And a paper bag. Dot, find the brandy. A large glass. Girls, you spoke to Lin Chung alone – you were sitting with him when I was called away to the telephone the last time we saw him. Did he say anything to you about his journey? Anything to indicate that it might be dangerous?'

'Yes,' said Ruth, edging closer to Jane. She had never seen Phryne look like that. An angel, perhaps. Or a devil. Something not quite human. 'You remember, Jane. About the pirates.'

'Oh, yes, so he did. We were asking which way he was going and he said that parts of the Chinese coast were dangerous now because China was in turmoil and the pirates of the South China Sea were operating again.' Jane stepped half a pace back under the force of Phryne's fierce regard. 'He ... he said that they were as organised as Henry Morgan's Port Royal and twice as cruel and that there was nothing romantic about pirates. He said they killed the crew and took

149

hostages for ransom and cut bits off them and sent them to their relatives...' Jane backed further away and came up against a table. 'But he said he was travelling on a big ship and they'd never dare attack a big ship. He said they preyed on small boats and fugitives, not on big ships which might have armed men onboard. That's what he said. That's all he said,' she added, and Ruth nodded in confirmation.

Phryne waved a hand to dismiss them and they escaped back to the kitchen. Ruth then escorted Jane to the outside lavatory, where she was copiously sick. Her scientific mind had just analysed the juxtaposition of what Lin Chung had said about pirates, Phryne's statement that she had received something from him, and the demand for coarse salt in a small jar. When she stopped retching, she told Ruth, and they went back into the bright kitchen, huddled together with their puppy and cried quietly, because Lin Chung had also told them that South China Sea pirates sometimes didn't release their hostages, preferring to take the money and kill them to save food.

'I liked him,' sobbed Jane.

'So did I,' said Ruth.

Molly, the puppy, whimpered and licked their faces.

'Madame Lin will see you at noon, Miss Fisher,' reported Mr Butler, treating his employer with all the caution due to an unexploded grenade. 'Will there be anything else?'

'Yes. Call Bert's landlady and get him on the phone. Tell him and Cec to find out all they can about the South China Sea pirates and report to me. Yesterday might be too late but I'll see them tomorrow at five. Tell him I'll pay anything he wants and – you may tell him not to fail me.'

Mr Butler nodded and went out. Phryne gulped some of the brandy. She needed to calm down. Scalding her household with invective would not help Lin Chung. And for the moment there was nothing else to be done.

She picked up the fragment of Lin Chung and laid it respectfully in the jar, shook salt over it, and enclosed jar, letter and envelope in the paper bag. She heard a partial conversation from the hall.

'No, I don't think so. She's looking like an avenging angel and asking you not to fail her. I shouldn't. I really shouldn't, unless you want to take your intestines home in a sugar bag. Both of you, and you'll go out right away? Good. I'll tell her. Good night.'

Phryne sat down carefully, as though she might break the chair, and stared into the fireplace. She heard someone's shoes crunching over the broken glass and looked up into Dot's plain, familiar, worried face.

'Miss?'

'Dot?'

'Is it Mr Lin? Have them pirates got him?'

'I believe so, Dot. I believe so.'

'Then you've done all you can for tonight,' said Dot sensibly. 'Come upstairs, now, have a nice bath with them chestnut-blossom salts and dress for dinner. You've got all them letters to look at after dinner, and I'll start a rosary for your special intention before I go to bed. Mr B says that Bert and Cec are going out now looking for your information and they'll be here at five like you said. Come along now,' said Dot. 'And let Mr B clean up all that broken glass with that new vacuum machine what he's so proud of.'

Phryne, suddenly drained, went.

Bert stumbled slightly as he went up the steps of the Courthouse Hotel. With sufficient thirst, enterprise and a little travelling, it was possible to drink for twenty-four hours of the day, following the variable opening hours of hotels near the railway stations, the docks and the markets. The only pub which deigned to open its door between the hours of four-thirty and six in the morning was the Courthouse, a fact which failed to endow it with any charms except scarcity. Market porters, carters, taxi drivers, lost sailors and solid hard-case lunatics were the only clientele and their wants were easily satisfied by the Courthouse, provided they only desired beer in profusion and sawdust to spit – or sleep – in.

'Just like 'ome,' commented Bert. 'I 'ope this bloke's 'ere, cos I 'ave to tell you, mate, I'm nearly buggered.'

'Me too,' said Cec. He drooped over the bar, ordered two more beers, and asked, 'You seen Pirates tonight?'

The barman, hands full, gestured with a free elbow.

'That's Pirates over there,' he said, slamming two pots down on the towelling and accepting Cec's coins. Cec was sober – one of them had to drive and the car was the bonzer new cab which they were both very proud of – and very bored. He never reckoned that he had seen the inside of enough hostelries before, but now he was beginning to wish for his own bed and the undemanding company of his cats. Bert, who had been drinking half the beer which they had had to buy in exchange for information, was staggering.

Cec helped his friend over to the table where a man in a dark cap and watchcoat was staring into an empty glass with mournful intensity.

'G'day,' said Bert, grabbing a chair and lowering himself into it with care. 'You Pirates?'

'Who wants to know?' demanded a gravelly voice, proceeding from a face leathery with weather and disfigured with scars. He had the watery, pink-rimmed eyes of the grog habitué, but they were webbed around by the kind of crow's feet which only came from staring across bright water to unimagined distances. Bert nodded to Cec. They had, at last, found their man.

'A bloke who wants to do you a good turn,' said Cec, putting down a pot in front of him.

'No one ain't done me one of them since the cook locked me in the stokehole when I went troppo,' said Pirates, draining the pot in one long, practised gulp. 'Off Rio, that was. What sort of good turn?'

'We want to pay you for tellin' us about the pirates of the South China Sea,' said Bert, belching behind his hand. Pirates began to laugh.

'You want to pay me?' he giggled. 'I been trying to tell blokes about the pirates since I got back and no one wants to know.'

'I do,' said Bert. 'So does an impatient sheila

153

who's gonna have our guts for garters if we don't have the full quid on South China Sea pirates by five this afternoon. Ten shillings to begin with, and all the whisky you can drink.'

'I reckon that old Father Reilly was right,' said Pirates reverently. 'In the end, you get your reward in heaven.' He waited until the note was in his pocket and the new bottle of whisky, opened under Cec's censorious eye, was on the table. 'It was the *Sunming*,' he began. 'Captain Foster, South China Navigation Company – British crew, out of Macao. Big ship, too. Three thousand or so tons, two hundred passengers, freight, and – we thought – a safe full of bullion for Honkers. Last year, this was. Good ship, good food. Lot of Chinks in the crew, though, stokers and stewards, and most of the passengers was Chinks. But we searched everyone coming on board for weapons and we checked all the baggage for arms. Them Bias Island pirates are monsters. Run it like a business, you see. Worst of 'em all is the man in tortoiseshell glasses, though Mountain of Gold runs 'im close. She's a widow. They say 'er 'usband died after a little domestic tiff.

'Anyway, since you're paying for the story; you can fill me glass again. We didn't know nothing about any trouble till they shut the engine room off and we changed course. Heading for Bias Island, we were. We heard shots. They grabbed a lot of women and children and sent 'em crawling up the companionway to the deck and from there to this grille which shut off the bridge, begging the captain to let them in. He refused and the pirates threw 'em all overboard. Babies and all.

154

They screamed as they fell but by then the water was full of *tiburones*. You know what *tiburones* are?'

'Nah.' Bert was finding the fast cockney-Australian voice hard to follow.

'I know,' said Cec. 'Sharks.'

'Yeah,' said Pirates. 'They followed us all the way after that. Good table for a shark, where pirates are. They just didn't care about people, not at all. They was tryin' to find the comprador, the liaison officer between the Chink crew and the officers. Ten coolies they lined up and asked each one, "Where's the comprador?" And they all knew he'd blacked his face and was hiding in the engine room, and they all said they didn't know, and they all went over into the mouths of the sharks. You know they turn belly-up when they surface to eat you? Pale bellies like tripe.'

'Have another drink,' said Bert, a little unnerved.

'Don't mind if I do,' said Pirates.

Phryne had bathed, dressed and eaten dinner, of a sort. The girls had elected to stay in the kitchen with Molly and Mrs Butler. Dot saw that it was no use urging Phryne to keep her strength up. Her mistress was in a cold, dangerous rage and although Dot was not frightened of Miss Phryne, she was not stupid either. She murmured some quiet banalities as Phryne sipped a glass of wine, ate two spoonfuls of soup, three mouthfuls of poulet ragout, a taste of Apple Charlotte and one chocolate mint. With all that rage inside her there probably wasn't room for anything more, Dot thought. No wonder she had scared the girls.

155

They hadn't seen her like this before. Neither had Dot. She was concerned about what Phryne was likely to do. Nothing seemed beyond the scope of such magnificent fury. In such a mood she might take on the entire pirate population of Bias Island, wherever that was. And she might win.

'I have brought a box of letters home,' said Phryne at last.

'Yes, Miss?'

'We need to find out who "Desperate" was, and Anne, and the others. Someone killed Miss Lavender carefully, with planning, on purpose. And I need to talk again to the people who live in the apartments. They all, it appears, have secrets and Miss Lavender liked secrets. She may have collected them because she was lonely and felt it connected her to the real world. Or because they gave her a sense of power.'

'Or because she was an interfering old busybody,' said Dot.

'That, too. I've got her dossier in the box as well. Jack delivered it just before I left *Women's Choice*. Dot, I don't want to wake any painful memories, but when you were kidnapped by anarchists, how did you feel?'

'Scared,' said Dot instantly. 'Of course. But I knew you'd be coming for me.'

'And as the time went on and I didn't come?'

'I knew you would,' said Dot with simple faith. 'I passed the time playing with the firing pin of that big gun and that gave me something to do. I just waited.'

'Lin Chung doesn't have that consolation,' said Phryne.

'Of course he does,' said Dot briskly. 'He knows you'll come, and he also knows his family will come. Very loyal, them Chinese families. They won't leave him there. If you don't get anything sensible out of old Madame Lin, you can always go to Hong Kong and get the British to take some action. They've got warships.'

'Send a gunboat?' asked Phryne with rising inflection.

'Why not?' replied Dot stoutly.

'Why not indeed?' repeated Phryne. It could be done. She was rich and titled, she had influence, and the British might have been waiting for a reason to clean out the nest of pirates only fifty miles from Hong Kong.

'You make me feel better, Dot. I can get to Hong Kong in a couple of days if I organise it with Bunji's flying chums. But I mustn't buzz off half-cocked into the blue without sufficient information. *"Ek sal en plan maak"*, as Peter Pienaar says in John Buchan. And the situation is very John Buchan, isn't it?'

Dot, who only read detective stories and devotional works, didn't know, but nodded. Phryne was losing some of her blue-tinted, cold aloofness and this was good. Dot ventured further.

'So maybe we can look at those letters, Miss, and then you'll take that sleeping draught Doctor Watson left for you last time?'

'I'll sleep,' said Phryne, pouring herself another glass of the good brandy. 'All right, Dot, bring on the letters and let's see what we shall see.'

Dot obeyed. Mr Butler cleared the table and Phryne spread out the dossier on Miss Lavender.

'Birth certificate. Marcella Joan Lavender born in Carlton on the seventeenth of September, 1877. She wasn't as old as I thought, Dot. Only fifty-one. Looked at least twenty years older than that. Father was a schoolteacher, mother also. That would explain the system of child-raising which caused her to break out in fairies in later life. Her parents were fanatical about facts, Mrs McAlpin says, and didn't allow any stories or religion at all.'

'No religion?' gasped Dot.

'Not a single bible story. Not one parable. Not even a fable, not a Mother Goose rhyme, nothing to soften the hard edges of reality. I see that Papa Lavender wrote a book. *On Scientific Child Rearing.* Jack hasn't been able to locate a copy. Miss Lavender might have had one, though I doubt it. Deservedly out of print. They only had one child. They turned poor Miss Lavender into a fiction-starved adult and then they died and left her, at twenty – yes, both death certificates in the same year, 1898. What do you think happened next, Dot?'

'She married a rotter,' said Dot. 'No religion, no principles. No priest to ask advice from. No relatives, by the look of it. No aunts.'

'What use are aunts?' asked Phryne, who considered herself over-aunted.

'They tell you what's wrong with your young man,' said Dot, and blushed. 'And I suppose that sometimes they're right.'

'But not in the case of a certain Hugh Collins?' teased Phryne.

'No,' said Dot.

Phryne smiled. This surprised her. She didn't think she was likely to smile at present. But Dot was right. Aunts and cousins acted as a chamber of review for family decisions. However much they might irritate the advised, they did at least relentlessly advise. And even though their advice was mostly ignored, it was another point of view. Marcella Lavender was alone in the world and seemed unlikely to have formed many friendships. When a pretty young man with no principles strayed her way, she was going to fall and fall hard.

'Here's the marriage certificate,' said Dot, extracting it. 'Captain James West, profession: gentleman.'

'Another word for idle layabout,' said Phryne. 'In some cases,' she added, seeing Dot's shocked look. 'Miss Lavender had a reasonable competence. I wonder how long it took the good captain to run through her fortune?'

'Not very long,' said Dot. 'This police brief says that she lived with him for about eight months. Then he left her and his whereabouts are unknown. She got a divorce for desertion seven years later. Then she took her own name back. In between she was living for a while in a spiritualist community in Eltham. When she came back to Melbourne she sold the family home and put the money into Funds. She was living in a private hotel in South Yarra for most of the time before she moved into Mrs Needham's.'

'Why did she move?'

'Here it is,' said Dot. 'The brief says that she needed more space for her art work. She was making a reasonable living with all that fairy stuff. They say she was good. Took classes in botanical drawing at the Mechanics' Institute and got top marks.'

'Yes, she was good, but only technically. See, look at this one.'

'A waratah,' said Dot. 'Just like a real one.'

'It's a really accurate waratah. Every petal just as nature painted it. Every leaf in place, every serration delineated perfectly. But it's got no life, Dot. Even the fairies are flat. Now you may not like May Gibbs, but her characters have life. Sentimental, sugary life, I admit. But they vibrate.'

This went entirely over Dot's head. As far as she could see, a good waratah was hard to draw and Miss Lavender had managed it. In matters of art, Dot liked to know what she was looking at.

'If you say so, Miss,' she agreed. Phryne thanked her stars that she was not trying to explain surrealism to Dot and went back to the dossier.

'Well, well, never mind. What else do we know about Miss Lavender?'

'Just that she's been getting a substantial payment from Marshall and Co. The police are still trying to find out about them. All the other payments come from her art work and her magazine work. Her account is at the Commonwealth Bank and it's healthy. She had a separate account for the Marshall and Co. payments. She might have been saving up.'

'She might have been blackmailing someone,' said Phryne.

'Do you really think so, Miss?' Dot was a little taken aback. She was feeling sorry for Miss Lavender. It seemed like a sad, aimless life.

'She liked secrets,' said Phryne. 'She liked to know what was happening. That can be a harmless fascination with other people or a lucrative trade. We really must find out about Marshall and Co., Dot. Well, that's Miss Lavender. Hello! What's this?'

'A photograph,' said Dot, wondering if Phryne's wits had gone astray.

'But what a photograph,' said Phryne.

Miss Lavender sat in an old-fashioned studio, one hand on a plinth, a violent thunderstorm behind her. But this was a modern photograph, taken in an instant. The photographer had clearly been talking to the model, for what was surprised on Miss Lavender's face was a pursed expression of shrewish ferocity.

'She's screwed up her face,' said Dot. 'Probably that flash.'

'No, I don't think so,' said Phryne slowly. 'She hasn't shut her eyes. What a picture! She looks like an inquisitor who's just found a whole village riddled with witchcraft, ordering the gallows to be built. And I know who took the photo,' she added. She told Dot the name before her assistant could turn it over.

'Right you are,' said Dot. 'McAlpin.'

'I wonder if I could get her to take me?' said Phryne. 'On second thoughts, not. She has a habit of taking pictures of souls and I don't think I want mine exposed this clearly.'

Dot, who had no idea what Phryne was talking about, opened the box binder. It contained letters.

'Half each,' said Phryne and they opened and

161

read in silence for some time.

'Miss?' asked Dot anxiously. 'I've found another letter from "Moderne". She says sorry for being cross and her husband has come back so it's all right now and she likes the new decor. And I've found Anne.'

'Good. I've found "Desperate". She shouldn't be here, of course. Her letter should have been returned or destroyed. Possibly the person who extracted the letter bunged it in here for destruction later. Surprised, perhaps, in the act. It hasn't got an envelope. What was wrong with "Desperate"?' Phryne read for a moment, then said, 'Oh dear.'

Dot accepted the letter. It was written in wavery pale ink. Each line drooped sadly down at the edge of the page.

'"I'm so tired all the time",' Dot read. '"I find it hard to get out of bed. I sleep all the time. I'm so miserable that nothing seems real. The house door, sometimes, is like a portcullis, keeping me prisoner. When I lie down to sleep sometimes I feel that the room is spinning and I am being dragged down into a black hole. The world is all grey. I have no joy. I keep going because of the children but I can't bear it much more. Help me. 'Desperate'." Poor thing! What happened to her?'

'She died, Dot, and I suspect she was a suicide. Those are all symptoms of depression.'

'Well, she could have taken a tonic,' said Dot.

'No, Dot, I'm talking about serious depression. The world is grey and there is no joy, only unplumbed despair. A few years like that and anyone would decide that death is preferable.

We'd better find out who she was.'

'The envelope you discovered at Miss Lavender's had a post office box,' said Dot. 'The cops can find out who it belongs to.'

'All right. What's Anne's problem?'

Dot pinkened. 'Her husband can't...'

'Can't what?'

'Just er ... can't. Here, you read it.' Dot handed over the letter. Phryne scanned it quickly.

'"I entered a companionate marriage. I didn't know what I was doing. My husband is an older man and he always said he didn't want children. Neither do I, so I went to the clinic and got some instructions and a contraceptive device. I told him about it and he didn't seem interested. What should I do?" Good question. I wonder if Miss Lavender gave her advice on how to seduce a man?'

'I shouldn't think so,' said Dot. 'I don't expect she knew a lot about it. She was only married for eight months and she must have been unhappy.'

'She would know about the mechanics,' said Phryne. 'That relentlessly factual education she received would have taken in the biological details. But there is a great deal more to it than that,' said Phryne.

'I'm sure you're right,' said Dot, trying not to blush. 'Do we have the answer to Anne's letter?'

'No, and it's another thing which does not belong. This box was supposed to contain the un-attributed or unaddressed letters for destruction. It has, Dot dear, been salted. Can we find Anne?'

'There's an address on the letterhead,' said Dot. 'It's embossed. She's scribbled it out but I might be able to read it in a good light.'

'If you can't the police laboratory probably can. One more mystery. We don't even know what the lady with the Kew postmark was going on about. Empty out the binder, Dot. It's likely to be at the bottom.'

'Why?'

'Because if you are trying to hide something, you instinctively push it to the bottom of the box and pile all the rest of the stuff on top. That way your secret is not disclosed to a casual survey. Anything from Kew which might draw forth a death threat for an unhelpful reply?'

'This one's about greasy hair and this one's about chickenpox scars,' said Dot. 'This one's about a child that won't eat its nice rice pudding and this one ... perhaps it might be this one,' said Dot, handing over a small piece of paper written in the same square handwriting of the unsigned threat. Phryne held the two letters together and compared them. Same paper, same handwriting.

'A match, I think?' she asked. Dot nodded.

'"Dear Artemis, I'm in awful trouble. I'm the mother of three children and I'm a widow. I work as a cleaning lady for a lot of different houses. One of my children is ill and the doctor says he has to have medicine and I can't afford it. I saw a ten shilling note on the floor of one house. It was folded up small as though it fell out of a watch pocket. I swept it up with the dust and used it to buy the medicine for my little Billy. Now he's worse and it's a judgment on me. What should I do?" That doesn't sound like it would give rise to threats of murder.'

'It depends on what Artemis told her to do,' said Dot.

'Well, whatever it was, it didn't work, did it? Any address on the letter?'

'Yes, Miss. Carlton. Lygon Street.'

'Good. Go there tomorrow morning, Dot, dear, she's more likely to talk to you. Take some money. If she's that skint she might respond to a little cash in hand. See if you can get the address from Anne's letter, too. The police should come up with the owner of the post box where "Desperate" had her letters sent by tomorrow. That's the five on my A list,' said Phryne. 'We may be getting somewhere, Dot.'

'I do hope so, Miss,' said Dot. 'What are you going to do tomorrow?'

'I'm going to find out about the residents of the apartments in the afternoon,' said Phryne. 'I will go to the Adventuresses in the morning. I need to speak to Bunji Ross. I might need to hire a plane,' said Phryne.

She put herself to bed and dreamt of nothing at all.

'Where you takin' me?' slurred Pirates as Cec lifted him not ungently out of the chair and half carried him towards the door.

'To my place for a bit of a sleep, and then we have to clean you up to meet a lady.'

'Took us all night to find you,' agreed Bert, colliding slowly with the doorpost, revolving once, and skidding down the steps. 'You're a slippery bugger, Pirates. Come on. There's another quid in it for yer.'

'Could do with a bit o' kip,' agreed Pirates.

Both he and Bert were fast asleep before Cec could start the bonzer new taxi.

CHAPTER ELEVEN

The third line, divided, shows one acting contrary to the method of nourishing. Let him take no action for ten years, for it will not be in any way advantageous.

Hexagram 27: I
The I Ching Book of Changes

The Adventuresses Club was always quiet in the morning. Most of the ladies had families, work or trades, or a combination of them all. Kate let Phryne in through the brass bound door, which had belonged to the good old lawless days of Melbourne, where if one wanted to re-enact the old Irish test, a virgin of either sex carrying the statutory baby and a crock of gold wouldn't survive unrobbed and unravished for more time than it took the local criminals to rehitch their jaws.

In the enlightened and modern year of 1928, the virgin might make it to the tram if he or she ditched the gold or the baby and was reasonably fit.

Phryne smiled slightly as she rode up to the library in the lift. Concentrated research might calm her mind. What did the library contain?

A very good map of the South China Sea, for a

start. Phryne spread it out on the table and pinned the corners flat with *The Life and Death of Scarlatt Blackbones, Pyrat*, a *Guidebook to Hong Kong*, volume nine of *The Newgate Chronicle or the Malefactor's Bloody Register* and a small shabby book called *Reminiscences of the South China Sea by A Lady*. This might, of course, prove to be pornography. A lot of tomes written by A Lady were. No one weeded the Adventuresses Club library and a curious collection of books had accumulated as members culled their own libraries or inherited or bought strange volumes. Phryne understood that there was an excellent collection on 'Magic in Theory and Practice' and quite a number of travellers' tales.

The members themselves were required to write copious notes, if not actually publish books, on their own adventures. These were frank enough to beguile even on a dark, sleety afternoon in July.

Borrowing books was simple. One wrote the titles in a large book. If they were not returned, the committee sent a deputation around to reclaim them. Unpublished books could not be borrowed. The committee had strong views on the way that amazing deeds done by women vanished out of the historical record, and they had a collection of the works of Mary Kingsley, Gertrude Bell, Flora Tristan, Mildred Cable and Francesca French, among others, to prove it. Phryne had heard that the club was intending to bring out small editions of the travellers' tales. Just so that no one could delete them again. So that no one could call an explorer, by definition, 'he'.

Phryne located Bias Island, its bay clearly marked, in a niche of coast not far from Hong Kong. The Chinese shore, which stretched up to Russia and down past Borneo, was riddled with little inlets in which a pirate might hide. Not to mention all those islands which dotted the ocean all the way to Australia. A place positively designed for piracy.

Phryne left the map and consulted *The Life and Death of Scarlatt Blackbones,* discarding it after a brief skim. Eighteenth century Port Royal scoundrels would not assist in her endeavours. She shut the book on the illustration of the 'pyrat's horrid fate', which was quite comprehensive, and opened the *Guidebook to Hong Kong.* No index entry on piracy. She flipped quickly through. The only mention was a footnote, in which the reader was told that 'travelling in a small coastal craft exposes the traveller to the risk of piracy. An expedition has long been mooted to clear out the pirates from Bias Island, a notorious pirate stronghold. Doubtless the authorities will take condign action in the near future. Meanwhile, tourists are asked to consider booking passage on the larger ships, which are not attacked.'

Nice, but not a lot of use to Lin Chung. During the 'strong action', the pirates would kill any prisoners so that they could not bear witness against them. Not encouraging. Phryne rang the bell and ordered coffee.

The Newgate Chronicle contained the awful story of the fate of the *Mignonette,* in which the shipwrecked sailors ate the cabin boy, Richard Parker. Interesting but not helpful. Phryne left it open at the other entry on pirates.

The little book by A Lady was treasure. The Lady had been the concubine of one of the White Rajah's young men, and he had taught her English while she had taught him the local language. Her grandmother had been a pirate with the famous Shap-'ng-tsai, whose fleets had been wrecked by an expedition under Commander Dalrymple in 1849. Steam had outmanoeuvred sail and superior firepower had decimated the fleet. Female pirates were not uncommon, it seemed. A Lady mentioned Ching Shih, widow of a notorious pirate, who had commanded an entire navy of junks and had later retired into smuggling as a less perilous life. The first clearing of Bias Bay, and the reason why the guidebook was so sure that the authorities would sooner or later act, was to extirpate the pirate Chui Apu in 1849. It had been successful. But the pirates had come back. After all, why abandon a strategically perfect island just because it was burned down? The island remained. The loss of ships had been great, but the fleet could be built up again by trade and theft. Commander Dalrymple had gone to his reward and the pirates were back in Bias Bay.

After all, what was a ship? A small floating prison. All its valuables were in one place and could not be otherwise hidden. One could not run away, especially in shark-infested seas. The pirates attacked the equivalent of the lonely farmhouse on the moor, far from help. Unless there was some strange stroke of luck, there would be no rescue. The sea was very big.

Despicable. Phryne slammed *The Newgate Chronicle* shut on a picture of the Notorious Female Pyrat Mary Read, closed the *Reminiscences* and rolled up the map. If she had to, she would fly to Hong Kong and lean on the Governor. Something had to be done.

Dot paused outside the small house in Carlton, gathering up her courage. Lygon Street was hot and busy. Dot had put on her most subdued clothes. She did not want to frighten Mrs Joyce, the cleaning lady. Dot had found out the name from the municipal register. The fact that Mrs Joyce was in there at all meant that she was alone. If she had been married, her husband's name would have been listed as the householder.

The house was shabby. It needed a paint job and the removal of the birds' nests from the spouting. It was one of those flat-faced stone houses with a heavy balcony above the front door, casting it into black shadow. The front doorstep, however, the housewife's pride, was scrubbed as white as snow.

She knocked. Slow footsteps dragged their way to the door, which creaked open. A middle-aged woman wiped her soapy hands on her red-flowered apron and said, 'Yes?'

The voice had not been born to be a cleaning lady. 'My name is Dot Williams,' said Dot. 'I've got a question to ask. Can I come in?'

'If you're from the landlord, I haven't got the money yet. I lost a cleaning job recently.'

'I know you did. On Artemis's advice,' said Dot gently.

'Do you come from that bitch?' demanded the woman, balling one fist.

'She's dead,' said Dot. Faded blue eyes scanned her face and what they saw must have satisfied them.

'Good,' said Mrs Joyce with deep satisfaction. 'Come in.'

'You're here alone?' asked Dot, following her down the hall to a small, sparkling clean parlour. There was a fresh frill of paper in the fireplace and every surface gleamed. Mrs Joyce clearly kept the same standards for her own house as for her clients.

'Just me and little Billy. He's asleep, so I've been getting on with the washing. Due to that Artemis, I lost my five mornings a week. I'll have to find another position, but work's hard to get when you can't live in. My other two are at school. What's your question?'

'What did Artemis tell you?'

'To go and confess,' said Mrs Joyce disgustedly. 'And me so soft and so worried about Billy, I did. And they fired me on the spot without a reference. They'd never have known if I hadn't told them. I managed to pay the ten shillings back so they didn't call the police but that meant I've got behind on the rent and that skinflint won't hesitate to throw me out on the street.'

'If you can give me some answers and Artemis's letter, I can pay you for them,' said Dot awkwardly. She was not happy offering people money. This consideration did not seem to bother Mrs Joyce.

'I've got it somewhere...' She rummaged in a

171

large straw basket with raffia flowers on it, sorted through a handful of unpaid bills and found an envelope.

'All right, now, Miss, some answers from you,' she said firmly. 'Who are you and why do you want this letter?

'Artemis was murdered,' said Dot. 'The police investigation was delayed. My employer is a private detective, Miss Phryne Fisher. She wants to collect the evidence in a quiet way and present the Detective Inspector with the result. Otherwise he'll be rummaging through everyone's private life and making scandals.'

'She's protecting someone,' declared Mrs Joyce.

'Probably,' said Dot. 'But I trust her.'

Mrs Joyce was captured by Dot's transparent simplicity. Here was a young woman who meant exactly what she said. Mrs Joyce stretched her aching back, folded her work-worn hands in the lap of her apron and surrendered.

'All right, what's the question?'

'Did you know Artemis? Where she lived, who she was?'

'No. How could I? I sent that letter, I was so wild, I can't afford to lose a job. Then I thought better of it, but it was too late. I never signed either of them so no one could find me, though your Miss Fisher did.'

'The letters were posted in Kew.'

'I've got a job in Kew. I just stuck them in the nearest letterbox.'

'Where were you on Sunday morning between seven and eight?'

'Getting the kids ready for Sunday School. We

go to Saint Joseph's, around the corner. Ask the priest if you don't believe me.'

'Early mass is eight o'clock,' mused Dot.

'So it is,' confirmed Mrs Joyce.

'I don't have anything else to ask,' said Dot. 'Will you sell me the letter?'

Mrs Joyce gave it to her. Dot opened her purse and handed over the five pound note Phryne had given her for bribes.

'Five quid?' asked Mrs Joyce, scanning the note as though she hadn't seen very many of them in her life.

'Miss Fisher is a generous lady. That ought to pay the rent and keep you going until you get another job,' said Dot. 'How's little Billy?'

'Getting on better now,' said Mrs Joyce, folding the note and secreting it in her corset. 'Doctor thinks he's turned the corner. Thanks. Tell your employer, thanks. Thanks very much. I'll...' Mrs Joyce scrambled for an adequate response, astounded by the wealth which had been lavished on her. 'I'll pray for her. This will make all the difference to us.'

Dot left on a wave of goodwill and walked away past the shops, mentally crossing Mrs Joyce off Phryne's list.

Now for Mrs Anne Corder, of Caroline Street, South Yarra. Dot took a tram, fumbling for pennies.

Little Bourke Street was not long enough. Phryne could have walked twice as far before her temper cooled, though even a foot race from Athens to Sparta, Sparta to Marathon and then

Marathon to Athens might not have had any appreciable effect. It did give her time to compose her mind.

Little Bourke was always busy and redolent of foreign scents and strange faces and unknown languages. On previous visits she had been with Lin Chung. They had been stared at and hurtful comments had been made; mixed marriages were not allowed in Little Bourke Street. Mixed alliances, between a fashionable and rich lady and the only grandson of Madame Lin, were allowable if that matriarch agreed, and so far, she had agreed.

Buddha only knows what she is going through now, thought Phryne as she knocked at the massive warehouse doors which enclosed the Lin mansion, like a wrinkled plum contains a nut, or a mussel shell its owner.

She was expected. The little door in the big ones opened and she stepped inside.

Out of the heat and glare into cool shade scented with gardenias. The Lin household lived in compounds contained within these sheet iron walls. It was ceaselessly patrolled. No burglar would have lived through his first 'Strewth!', assuming that he could be heard over the baying of the guard dogs.

Two of the uniformed men fell in on either side of Phryne and led her through deep shade, under an arch, and up several stairs into the main house. Carved, red lacquered doors opened. Frightened faces were glimpsed as she passed several rooms hung with different silks: aquamarine, copper, the yellow gold of the emperor, the green of emerald,

174

the rich red of wine, garnet or blood.

The guards conducted her into a small room. It was hung in azure and white, embroidered with phoenixes. Gauzy curtains were drawn back to reveal a richly green, scented garden. There were two carved blackwood chairs set on either side of a small table which bore only one ornament. It was a celadon pot of orchids as white as jade.

Madame Lin was standing as she came in. Phryne held out the satchel. A guard took it and placed the paper bag on the table. The orchids were heavily scented. Phryne felt almost dizzy.

'If you will sit?' asked Madame Lin in her quiet, cultured voice. Almost, but not quite, a perfect Occidental accent – she still stressed incorrectly, so that her speech was subtly, fundamentally, off-key. She was a gaunt woman no taller than Phryne. Her dress was Eastern, perhaps to emphasise the distance between the Chinese lady and the Western one. It was of the finest silk – in fact Phryne had never seen silk so glossy – but it was unfigured and the cut plain. It was white. She wore no jewellery. Her snowy hair was dressed in a smooth chignon held by invisible pins.

'You have something for me,' she said. Phryne indicated the bag. Madame Lin unfolded the top. The absence of conversational openings was very significant. Madame Lin was worried enough to appear discourteous, even though she was dealing with a *gangin*, a foreign devil.

Phryne was watching her as she turned the jar around and caught sight of what it contained. She gave a small gasp, instantly contained. So,

Madame had not been expecting this. Then she examined the letter and the envelope. Such loss of composure as there had been was repaired by the time she spoke again.

'On the outside, it is merely a message to the carrier to pass the letter on, because it is of importance to the Lin family and they will pay well for it. But it is addressed to you. Why is that so, do you think?'

'I don't know. He says he fears that you will not pay what these pirates want. Perhaps he thought that I might pay it.'

'That is something you cannot do,' said Madame Lin. 'What they want is something only the Lin family can give.'

'And will they give it?

'Is that for you to know?'

'Madame, this letter was sent to me,' said Phryne. 'As far as I knew, Lin Chung was in China on a silk-buying trip. Now I am told that there have been negotiations to set him free. How long have you known that he is captive, who's got him, and why? And did no one owe me the courtesy of telling me? I have abided by the deal I struck with you, Madame. That I would not take Lin away from his family, that I would give him back when you needed him to marry. That gives us a contractual relationship, at least.'

'You are correct,' said Madame. Phryne almost fell off her chair. 'It was a grave discourtesy not to inform you. But we received the demand, we transmitted a reply to our agents in Hong Kong, and we thought all would be well. It may still be well.'

'But you don't think so,' offered Phryne.

'He is my grandson. My heart misgives me. I am in mourning, as you observe, in a superstitious attempt to distract the demons who are bedevilling us. If they think that he is already dead they may take their eye off him.'

The door behind Phryne opened a crack. A quiet voice was insisting and the guard was asking Madame a question.

'Very well, if he must,' said Madame. She took a white handkerchief out of her sleeve and dabbed at her eyes. They were wet. Phryne was suddenly cold, as if she had been plunged into iced water. Madame Lin was crying. That formidable dragon was weeping. Things were terrible. They would almost certainly not be well.

'Silver Lady,' said a voice, and Phryne found a man kneeling at her feet. His hands were clasped together. His sleeves fell back to reveal a dragon brand on the inside of both forearms. She had only seen that once before. A Shao Lin monk from the temple of Confucius. There couldn't be more than one in Melbourne.

'Li Pen!' she exclaimed. 'You left Lin?'

His face turned to her. He had been beaten, badly, over a long time. Even now his bruises were yellow and he had stitches in a cut across one cheekbone.

'They made me their messenger,' he said. Lin had clearly kept up his bodyguard's English lessons. His voice was stilted but perfectly accented. In fact he sounded like Lin Chung, and Phryne had to suppress a sob which rose unbidden from some depth.

'Otherwise I would not have left him, even in death.'

'And you came home and showed Madame the message? How long did it take you to get here from the South China Sea?'

'A week. When I came to Hong Kong, I chartered a plane and came as fast as I could. But I could not lose the message.'

He opened his shirt and showed Phryne several characters cut into the smooth muscle of his chest. They had scabbed over and were healing. Li Pen was strong.

'They say, "Lin family lands",' said Madame. 'I cannot give them on my own. I have called a family council. The cousins will be here tomorrow. Our lands in China are worthless now. War and famine rage over the country. Most of our people are dead or fleeing. I will attempt to prevail over the council. But they may argue that land, once lost, cannot be regained, and the life of my heir is not worth the loss.'

'Li Pen, how is he? Will they kill him?' asked Phryne urgently. Li Pen took her hand. His touch was extraordinarily alive.

'Not unless the negotiations fail. He is safe while they are still talking. This letter and this offering are just ... an inducement to speed. If he was given a chance to write, Silver Lady, he would write to you. You do not understand about pirates.'

'No, but I will. Madame, send Li Pen to tell me how these negotiations go. I will always be at home to him. Will you allow this?'

'Yes,' Madame bowed her head.

'If there is anything I can do – anything – send for me. Madame,' Phryne rose and bowed slightly. Madame echoed the gesture.

Li Pen escorted Phryne out of the house and into the street. At the door she paused.

'Come anyway,' she whispered. 'I wish to talk to you.'

Li Pen bowed.

Phryne walked back to the Adventuresses the long way, to give herself time to adjust. She felt that she had just visited a very alien, very cold, very dangerous world. It had mutilated Li Pen and eaten up Lin Chung and, from Melbourne, there didn't seem to be a lot she could do about it. In fact there was nothing anyone could do until the Lin family made up their minds to pay the ransom. Phryne was not going to think about what would happen if they didn't pay it. Anyone strong and numerous enough to carve characters into Li Pen was not going to let Lin Chung go with a 'So sorry'.

She was thinking furiously. Two lots of pirates. That is what Madame had implied. Lin Chung had first been taken by one lot, who had demanded money which Madame had paid. Then he had been captured again by a second lot, who wanted the Lin family lands. They were the ones who had cut off his ear and recorded their demands, in fine calligraphy, on the living manuscript of Li Pen's chest. This was an insult which ought to be expunged in blood, and would be, if Li Pen ever got his hands on whoever had done it.

Phryne became aware of a Chinese man dogging her footsteps. He was dodging through the crowd, getting closer. If he laid a hand on her, she vowed, if he even thought a single assailant's thought, she was going to do something permanent to him.

He was now beside her, another of those anonymous serfs in blue, so ubiquitous in Little Bourke Street that no one noticed them. Without turning his head he said, 'It would be safer to leave Lin family matters alone.'

'Probably,' said Phryne.

'Shall I tell my master that you will do so?'

'If you like,' said Phryne.

She had slowed her pace, and right at the mouth of an alley she lunged and forced him out of the stream of foot traffic. He came up shocked with his back against a wall. A tigress was confronting him, baring her teeth.

'Who sent you?' she demanded, one heel grinding into his instep, one fist pulling his shirt collar chokingly tight around his throat.

'I can't tell you,' he whispered.

'You can,' she informed him. His eyes bulged. Phryne only relaxed her grip when he was about to pass out. It would require more time and more privacy to get any information out of this loyal servant, and the alley was hardly the place. She was already attracting attention from the passing trade.

'All right, you can't. Tell your master to stop these attacks on me or the next attacker will be taking his testicles home in a paper bag,' she snarled. Then she shoved the man so that he stumbled, unable to grab her. He exited the alley at speed and vanished into a side street.

Phryne shook herself into order, reseated her hat, and walked on.

The Adventuresses Club luncheon had improved. Crayfish, sole meunière and filet bordelaise were on the menu. Phryne ordered a lavish meal: bouillon, lobster mayonnaise with salad and an iced orange pudding. The installation of a larger ice-chest had obviously been a good investment. She was toying with Camembert and water biscuits with a strong fragrant coffee when Bunji Ross seated herself at the table and helped herself to a biscuit.

'Bunji dear!' exclaimed Phryne. 'Just the person.'

'Kate told me you were looking for me,' said Bunji. 'You know, this cheese is all runny.'

'It's supposed to be. Bring Miss Bunji some mousetrap and some more biscuits, will you?' asked Phryne of the waitress. 'It's about Lin Chung.'

'Your beautiful Chinese chap? What about him?'

'Pirates,' said Phryne.

Bunji looked grave. Her round, cheerful face lost its cheer. 'Gosh, Phryne, that's bad. Nasty people, pirates. Where?'

'Bias Island, South China Sea,' said Phryne, abruptly losing her appetite.

'Done a bit of flying around there,' said Bunji. 'Could probably get you there. Couple of days. Faster if we can risk flying at night. But it's a bit tricky, Phryne, old thing. Nowhere to land except bang on a nest of pirates. And Miss Jane – you know, the missionary, she's just finished her book

181

on Sarawak butterflies – she told me that the Dyaks attack anything smaller than a liner and just kill everyone and steal the ship. Rajah Brooke wiped them out in the nineteenth century, but they're back now that China's gone boom. Nervous part of the world. Nothing much you can do on your own. Might be better to go to Honkers and see what the navy can do.'

'Unfortunately, Bunji, that's the conclusion I had come to,' confessed Phryne.

'Still, far be it from me to stop a pal who wants to break her neck in a good cause,' said Bunji, halving a biscuit with a snap. 'If you want to fly, Phryne, I'm your flyer.'

'Thank you, Bunji,' said Phryne. 'But much as I am dying to do something, I'd better get on with finding out who murdered an old lady who liked secrets. That, at least, will give me something to occupy my time.'

'Do tell,' said Bunji, agog.

Phryne told. Bunji summed up.

'So you've got three groups of suspects. The ladies of the magazine. The people of the house. And the writers of the furious letters.'

'That's about it. A huge cast which has to be narrowed down or I'll never get anywhere. And of course there are some overlaps. Miss Grigg and Miss Gallagher, Mrs Opie and Mr Bell are all co-tenants with Miss Lavender, as well as working at *Women's Choice*. Some of the letter-writers may be co-tenants as well.'

'Good luck, then,' said Bunji, mopping up the last crumb of cheese. 'I'll be around for a couple of weeks before we start the ferry service over the

Tasman. Call me if you need me,' she said, and went away.

Phryne stayed, thinking about the odd web of relationships around the dead woman. Who had Miss Lavender been, anyway?

CHAPTER TWELVE

In the fifth line, undivided, we see the dragon on the wing in the sky. It will be advantageous to meet with the great man.

Hexagram 1: Khien
The I Ching Book of Changes

Dot paused with her hand on the iron gate, gathering courage. This was a nice house in a nice street. The sloping lawn was immaculate. The bright beds of pansies and sweet william were sparkling with water. The two-storey house was as bright as new enamel and as clean as a seashell.

Dot was daunted. This was not the same as bribing a downtrodden cleaning woman to part with a letter. But Phryne needed to know about Anne and Phryne was terribly worried about Mr Lin and therefore Dot needed to find out about Mrs Anne Corder.

She forced herself up the steps and rang the front door bell. It was answered by a woman thrumming with nerves. She was thin as a wire and seemed to vibrate. Her flyaway dark hair was alive with static and Dot fancied that electricity had given her such vivid grey eyes.

'Mrs Corder?'

'Yes,' said the woman. 'What can I do for you?'

'I need to know...' began Dot. Mrs Corder started to shut the door.

'I don't buy anything at the door, nor do I answer questions,' she snapped. Dot grabbed at the only advantage she had.

'Artemis,' she said.

Mrs Corder darted out, saw that no one was watching, dragged Dot inside and slammed the door.

'Have you come from her?' she hissed.

'She's dead,' said Dot.

'Dead?' said Mrs Corder.

'Murdered,' said Dot.

'I can't say I'm surprised,' commented Mrs Corder.

'I work for Miss Phryne Fisher,' said Dot, handing over one of Phryne's engraved cards. 'She's helping the police with their enquiries. She wants to eliminate as many people as she can so the police won't make a scandal.'

'She's protecting Artemis,' declared Mrs Corder. Her hands, Dot noticed, had a slight tremor. A small heap of off-white fur revealed itself to be a Scotch terrier, which began to sniff Dot's ankles suspiciously.

'And Artemis's clients,' said Dot.

'God, yes,' Mrs Corder passed a hand over her forehead. 'The Hon. Phryne Fisher, eh? Very well, I'll talk. Isn't that what they say in the movies?

Come into the kitchen, the girl's just gone. Would you like some tea? And there are gingernuts. I think there are. Come along, McTavish. This is my little friend, McTavish. Isn't he divine?'

The terrier, still sniffing Dot as though his Presbyterian ancestors had endowed him with the ability to scent out Catholics, trotted at her heel. Dot tried not to wonder how much value was about to be bitten out of her stockings. Mrs Corder was leading the way through an immaculate hall. Every picture was exactly square to the wall and every surface gleamed. 'Come and sit down, Miss Williams. I'm sure that she put the tea somewhere.'

Mrs Corder appeared so unhinged that Dot made the tea, finding the crockery, the ingredients and even the gingernuts by a sort of psychic echo-location. Dot had spent so much time in other people's kitchens that she divined where they might put the tea caddy without thinking. McTavish accepted a gingernut with a reluctant growl, probably considering that a decent Kirk Elder should not be asked to take food from the hand of the Scarlet Woman.

This was a very modern kitchen, spare and elegant. The linoleum was new, the sink and sink-heater still had labels attached to the pipes and the room smelt faintly of paint. The tea set was unchipped, fine German china of the flowing Art Decoratif lines which Phryne favoured. Mrs Corder had just completed the redecoration of her kitchen. A bribe, perhaps, from the impotent husband?

Dot poured the tea and sat down. Mrs Corder

185

took a deep sip and declared, 'I can't imagine why I wrote to Artemis. I wanted to have a companionate marriage. I don't like being ... being messed around. And Donald is a good man. We have the same tastes, read the same books, like the same plays and music. We like good food and wine and small parties. He has his group of men who do men things and I have my girlfriends. We go out together, shopping and so on. But I was listening to Julia talking about the body-urge, the poetry of the flesh, and I thought I'd like to try it, but I had no idea of how to go about it, so I asked Artemis and she told me...'

'What did she tell you? Do you still have the letter?'

'No, no, I burned it. It was so humiliating.' Mrs Corder shuddered. 'She said to buy a pretty negligee and have a scented bath and make a nice dinner with wine and then to snuggle up to him and touch him.'

'And?' asked Dot, not knowing whether she could cope with the reply.

'Disaster,' said Mrs Corder. 'He told me to stop behaving like a tart and stormed out and didn't come back for two days. Then he wouldn't talk to me for a week. And when I finally swore I would never, never do such a thing again, he told me to forget it and I suppose it's all right but I'll never forgive that Artemis for telling me to do such a thing. I was so embarrassed. He looked at me as though I was a ... a...'

'It's all over now,' soothed Dot. 'Drink your tea.'

'But if this should get out,' wailed Mrs Corder. 'If this should get into the papers, it will be the

186

end of it, I swear, he'll leave me and then what will I do?'

'It won't get into the papers,' said Dot. 'Not if you help Miss Fisher. Now tell me, did you know Artemis? Who she was, where she lived?'

'I tried to find out,' confessed Mrs Corder. 'I called at *Women's Choice* and asked to see Artemis and they told me that she didn't work in the office. They said they sent the letters to her. I followed a little blonde office girl up the road to the GPO but I couldn't see over her shoulder without attracting too much attention. So I gave it up. Anyway, Don had come home by then and everything was back to normal. Except that I felt like a wrung-out rag.'

'Indeed,' murmured Dot. 'Where were you on Sunday morning?'

'I don't see what business–' began Mrs Corder, then realised. Dot caught a glint of excitement in the grey eyes. 'Of course, I am being asked to account for my movements. How thrilling! I rose late on Sunday and made a nice breakfast for my husband and myself. Sausages, eggs, grilled toma-toes and bacon, if you must know. I must have got up at about nine and we breakfasted at ten.'

'And, er...' Dot was unsure how to phrase her next question. 'There was no one ... with you?'

'Only McTavish. He always sleeps on my bed, don't you, darling?'

McTavish was not a compellable witness. 'Do you drive, Mrs Corder?'

'No,' said Mrs Corder. 'I can always take a taxi if I need to get somewhere in a hurry. But on that Sunday morning I was being lazy. My husband could confirm that, but please don't ask him.'

'I can't promise,' said Dot honestly. 'But I don't think we'll need to. Thanks for the tea, Mrs Corder. Goodbye, McTavish.'

McTavish gave Dot a glare which told her that she had not been forgiven for the Counter Reformation. Dot left, in need of a tram to the city and the Travellers' Rest. From thence she would go to Russell Street to see if Jack Robinson had found the post office box used by 'Desperate', deceased. Then she would have a modest lunch in Coles cafeteria and follow the path. Wherever it led.

Phryne Fisher was halfway to South Yarra on the tram. She was making a list of what she still needed to know. Who was Marshall and Co.? Who was 'Desperate'?

The tram inched across St Kilda Road and turned into a street lined on one side with the massive, ancient trees of the Botanical Gardens and on the other with the walls and buildings of Melbourne Grammar School. Fortunately the scholars were still virtuously pursuing their studies and not gadarening onto the tram trampling all before them, as was the way of boys.

Phryne loved tram travel. It combined the convenience of not having to drive (which nowadays meant keeping a continual alert for madmen, trucks, straying bicycles and instant children, dogs and footballs), with the airy confidence of a vehicle which weighs nine tons moving on its own predestinate tracks. Anything, short of a tank, which hit a tram would regret it.

In the summer it was very pleasant to sit in the wood-lined, open part of the tram, smoking a reflective gasper and meditating on the universe. Or, in Phryne's case, the complicated matter of Miss Lavender, Artemis, and the threatening letters. Phryne still had no clue as to who had sent Miss Lavender the 'you bitch' letters, though she suspected that the writer was not as illiterate as he or she wished to appear. Were not anonymous letters, like poisoning, a province of female criminals?

'So they say,' said Phryne to herself, with Nellie Melba. 'What say they? Let them say.'

A very well-dressed lady with shoulder blades you could have used to cut cheese moved away from Phryne and ostentatiously turned her back. Phryne grinned. The tram rounded another corner and clanked past respectable lodging houses and apartments. The notebook snapped shut in Phryne's hands. She closed her eyes.

She had only drowsed, it seemed, for a moment, when she woke and realised that she was past her stop and heading for pastures new. She pulled the cord and got out, crossing the road and walking back toward Tintern Avenue. The sun was hot and her shoes were not well designed for tramping. She was tired when she reached the huge gate in the wall and was admitted by a parlour maid in a well-washed uniform with a token wisp of white net attached to her forehead, apparently with strong glue.

'Hello,' said Phryne. 'I'm Phryne Fisher, and I need a place to sit down, a glass of cold water, and Mrs Needham.'

'Yes, Miss. If you'd come this way. Mrs Needham is expecting you.'

'Are you Mercy Porter?'

'Yes, Miss. I found the body,' said Mercy with some pride. 'And I fainted, too, and I never fainted before. Didn't think I'd be such an idiot. I was that embarrassed when I came round and found them all staring at me.'

'Did you feel anything odd, smell anything, when you felt faint?'

'Miss Lavender's cottage always smelt strong,' said Mercy. 'All them different scents, roses and almonds, enough to make anyone come over all unnecessary. Anyway, Miss, if you'd like to sit here,' she pulled out a chair at the parlour table, 'I'll just go and get Mrs Needham and your glass of water. Hot today, isn't it?'

Phryne assented. In due course, Mercy came back with a glass of iced water on a small silver tray. Behind her came Mrs Needham.

Murder in her household had not been kind to Mrs Needham. Her eyes were pink-rimmed and her hands plucked incessantly at her belt, the tablecloth, the seam of her left sleeve and her buttons, which were loosening under the strain. Phryne hoped that she could solve this case before Mrs Needham quite ruined her wardrobe.

'Miss Fisher?' she asked in a hollow tone. The respect due to a titled person was the only consideration which stopped her from saying, 'You again?'

'Like a bad penny,' said Phryne, answering the thought. 'I'm just going to talk to some of your residents, Mrs Needham, nothing to worry about.

I'm as anxious as you are to conclude this matter quietly.'

'Have your enquiries ... progressed?' demanded Mrs Needham.

'They're coming along nicely. Tell me, who is at home?'

'Mr and Mrs Hewland. They've just come back from their walk. They always take a walk at this hour. Then they have a little nap until tea. Such nice, quiet people.'

'So they are,' said Phryne. 'Anyone else?'

'I believe that Mrs Gould is in. She was in for lunch, I believe. Mr Bell is pottering in the garden. Otherwise they are all out. Mr Carroll and Mr Opie are in the city, Mrs Opie, Wendy, Miss Gallagher and Miss Grigg are at that women's magazine. Oh, dear! I am forgetting Professor Keith, how dreadful. He's in. Miss Keith is at the hairdresser's. She always gets her hair done on Wednesday.'

'I'll wander up to see the good professor when I've finished this glass of water. Thanks, Mrs Needham. I think I can see a pattern developing. Won't be long before we are all out of your hair.'

'Do you think so?' Sudden hope made her hand jerk and she pulled off the button she had been fiddling with. 'It's awful about poor Miss Lavender, but I need to make a living. I can't leave the Garden Apartment empty for too much longer.'

'I understand.' Phryne stood up, missing Ping's tail by one-eighteenth of an inch. She had detected the dog's plot when she heard him shuffling around under the table, arranging his plumed tail within easy reach. He would garner an oodle of sympathy if someone stood on him, and this visitor was a good reliable tail treader. She smiled slightly at his snuffle as she went out into the sunshine again. Ping had found Miss Fisher a disappointment.

Professor Keith so resembled a stage professor that it was hard to look beyond the bald head, the white beard, the pipe, the shirtsleeves, the tweed waistcoat stuffed with notes and the fountain pen. He was holding it in one ink-stained hand as he answered the door, scowling. Phryne had been scowled at by experts.

'Bit of trouble with the fountain pen, Professor? Lead me to it,' said Phryne, taking it out of his grasp. 'There is a lot to be said for fountain pens – one is not forever dipping, but they do take careful handling, particularly the expensive ones. Presentation, was it?'

Phryne perched on the desk in a large, sunny room full of potted plants and books. The professor sat down in his big leather chair and looked bemused. His office had just been augmented by a beautiful young woman with a daring red hat who was, moreover, very good with fountain pens. He watched her sure hands as she filled the little rubber thingy, unscrewed the intractable metal gadget, swooshed up the ink and reassembled the pen, all without getting a drop of ink on her person or her hands.

'Thank you,' he said. 'I've never managed that.'

'You're used to being looked after,' observed Phryne. 'No one is mollycoddled like a professor. No one works harder, either,' she added before Keith could reply.

'Who are you?' he asked instead.

'Phryne Fisher.' She held out her hand and he shook it. 'I'm looking into the Miss Lavender matter for the police. Trying, for a wonder, not to make a scandal. I've read your police statement.'

'Then you'd better have a drink. What's your poison? Gin, like all these young women?'

'Whisky,' said Phryne. 'With a little water.' She waited until the professor had made her a small drink and himself a larger one and asked, 'I gather you didn't take to our Miss Lavender?'

'She was an interfering old busybody,' said the professor.

'Tact,' suggested Phryne.

'That's Sunday school language to what I would have said if you hadn't been a lady,' said the professor frankly. 'It's no use hiding my opinion. It would look suspicious. Police might leap to the wrong conclusions.'

'They have been known to do that,' said Phryne. 'But not when I am advising them. So, tell me, what was she being nosy about?'

'Me and my niece Margery,' said the professor. His moustache twitched when he was cross. Phryne found it hard to take her eyes off it.

'What about you and your niece?'

'Whether she was my niece, dammit, or my mistress.'

'And what is she?' asked Phryne in a friendly tone.

'My brother's daughter,' said the professor. He found it hard to take offence when the questions were being asked by such a stylish young woman. 'She's had a bad time and I won't have her ballyragged. I used to play peekaboo with her when she was a baby, taught her to swim, gave her her first doll. I wasn't very close to my brother, but I always loved Margery.'

'What sort of bad time?' asked Phryne, so quietly that the professor carried on his train of thought without appearing to notice.

'There was a young hound... There was trouble of the usual kind, Miss Fisher. When her parents threw her out – threw her out, by God! – she came to me. She was sick and miserable. She's always helped me with my specimens so I asked her if she wanted to help again. Just like when she was a child. See. She does lovely work.'

Phryne inspected a hortus siccus, a collection of dried plants. Each one was laid out in perfect order, seeds, fruits, flowers and leaves. It was labelled underneath in black marking ink – in easy capitals, using fine lines and the Greek E – with its botanical reference, its Linnaean name and its common name. She took a swig of whisky to cover her slight hesitation as she handed back the book.

'Did Miss Lavender ask you about the plants? She was a very accurate botanical artist.'

'Was she?' grunted the professor, clearly regretting his hospitality.

'Yes, have a look.' Phryne produced the drawing from her satchel.

'It's not a bad waratah,' he said grudgingly, pulling his spectacles up on their cord and inspecting the drawing. 'In fact, it's not bad at all. Quite good. Better than most of the rubbish they print. I found an illustration in a text the other

194

day where the common daisy had two sepals. If you can believe that. Two! The old bat could have made a living in a museum. They use botanical artists. Pity about the fairy, though.'

'Yes, she wasn't good at fairies. Or rather, she was too fond of them. A strange lady. Are you writing a book?'

'My life's work,' said Keith. 'Indigenous dicotyledons of the Otway forest, and what I have to say will shake some dovecotes. My word it will.'

'I'm sure,' said Phryne, resolving to look up 'dicotyledon' when she got home. 'Di' meant two. Two cotyledons. Better than one, I suppose, she thought. Though that hadn't been the case with the common daisy's sepals.

The door opened and a plump young blonde woman bustled in, taking a hat off hair which had just been cooked to a crimped crisp.

'Sorry I'm late, Unc, it took simply ages for my hair to dry. Who's the lady? You been flirting again, Unc?'

'Don't call me "Unc",' grumbled Professor Keith comfortably. 'Miss Fisher, my niece Margery. She's asking about Miss Lavender on the QT.'

'I know you didn't like her, Unc, but she was murdered,' said Miss Keith. 'That's awful.'

'Yes, yes, m'dear, but nothing we can do about it now, is there? No use me saying that I loved the old bi – biddy like a mother when I couldn't stand the sight of her. Neither could you,' said the professor complacently.

'Oh, uncle,' said Margery Keith in the voice of all young persons oppressed by the embarrassing loquacity of the aged. Phryne now knew that these two were not, and never had been, lovers. There is a psychic fingerprint, an electric charge, when intimacy has been established. Miss Lavender must have had insufficient experience of the flesh to recognise this if such was her plan of attack for the Keiths.

But Phryne had seen the Greek E and the flowing capitals before.

'Sit down, Miss Keith,' she instructed. 'Your uncle was kind enough to show me the hortus siccus you arranged for him. Very pretty work.'

'Thank you,' faltered Miss Keith. She was already afraid. Being taken in by a rotter and thrown out by one's parents to miscarry, possibly illegally, did not build the confidence.

'And I have seen that lettering before,' said Phryne. She drew one of the threatening letters out of her satchel and laid it on the table. Miss Keith stared at it as though it was an unexpected cobra, and she without a mongoose to her name.

'The police can get fingerprints off paper, sometimes,' Phryne insinuated.

'They can't,' said Miss Keith through frozen lips. 'I always wore gloves.'

'Margery!' exclaimed the professor. Phryne put a hand on his arm.

'It's all right,' she said. 'She didn't kill Miss Lavender. Not unless you've got some cyanide in your botany supplies.'

'No, that's entomologists,' said Keith distractedly. 'Chaps who chase butterflies. Though you can distil cyanide from apple pips. Some idiot did it. Anyway, if she did kill the old bitch

196

she was no loss. Though I'm sure she didn't. Are you sure that Margery sent those letters?'

'It's her writing. There is also something wrong with someone who spells deserve, "disserv". No illiterate would do that. What was Miss Lavender doing to you, Margery?'

'I can't tell you,' sobbed Margery.

'You really must, you know,' said Phryne quietly. 'Me or the cops and, really, believe me when I say that I would be better. Unless you want to end up as page one of the *Hawklet*, my girl, spit it out.'

'I can't,' wailed Margery, and threw herself into her uncle's arms.

'Now, now, May,' he soothed. 'Now, my little May, it doesn't matter what it is.'

'Yes, it does,' said Margery, stopping on a sob and wiping her face. 'I've been so happy here with you, Unc, it's been so nice, so quiet, and I love working on the book.'

'And it will continue,' he said. 'We haven't finished yet. I still need you.' She tugged at his beard.

'Not when you find out. You won't want me anywhere near.'

'Find out what?' asked Professor Keith.

Margery wailed again. Phryne sat down close to the young woman's ear.

'The last time you fell in love, you were thrown out of your house and lost your baby,' she said. 'So you're afraid that this will happen again. Now it's really unlikely to have been Mr Hewland, so who was it, Margery? Mr Bell? Mr Opie? Mr Carroll?'

197

At the name Hewland Margery managed a shocked gasp. She repeated it with every name but the last. Phryne nodded.

'Mr Carroll, who likes late nights, dancing, drinking, and flirting. Not surprising that a young woman would like some fun.'

'Stuck here all day with an old man,' said Professor Keith heavily, 'who falls asleep at nine o'clock every night.'

'Thus releasing your niece for a night of relatively harmless pleasure,' said Phryne.

Margery clung to her uncle, burying her face in his tweed waistcoat.

'Unc, that's what I didn't want you to find out because I knew that's how you'd feel! I really love you and you've been so kind to me and I really want to stay here and she said ... she said...'

'That she'd tell your uncle that you were having an affair with Mr Carroll unless you did as she bid,' said Phryne.

'And she would have made it sound awful, as though I was a tart,' wailed Margery. 'I thought I might scare her off so I wrote her letters. It didn't work,' she said sadly.

'Were you having an affair with Mr Carroll?' asked Phryne.

'No, of course not! He goes to all the shows, and he usually has two tickets, and he's funny and he isn't in love with me and it was harmless, Unc, like she said. Anyway, he's got a mistress. One of the Green Mill girls.'

'What did Miss Lavender want from you?'

Margery blushed like a Rosacea Gallica. 'She wanted me to spy on the others. Not you, Unc.

She wanted me to find out about Miss Gallagher and Miss Grigg, and especially about Mr Bell. She even told me to go and visit him in his room,' said Margery, blushing harder.

'What did you say?' asked Phryne.

'That I wouldn't do it. Then she said she'd tell Unc, and I'd had enough so I told her to tell him and be damned.'

'What did she want with Mr Bell?'

'Don't know,' said Margery.

'So the morning that Miss Lavender was found dead, you came home with Mr Carroll, went to bed for a couple of hours, then rose at your usual time to make the coffee,' said Phryne, marvelling at the stamina of the young.

'Yes,' said Margery.

'Did you see anyone in the garden when you came in?'

'No one,' said Margery. 'I didn't see anyone, and I was looking carefully, because sometimes the tenants sit in the garden when they can't sleep. I had to hide in the bushes for almost an hour one night when Mrs Opie couldn't get Wendy to sleep and Mr Opie sat there next to the fountain like a statue.'

'Oh, Margery,' said Professor Keith with infinite affection.

'Uncle, can I stay another month? I have to find somewhere to go. I'll need a job, too.'

'You've got one,' he said. 'You don't think I want to leave my work unfinished, do you? You can go out to the dance with Carroll one night a week,' he said severely. 'But don't expect me to wait up for you.'

'Oh, Unc!' Margery threw herself into his arms again. He kissed her on the top of the head as she burrowed beneath his second waistcoat button.

'Well, that seems to have solved that,' he said to Phryne over his niece's metallic coiffure. 'Is there any need to tell the police about this?'

'No, but we might need Margery to testify that there was no one in the garden when she came in.'

'She can do that,' said Professor Keith. Margery, in a flood of happy tears, agreed.

Which was all very nice, Phryne thought, crossing the anonymous letters off her list. Margery hadn't seen either Opie or Bell, though she could not have seen Miss Grigg from the direct path between the front door and the Keith apartment. That meant that at seven the garden was empty.

Someone was lying. Possibly everyone.

Phryne hurried home. She had an appointment with a pirate.

CHAPTER THIRTEEN

The second line, undivided, shows the subject exercising forbearance with the ignorant, in which there will be good fortune; and admitting even the goodliness of women, which will also be fortunate.

Hexagram 4: Mang
The I Ching Book of Changes

Phryne dead-heated Dot at the door and said, as they were admitted to the house, 'Well, fellow sleuth? How did it go?'

'I found two of them,' said Dot. 'The cops still haven't got the post box address. Something about the sanctity of the mail.'

Phryne muttered something about the sanctity of the mail which could not have been written down and sent through it.

'I found out who was sending the "you bitch" letters,' she told Dot. 'Not a lot of use, I admit, because she isn't the murderer.'

'Neither are Anne or the cleaning lady,' said Dot. 'But that takes them off the list.'

'The rate people are being crossed off this list, we won't have anyone left,' said Phryne. 'And we'll have to put the death down to divine intervention. Never mind. Well done, Dot, dear. Did you have any trouble?'

'No, Miss. I gave the five quid to the cleaning

lady. She was in real trouble from taking Artemis's advice. I got the first letter, but Anne had burned hers. And you were right, Miss. Artemis had told her how to seduce a man. Only it didn't work.'

'There are reasons for entering into a companionate marriage, Dot, dear, with which I will not sully your ears.'

'You never worried about sullying them before,' objected Dot, taking off her hat in front of the hall mirror. Behind her she saw Phryne's narrow, cat-like face and the quick fingers removing hairpins. 'Do you mean that the husband's one of those men who don't like women but like men instead?'

'Neatly put,' said Phryne. The reflected face looked worried. 'Now, Dot, if Bert and Cec haven't failed me, and they had better not have failed me, we should at any moment be visited by...'

The door bell rang.

'Shove him up that last step, mate,' said Bert's voice. 'That's the ticket. Well, Miss,' he announced as Phryne opened the door, 'we've got your pirate. But he got away from us this arvo and got on the giggle-juice, so if you don't mind, we'll take him out the back and get him sobered up a bit.'

Cec hauled in a dishevelled man who had obviously been forcibly dressed in a coat and hat. The coat was askew and the hat was planted so far down on his forehead that he could not have seen out from under the brim.

'Drunk?' asked Phryne, scenting a medicinal smell which she could not quite identify.

'Worse. He did a sneak on us and got on the Fitzroy cocktails. Mrs B in the kitchen? We'll get some coffee. We should'a turned him over to the Salvos. But you said five pm and five pm it is.'

'All right, Bert, dear, carry on,' said Phryne.

The extinguished figure heard this and threw really quite a good salute, which almost tipped him over backwards.

'He's a sailor,' said Dot. 'My uncle says that as long as they can get up the gangplank and salute the bridge by themselves, they won't be booked for drunkenness no matter how tipsy they are.'

'That's gone beyond tipsy, Dot,' said Phryne. 'What's a Fitzroy cocktail?

Dot shrugged. 'Only cocktails I ever heard about were Mr Butler's – onions, frankfurts and hats,' she said.

'Come along, I've got to get out of these shoes. I've walked altogether too far in them today. Tell me all about Anne and the cleaning lady, and I'll tell you all about Professor Keith's niece. By then, Bert and Cec ought to have emptied the grog out of their sailor and filled him up with strong coffee. I could do with some, too.'

Phryne and Dot were sitting in the parlour, discussing Miss Keith's desire to see some bright lights, when Bert and Cec came back, escorting a shaking, damp, sailor's ghost. They plumped him down in a chair and stood either side of him like cattle dogs that have brought in not only their target steer but three other strays.

'Here he is,' said Bert with some pride. 'Clean as a baby and sober as a judge. Miserable as a bandicoot, too,' he added. 'This is Pirates,' he introduced the evanescent figure. 'Say hello to the nice sheila, Pirates.'

'H'lo,' muttered Pirates.

'Hello. What's a Fitzroy cocktail, Bert?'

'Metho, ginger beer and boot polish,' said Bert. 'Puts hairs on your chest. While you still have a chest, o' course. Trouble with metho is, it makes yer into a dingbat and he's well on the way to being dingbatted. But we was talking to him last night and he knows what you wanted to know,' said Bert righteously.

'Then he will tell me,' said Phryne.

Something in the tone of her voice penetrated Pirate's alcoholic fog. He raised his head as though the weight of all those dead brain cells was biasing it like a bowling ball. Phryne looked into eyes which had seen too many horrors and had never been able to drink them away.

'Tell me,' she said, 'about South China Sea, Pirates. I want to know about Bias Island, and about a woman pirate who runs it, and about how they take over a ship.'

'I was on the *Sunming*,' said Pirates. 'I can't never forget. I been tryin' to forget ever since.'

'But for me, you will remember,' said Phryne.

''Er name's Lai Choi San. Means Mountain of Gold. Good name.' Pirates was about to lapse into semiconsciousness again when Bert held a cup of coffee to his mouth and he gulped. His voice strengthened. 'She runs the whole of Bias Island. She's Queen. She's got a whole fleet of junks. They even take on big ships now. They took the SS *Irene* last year and would have got her away but the navy torpedoed her and got all the passengers off. And the SS *Hopsang*. She disappeared. They say Lai Choi San's a tiny madam with a golden crown and a mean hand with a rifle. But I never seen 'er. I only seen what they did to my ship.'

'Tell me,' said Phryne.

As though he had been wound up like a music box, Pirates told the story of the *Sunming*. Bert noticed that the words, even the phrasing, were identical to the story he had told the night before. The dreadful story of the *Sunming* had etched itself on the poor bugger's brain, Bert thought. You just put on the gramophone and it played the record all the way through. Phryne listened, making notes.

'What happens to the hostages?' she asked.

'They call 'em *p'iao*,' said Pirates. His recitation had made him more confident. 'Tickets, you know, like a lottery ticket. The family pay up, they let 'em go. No hard feelings.'

Phryne bit a fingernail. 'What could interrupt this exchange?'

'Nothin' I know of. They 'ave to deliver the package, or they'll lose face. And trade. No one's gonna give money to a pirate if he's not gonna deliver the ticket back. The families might just talk to the British and get the navy to drop in with a warship and burn the settlement. That's what they did last century. Set piracy back fifty years. Course, if Queen Lai wants your ticket, then you 'ave to give him to 'er.'

'Why would she want him?'

'I dunno. Fancy boy? Better offer? Some families might pay to have him killed, if they don't like 'im. But if your friend's been in China, they could have got rid of 'im there easy as kiss your 'and. Terrible place, now, China. Even the treaty ports are none too safe. Seems like a lot of trouble to go to just to get rid of one man.'

'Yes, it does,' said Phryne thoughtfully. 'What do the pirates do with the ships? Burn them?'

'Nah,' said Pirates scornfully. He was on his fifth cup of coffee now. The strength of the brew was such that it had obliterated his trademark scent of methylated spirits. 'They phantom 'em.'

'Ghost ships?' asked Phryne.

'Phantoms,' said Pirates. 'They steal the ship, strip off all the identifying marks, repaint 'er, maybe change the superstructure so she don't look the same, and then they send off for a registered name in Algiers or Liberia. Then they doctor up some false logs in the new name. The Chinese are real good at false logs. Then they take up a cargo contract from Honkers, say, or Bangkok, and deliver it and then they sell the ship. She's got papers and a registration and she's completed a cargo voyage, so it's ryebuck and they've got a deal. Lot more money in your actual ship than there is in cargo, unless it's gold. 'Course, if the ship's a real rust-bucket they can just insure 'er for a lot and then scuttle 'er. Lot of good sailormen go down in insurance frauds. They say you can stand on the Peak in Hong Kong and see one phantom for every ten straight ships.'

'I see,' said Phryne thoughtfully. An inkling was itching at her mind. Ordinary pirates wanted money for their ticket. They got it. A sound commercial transaction. We have something you want and we will sell it to you for so much. But then the Queen of Pirates suddenly interrupts this time-honoured procedure, seizes the prisoner, and asks for the Lin family lands. Breaking the contract with the original kidnappers. She would not do that without a good reason because, as Pirates said, pirates needed to be trusted to keep their word or no one would deal with them. Did Lai Choi San want to set up her own little kingdom in disintegrating China? Piracy seemed to be a good business with expanding horizons and many opportunities for increasing profit. Why should she leave it? The possibility of the royal navy visiting with big guns? Or had she fallen in love with Lin Chung? He was definitely worth the effort and the Queen was a widow.

For a person of this lady's acumen, that seemed unlikely. And why were the Lin family trying to kill Phryne?

'Pirates, I want to employ you,' said Phryne. 'I've looked through the shipping lists and there's no sign of SS *Gold Mountain*. She was supposed to be on her way from Hong Kong but she never arrived. I'm interested in what you say about phantoms. The cargo they would have stolen isn't of much value in Chinese waters, but would command a big price in Australia with one of the rival silk firms. So I want you and my colleagues here to comb the waterfront for *Gold Mountain*. Would you know her if she had been phantomed?'

'Know 'er like the back of me 'and,' said Pirates, examining the back of his hand with great interest, as though it were a novelty. 'Did two voyages on 'er.'

'All right. I'm giving Bert drinking money for

207

you. No more Fitzroy cocktails for the duration, Pirates. Stick with beer. I'll give you a pound if you find her. But you have to be positive and that means you have to stay off the metho. If you sneak out on Bert and Cec again and fill yourself full of poison, then the deal's off. And the horrors you'll get from metho will be pleasant dreams compared to what I'll do to you,' she added with a sudden cold ferocity which took all of the company by surprise.

'Yessir,' said Pirates automatically. 'Beer it is, sir.'

'Double rates,' said Phryne to Bert and Cec. 'This will not be amusing.'

'Fair enough,' said Bert. 'On the wharf, we get dirt money for handling noxious cargoes.'

'They don't come a lot more noxious,' said Phryne. 'But if he can find Lin Chung for me, I'm willing to kiss him.'

'I don't reckon we need to go that far, Miss,' said Bert. 'If yer feel like kissin' anyone, it might as well be Cec and me. Yer might catch something offa Pirates.'

Phryne admitted the truth of this and watched them cart their prisoner away, one on each side, like jailers.

Jack Robinson passed them on the steps.

'Taking him in for questioning?' he asked, struck by their resemblance to two arresting officers and a miscreant.

'Nah,' said Bert, who did not like policemen. 'We leave that to the jacks. Miss Fisher's just given him a job, and we got to keep him sober to do it.'

'Good luck,' said Robinson, noting that their prisoner had all the earmarks of a man so far down the road to Grog Country that Sobriety couldn't have reached him unless it was on the telephone.

'Thanks,' Bert grunted. As Robinson was admitted, he heard the drunk begin to sing in a high, sweet tenor, 'Show me the way to go home, I'm tired and I wanna go to bed, I had a little drink about an hour ago, and it's gone right to my head...'

'Strange visitors,' he commented to Dot.

'Another case,' replied Dot. 'Come in and let's swap stories. I've been investigating,' she informed the Detective Inspector.

'Did you like it?' he asked.

'Sort of. It's interesting. But it takes a lot of front to just go up to someone and demand that they tell you all their secrets.'

'I know,' said Robinson, handing over his hat and coat to Mr Butler.

Ten minutes was enough to summarise the developments so far.

'So it's not the Keiths. We know their secret. It ain't Anne or the cleaning lady. Or so Miss Dot says, and I trust her judgment.' Dot blushed at the compliment. 'And here's the address of "Desperate".'

'Oh, well done, Jack, dear!' exclaimed Phryne, shaking herself bodily out of Pirates' horribly vivid narrative. 'However did you manage it?'

'My chief and the Postmaster General play golf together,' said Jack. 'I also brought what was in the safety deposit box in the Commonwealth Bank.'

'The manager is another golf partner?'

'Every Saturday,' agreed Jack. 'If the chief takes up chess instead, like he's always threatening to do when he has a bad round, we'll be in dead trouble. Mind you, the chaps who've had to go and fetch him from the tee reckon that you can only look at his knickerbockers through smoked glass, so it might be a bit of a gain for the aesthetic life of Melbourne. But we had the key of the safety deposit box. They had to let us look at it.'

'Good,' said Phryne. 'I hope we have a will.'

'We have. Drawn up by herself, I think. Typed on her Corona. Documents don't reckon it's been tampered with. Trouble is, she leaves all her money to the Lost Dogs' Home and the Presbyterian Church.'

'Oh dear. Not a lot of motive there, is there? I've heard of fanatical dog people, but I doubt they'd kill someone just to get the money. Though there have been a lot of dogs in this case. That awful beast Ping, and Mrs Corder's McTavish. I don't think it's relevant, however. The only people we know who go to the Presbyterian Church are Mrs McAlpin and – are the Hewlands Presbyters? We'd better find out. That reminds me, Dot, we need to look through the letters I brought home the first time. Which one, I wonder, was Mrs Opie groping for? She's not in the clear. In fact, none of the cast is.'

'Especially now we know that Miss Lavender used her knowledge of someone's secrets to put pressure on them,' said Dot. 'That's not a good idea. What if someone gets angry?'

'Yes, but she would have known when to draw back,' Phryne mused. 'When Miss Keith defied her, she did nothing. Though of course we don't know what she intended to do. What else is in the box, Jack?'

'Bundle of letters, a couple of photographs and this.' Robinson exhibited a scrap of cloth with some dark reddish marks on it.

'Blood?' asked Phryne.

'I don't think so. Wrong colour. Blood as dry as this turns black. Feels like canvas. Might be paint.'

'The edge of a painting, perhaps,' said Phryne. 'And she was trying to force Margery Keith into spying on Mr Bell. We need to know more about that interesting young man. Add him to your list, Jack, if you please. Have you found Marshall and Co. yet?'

'Got a clerk onto it at the Companies Register. Not a Victorian company. We've called Sydney and they're searching.'

'More letters,' said Dot.

'Yes, this is an excessively epistolary case, isn't it? I never want to see another missive, Dot, I agree. Now what have we here? Letter from Pater to Mater about education. Letter in superfine linen envelope with splashing red seal on the back It's from...' Phryne's eyebrows rose. 'A lady who signs herself "Devoted" to an unknown gentleman. Nice turn of phrase, if a little gushing. "If I can't see you and touch you, I go cold and blank. The world turns grey and the people are all sad. Even the birds do not sing, the fish sleep in the water and the trees shed their leaves in the autumn of your absence. Lacking you, I have nothing at all." Not Miss L's writing, posted in Sydney. Is that why you are looking there for the company, Jack?'

'Partly. It's always a next step.'

'Letter from "Devoted" complaining of her lover's cruelty in staying away so long across the sea. How provoking. She doesn't say which sea. Not much to identify the lover. Chestnut hair. Eyes like stars. "Come back before the vine bears grapes".'

Dot gave a squeak of excitement. 'Miss, it sounds like she's talking about the garden at Tintern Avenue. Fish in the pool, leaves on the trees, the vine. Miss Grigg has a vine.'

'And I cannot imagine Miss Grigg writing this, Dot. Though love makes poets of us all, I believe.'

'Miss Gallagher,' suggested Robinson.

'Bingo,' said Phryne. 'Just her style. Check it with her handwriting. But the letters are not recent. Postmark's illegible but I can just see the twenty-six at the end. Two years ago. One would have thought that the lover would have come back across the sea by now.'

'Maybe he has,' said Robinson. 'But Miss L kept these letters for a reason, we may be sure of that.'

'True, and tied with a blue ribbon. And what we have here is a bundle of bills of lading for the Melbourne waterfront. Marshall and Co. Delivery of various crates containing, and I quote, "art objects". Despatch note says "Origin: Napoli". Marshall and Co. buy things from Naples. Seems an unobjectionable practice.'

'Depends on what they buy. Would it be drugs, perhaps?' asked Robinson.

'Perhaps. Is Italy a well-known source of illegal drugs?'

'No, Miss, it don't have to be. Drugs from other places come into Naples, a rough port, they say, and they are transhipped here.'

'It must be something illegal,' Dot pointed out, 'or Marshall and Co. wouldn't be paying Miss Lavender to keep quiet about the trade.'

'True. Well, Jack, thanks for the display. I'll go and see "Desperate" tomorrow.' Then, observing Dot's disappointed face, she said, 'Or rather, I will go to *Women's Choice*, where they should be all relaxed because the paper's gone off to the printer. I'm meeting Madame Fleuri there, to start remaking the Worth. Dot will go and see what happened to "Desperate". Poor girl. Will that suit?'

'Yes, thanks, Miss,' said Dot.

'You keep looking for Marshall and Co. and get Mr Bell's service record, and I'll go over those letters and find Mrs Opie's. Someone is fibbing to us about what went on in that garden the night Miss Lavender died, Jack.'

'Of course they are, Miss Fisher. But the fact that they're lying doesn't make them a murderer, and we've made some progress to tell the chief. At least we're getting a better idea of who it wasn't.'

'That's what my mother used to say,' said Dot. 'You always find the thing in the last place you looked.'

'Because that's when you stop searching,' said Jack, and took his leave.

When he'd gone, Dot brought the box of letters and sat down next to Phryne as instructed.

'Look at me,' said Phryne. 'You're sitting on a rustic bench and it's nearly dark so you can't see, and in any case you don't want me to notice that you're feeling around in my … er … property. Feel over the letters and take out each one which seems different.'

Dot rummaged for a few minutes and produced an unusually large envelope, a very small one, one with an elaborate seal and one embossed with for-get-me-nots. 'And this one, I suppose,' said Dot. 'It's the same size as the rest but it's ripped at one corner.'

'Good. Now, what have we here? This one is about dry hair. This one is about greasy hair. This is the one who had gynaecological problems. Scrub those. This is the one about the difficulty of growing primroses in an Australian climate that has "refer Agricola" on it. Keep that aside, Dot. And this is the one,' said Phryne. '"My child will not sleep and my husband doesn't under-stand." That's been Mrs Opie's burden all along. Small envelope with raised forget-me-nots all over it. We'll need to match the handwriting and the stationery. There's a draft of Mrs Opie's float-ing around the office at this moment. All right. That's enough for one day. We need a good dinner, Dot. What has Mrs Butler made?'

'Cold steak and kidney pie, Miss, and I think there's ice cream for dessert.'

'Good,' said Phryne. 'We will enjoy that.'

Despite a lurking memory of horrors, she did. Dot, excited by her elevation to fellow sleuth, was chatty and the girls came back from their self-im-posed exile in the kitchen, not bringing Molly the

214

puppy (who was still unsafe on carpets). Ember floated in, curled his black length into a chair, and allowed Phryne to scratch behind his ears.

After dinner they played a game of cards. Jane, who had been taught the rules and technique of poker by Bert and Cec, won two boxes of matches, match by match. The only diverting aspect Phryne could see in playing with Jane was wondering how long it would take you to lose your under-garments.

The girls went to their room to do their home-work.

The knock came not at the front door but at the parlour window. Tap, tap, a pause, then tap, tap, tap. Phryne turned off the light and opened the French window and Li Pen wafted through.

'Good evening,' said Phryne.

'Silver Lady,' said Li Pen, bowing.

'Will you have tea?'

'I will be missed if I am away too long,' he said. 'I came at your orders, Silver Lady.'

'Are you familiar with the practice of phantom-ing a ship?' she asked.

'You think that this has happened to *Gold Mountain?*'

'Yes. I hope that they might come back to Mel-bourne and try to sell the silk. They might even be bringing Lin Chung back. If Madame Lin can prevail on the family council to hand over the land, the pirates will need to have him on hand to exchange, and they can improve the shining hour by selling your silk to a rival.'

'Your mind is, as always, of the finest calibre,' said Li Pen.

'I've found a man who sailed on *Gold Mountain* who thinks he can recognise it, no matter how they may have altered it. Bert and Cec and this man will be combing the waterfront for it. If – when they find it, I will call for you and we can take some action.'

'You have not considered how illegal this action might be?'

Phryne stared straight into the dark, unfathomable eyes.

'I don't care,' she said flatly, and Li Pen realised the essential truth in her statement. 'If Lin is on that boat we will retrieve him or die trying, though of course I would prefer that someone else might die trying to stop us. Are you with me?'

'To the death,' said Li Pen softly. 'Only thus may I retrieve my lost honour. There will be a stain even on my great grandchildren if I allow this piracy to succeed.'

'Tell me about Lai Choi San. What did she want with Lin?'

'I do not know. She is a small woman, much your own size. She wears very fine garments. She is ruthless and obeyed without question. Her punishments are feared. She rules her pirates with a rod of iron. The rape of a female prisoner, for instance, is punished by the castration of the whole crew of the offending junk. Female prisoners who cannot be ransomed for sufficient profit are sold as concubines or killed. She is very successful. When the first pirates released us on payment of the ransom, she had us seized on the shore and conveyed to her palace. There she ordered these marks to be set on me. There she kept my master.'

'Isn't this unusual behaviour for a pirate? Why would she want land?'

'I do not know. I can only think that she wishes to retire, or that she is acting on behalf of someone else. She is rich enough to buy as much land as she wants in China, so I think it is reasonable to assume that she is acting on instructions, however unlikely that may seem.'

'Who wants to kill Lin? And, moreover, who in the Lin family wants to kill me? They've been lining up lately.'

'I know of no orders about you,' said Li Pen, taken aback. 'Madame Lin would not issue such orders, Silver Lady. She might not approve of your association with Lin Chung but she would not order an assassination.'

'Sounds like an attempt at a take-over, doesn't it?' mused Phryne.

Li Pen raised an eyebrow. He was not familiar with the term.

'I mean, it sounds like one company attempting to force another company to sell its assets at less than their market value. Who is mounting a take-over on the Lin family in China? Because they've suborned this pirate queen and they've been trying quite hard to kill me.'

'I will think about this,' said Li Pen. 'If you need me, telephone this number and say to the person who answers *"Li Pen gaumehng a"* and I will call you.'

Phryne took the piece of paper, repeated the phrase to his satisfaction, then wrote it down phonetically. He congratulated her on her mastery of Cantonese, apparently without irony, and vanished through the French window like a phantom.

Phryne sat in the dark, watching the moon. Lin Chung was not there.

CHAPTER FOURTEEN

The fourth line, divided, shows the subject waiting in the place of blood. But he will get out of the cavern.

Hexagram 5: Hsü
The I Ching Book of Changes

Morning brought a telephone call for Miss Fisher.

'I wonder if you could look in at *Women's Choice* this morning a little earlier than you intended?' asked Mrs Charlesworth's calm voice. 'There has been a development.'

Phryne could hear someone sobbing in the background.

'Miss Nelson has confessed?' she asked.

'Partially,' said Mrs Charlesworth dryly.

'And you think I can make that into "fully"?'

'Oh yes, Miss Fisher, I have a very high opinion of your talents.'

'Right with you,' Phryne replied. She rang off. 'Unleash the Hispano-Suiza, Mr B,' she shouted. 'Ten minutes?'

'Yes, Miss,' said Mr Butler from the kitchen. 'Into the city?'

'Yes,' said Phryne, 'and I'm in a hurry.'

'Ten minutes,' promised Mr Butler, taking his chauffeur's hat and coat off their peg. 'Going for a little drive, Mrs B,' he called.

'You mind the speed limit,' said Mrs Butler.

'I mind it,' he replied. 'It's just that the boss doesn't.'

'Dot!' Phryne called. 'It occurs to me that you might like a little assistance. Mr B will take you on to "Desperate's" house after he's taken me to *Women's Choice*, where Mrs Charlesworth says that we have a confession.'

'Who's confessed?' Dot came down the stairs in a beige summer dress with a light jacket the shade of old terracotta bricks. Her resemblance to a cottage garden was increased by the bunch of geraniums on her hat.

'Miss Nelson. But only to stealing letters, I bet. You do look nice, Dot. So summery. After you've finished with "Desperate", get Mr B to bring you into the city. Madame Fleuri is remodelling the Worth so I have to stay for a little while. Mrs Mc-Alpin is taking the photographs. Then we shall see what to do next. Ready? Then off we go.'

Mr Butler's driving was effective and sedate. Phryne lit a gasper and stared out of the window. The case was breaking. She knew the feeling. The matter would be as obdurate as a big stone block for ages, utterly resisting all chipping and tapping, then just when you were about to give up and take to it with a sledgehammer, it cracked into a lot of pieces and fell away, revealing the gold egg of the solution in the middle.

Feeling that she had extended her metaphor

beyond its coefficient of expansion, she blew idle smoke rings all the way to the city.

Dot reread the address, written in Jack's policeman's writing, which was square and easy to read under cross-examination. 'Desperate', otherwise known as Mrs Robert Green, Christian name Alexandra, had lived in Seddon, a respectable suburb between Footscray and Yarraville, on the other side of the river. She had died in a manner still under examination by the Coroner's Court. She had left two children and a husband. Her maiden name was Hewland.

Hewland? An uncommon name. But the first rule of detection, Dot's novels had told her, was not to leap to any conclusions. Of course, the detection methods of Miss Phryne Fisher consisted of leaping to any available conclusion and then following the fancy wherever it led. That seemed to work just as well. The rule appeared to be that as long as one was pursuing some line of enquiry, one would reach the end, in the end.

Phryne alighted and blew a kiss to Dot. Mr Butler inched the huge car down Hardware Lane and into Bourke Street, making an illegal right-hand turn and heading for Spencer Street, the Swamp Road, and Seddon.

Dot brooded.

Phryne ran up the steps to *Women's Choice* and found a room full of women working very ostentatiously at their proper duties. They reminded her of a room full of schoolchildren warding off fate. A litany of grief was audible from Mrs Charlesworth's office.

'She said that you should go in right away,' said

Miss Grigg, wiring a magneto with precision. Miss Gallagher, beside her, was copying recipes and keeping her head down. Miss Prout was typing, Miss Phillips sketching an art deco pot, Mrs Opie feeding Wendy ice cream, Mrs McAlpin cleaning slides and Mr Bell brushing and sorting a box of bulbs.

'What's going on?' whispered Miss Herbert. She had come in to work wearing higher heels and more make-up than usual, for her debut as a model, and found something which sounded like the Wailing Woman of Willow Glen, as described in the ghost story she had been reading.

'I'll let you know when I find out,' said Phryne.

Mrs Charlesworth directed Miss Fisher to a chair and showed her Exhibit A: Miss Nelson's letter book. Exhibit B: the empty envelope from 'Desperate' and Exhibit C: Miss Nelson, crying her eyes out, a pulpy lump of misery. The girl had a crumpled handkerchief in her fist and an inexhaustible supply of tears.

'Tell Miss Fisher what you told me,' said Mrs Charlesworth.

'I took the exciting letters out of the pile and kept them,' sobbed Miss Nelson.

'Why?' asked Phryne.

'Because ... they were interesting,' said Miss Nelson.

'And then what did you do with them?'

'I put them in the dead letter binder to be thrown in the fire,' said Miss Nelson.

'Well, well, that's true enough,' said Phryne. 'And you extracted "Desperate's" letter and re-glued the envelope. Why did you do that?'

Miss Nelson gaped, puffy-faced, and did not answer.

'Who asked you to do that?' prompted Phryne.

Miss Nelson shook her head.

'You won't tell? What has she got on you, girl? Blackmail's a crime, Miss Nelson. You aren't expected to keep silent if you've been pressured. What was it? A small theft? Took a pair of scissors home, did you? Or a boy? Or a phone call? Tell me,' said Phryne compellingly.

'I promised,' Miss Nelson burst out. 'I promised I wouldn't tell, I gave my word.'

'There's a good girl,' said Phryne gently, calling forth another burst of tears. 'It's all right. I understand. So does Mrs Charlesworth. We recognise the pure adolescent honour which drove Joan to the stake, inconvenient though it is at this juncture. Now you stay here. I won't be a moment.'

Both Miss Nelson and Mrs Charlesworth nodded. Phryne went out and shut the door behind her.

'Poor little creature,' she said carelessly to the office at large, bending her head to light a gasper. 'Plenty of backbone, but she broke at last.'

From a standing start Phryne then executed what the *Ballets Russe* would have recognised as a *grande jete,* arriving at the door to the stairs a microsecond before Miss Prout. Miss Grigg noticed with admiration that Miss Fisher's cigarette was alight. She had the reflexes of a cat.

'Urgent appointment, Miss Prout?' she asked, waving the Sobranie in a hypnotic pattern inches from Miss Prout's nose. 'You will shortly have one at the Labour Exchange, I think. Come along. I know all – at least, most. Mrs Charlesworth, however, doesn't. And your staunch accomplice didn't betray you. She was willing to be sacked in disgrace to protect you, which is one of the most disgusting things you have done.'

'You can't keep me here!' gasped Miss Prout.

'Can't I?' Phryne grinned. Miss Prout took an involuntary step backwards. Phryne nudged her into a chair and perched on the desk beside her.

'Fetch Mrs Charlesworth,' she told Miss Gallagher, who obeyed instantly. 'Now, Miss Prout, we are going to have an *éclaircissement*. I want to know all about this, and I am going to be put fully in the picture, or I shall arrange for you to spend a few nights in a cell, under suspicion of murder.'

'Murder?' Miss Prout paled to the colour of a Rosa Gallica.

'Miss Lavender received death threats because of your interference,' said Phryne. 'I'm sure that Detective Inspector Robinson will see it my way. Miss Lavender being, as you know, very dead.'

Someone in the room was holding their breath. Phryne, facing Miss Prout, tried to triangulate. Who was under such tension that they weren't breathing? Only the ears of a bat could detect them.

Mrs Charlesworth brought the sobbing Miss Nelson into the main office and planted her down in a chair. Miss Gallagher offered her another handkerchief. Wendy, with that curious empathy which children sometimes show, put a sticky hand on her skirt.

'All right, Miss Prout. Your accomplice has stuck

to her guns and refused to name you, but you gave yourself away. Do you hear, Miss Nelson? When Miss Prout speaks, you may speak. Now, Miss Prout, if you please, when did you suborn Miss Nelson into extracting the juicy letters for you?'

'Six months ago,' said Miss Prout sullenly. 'I noticed that Artemis never handled the really important letters, the ones about sex and death, the ones about life. She stuck to divorce and interior decorating and advice about the complexion. The readers needed to know about the real things.'

'So you got Miss Nelson to take out the "hot" letters and give them to you. What did you do?'

'I couldn't get them published, so I answered them,' said Miss Prout. 'Better than Artemis would have, with real advice.'

'And froze onto the fees, as well?'

'Well, yes, I was earning it.'

'It never occurred to you that there was a reason why Artemis didn't answer the "hot" letters?'

'Just timidity,' said Miss Prout scornfully. 'She was too scared and too old-maidish to tackle the real things.'

'Let's see what your track record was,' said Phryne with ominous gentleness. 'You advised Anne to seduce a husband who had entered into a marriage on the understanding that it was to be companionate, which means, of course, no sexual contact. You counselled her to break her word, compromise her husband's trust and behave, as she said, like a tart. Do you know what happened?'

'No,' said Miss Prout.

'Her husband walked out on her,' said Phryne.

224

'And she sent a letter threatening death to Miss Lavender, who was the stalking horse for your mistakes. That is how I found out about you. I was reading the returned post, looking for murderers. Anne was not only misadvised, but laid herself open to the danger of being accused of murder.'

'It was good advice,' muttered Miss Prout. 'She must have done it wrong. All men can be attracted by a pretty gown and a nice dinner.'

Miss Grigg giggled. It was such an unexpected sound that everyone's eyes turned to her. She hid her face in her wiring.

'You know very little about the big bad world,' said Phryne. 'And then when a cleaning woman who desperately needed some money asked what she should do about the ten-shilling note she'd found, you counselled her to 'fess up.'

'Yes,' said Miss Prout, aggressively.

'And she lost her job, as might have been expected, and she wrote to Miss Lavender saying she was going to kill her, thus exposing herself to the same charge as Anne.'

'It's better to confess,' said Miss Prout pompously. 'Theft in the lower orders cannot be condoned.'

'Your moral standards do you credit,' said Phryne with frightening irony. 'Are you beginning to see a pattern here, Miss Prout? From your very minor knowledge, you are presuming to advise women on all manner of problems of which you know nothing. You've never lain down with a man, you've never borne a child, you've never kept a house, you've never been poor or hungry or tempted beyond bearing. Miss Lavender gave safe advice, which could not cause harm. Counselling Christian resignation to a beaten wife is only what society is saying to her and perhaps may be what she wants to hear. If she is to take action, she must do it on her own, not because some magazine sibyl tells her to. What did you say to "Desperate"? Because that's what brought the wrought undone, isn't it? Getting that returned letter with "Deceased" on it?'

'She wrote to me seven times,' said Miss Prout defiantly. 'I was encouraging her. Telling her to pull her socks up.'

'Yes, I thought you might have been,' said Phryne.

The rest of the office was staring at Miss Prout in silence. She looked around for the first time, from face to face. Miss Gallagher avoided her eyes. Miss Herbert stared at her in horror. Mrs McAlpin looked disgusted, Miss Phillips blank, Mrs Opie nervous, Mr Bell ironically amused. Miss Grigg, after her lapse, kept her regard on her magneto. Miss Prout's gaze was drawn to Mrs Charlesworth's face. For the first time the younger woman registered fear. Her defiance drained away. Mrs Charlesworth was beside herself with rage.

'Get out,' she said through her teeth. 'Pack your things and get out. Your actions have brought women into danger and my magazine into disrepute. You are a fool. What's more, you are a malicious, hot-headed, self-important fool. You have influenced the most easily led of my staff to betray her duty and exposed my magazine to calumny. Who will believe in our assurance of confidentiality now? If it had not been for Miss

226

Fisher you might have continued in this course and caused more deaths. Why did Miss Lavender give anodyne advice? Because that is the only safe advice to give. Even the Delphic oracle wrapped her words in obscurity.'

'But what will I do?' asked Miss Prout.

Mrs Charlesworth grew another inch in height and said, 'I do not care, but if you are not out of my office in ten minutes I shall–'

'Call the police?' sneered Miss Prout. 'They'd like to hear what I have to say.'

'Would they?' asked Phryne. 'Tell me. What have you to say?'

'About all this,' said Miss Prout, growing desperate. 'About the letters.'

'Is there anything else about the letters to which you would draw my attention?'

'I wasn't the only one who took letters out of the book.'

'Oh? Who else?'

'All of them.' Miss Prout made a broad gesture.

'If there was a gardening letter, it was sent to me,' said Mr Bell in weary explanation. 'If there was an enquiry about child care it went to Mrs Opie, and so on. Is that what you mean, you silly woman?'

'So all of you wrote replies to letters relating to your special interests,' said Phryne. 'Nothing else to tell the cops, Miss Prout?'

Miss Prout subsided, shaking her head.

'Right, then. Off you go,' said Mrs Charlesworth. 'Miss Phillips, make up her pay. Miss Grigg, make sure that she only takes what is hers.'

'I'll help you with your things,' Phryne offered.

Miss Prout, who seemed stunned, allowed Phryne to assist her with a large straw basket and a handbag. Miss Grigg, embarrassed, had nevertheless watched it being packed. It contained no letters or documents. Miss Phillips handed over a small envelope containing her pay up to that day, calculated on the outside in black ink.

From the exclusion order to the stairs, Miss Prout was out of the office in under ten minutes. Behind her, Phryne felt the tension ease. Whatever the person had feared had not come to pass.

Phryne hefted the basket, looked both ways in case of Chinese assassins, and helped Miss Prout across the road and into a tea shop.

'I only wanted to help,' wailed Miss Prout, the full horror of her situation dawning upon her at last.

'I know,' said Phryne. 'But you didn't help, did you? "Desperate" is dead. You must not tell depressives to buck up and stop blubbering. Anne's marriage nearly broke up. The cleaning lady was sacked and she has a sick child. If you want to give advice, you have to know something first. Now drink your tea,' said Phryne, 'and tell me what you wouldn't say in that office with them all staring at you.'

'Why should I do that? You got me sacked.'

'No, you got you sacked,' said Phryne patiently. 'And if you'll allow me to say so, you have no talent for intrigue. You gave yourself away by reacting when I said that Miss Nelson had confessed. I'll give you a pound to tide you over until you can get another job. And an introduction to the editor of the first Australian *True Confessions*

Magazine, which is starting up as we speak. You ought to find a niche there. Here it is,' said Phryne, laying a letter and a pound note on the table. 'Now, talk.'

Dot drew confidence from the big car and the presence of Mr Butler, as Phryne had hoped that she would. As the Hispano-Suiza rolled along Dynon Road past the railway yards, she rehearsed some platitudes which might get her past the door. Nothing like a smooth sentence which might slip past a sore mind without rasping the nerves. The sort of thing one always said. Regret. Sorrow. Resignation. God's will.

Mr Butler drew up at the door of a large house on the road which curved past the Williamstown railway line. There were mock orange bushes blooming as Dot walked up the path to a front door shrouded in black crepe.

'Yes?' a man opened the door. 'If you're from the newspapers you can bloody well go away.'

'I'm not from the papers,' said Dot. 'I come from–'

A wail inside turned into a shriek and a crash. Dot sprinted into the house and extracted a small child from the remains of a large jardinière which had been filled with ferns. Now it was broken and the child was emerging from the compost, bleeding from the forehead and screaming with shock. A baby yelled in the back of the house. The noise was appalling.

The man sat down abruptly in an easy chair and began to cry.

Knowing that he would never forgive her if she

took any notice of his tears – it was well known that men did not cry – Dot hefted the child out of the shattered china, brushed it off, and carried it into the kitchen. The house was not filthy but dingy, as though it had been years since it had been properly cleaned. Dot sat the child on the sink and washed its forehead. There was only a small cut and a big bump. The child stopped screaming and settled down to a solid, cadenced sobbing.

'There now,' said Dot. 'We'll just patch up your head and then we'll see if we have a biscuit.'

'Mummy!' sobbed the child.

'Oh dear,' said Dot. 'Here's a biscuit,' she said, finding an ancient ginger one still in the grocer's bag. 'Now you shall go back to Daddy while Dot goes and finds that baby.'

'Dot?' hazarded the child, trying out the new word. He walked beside Dot and scrambled up into his father's lap, demanding that he kiss the bump better. Dot left them there and located the baby by sound. It was wet, hot, cross and hungry.

These faults could be mended. Dot found the means and worked with unthinking efficiency. She took the baby and the bottle into the parlour and sat down in a straight backed chair to feed it. The hungry gums clamped onto the teat and the bottle emptied rapidly. Silence filled the house.

'Are you an angel?' asked the man.

'No, I'm Dot Williams. I'm investigating another matter and I need to ask you some questions. But haven't you any assistance?' she asked, which was not on her brief.

'My sister was supposed to be here by now,'

said Mr Green helplessly. 'I haven't ever touched the children. Alex wouldn't let me. Said men couldn't know anything about it. Now she's gone and I'm useless.'

'Just unpractised,' Dot said. 'Your sister will show you what to do. But until she comes I have to tell you never to leave a two year old alone. It's amazing how fast they move and they're always pulling things down. They can get anywhere, climb like a monkey, and they've got no sense of danger at all.'

'I can see that. I only looked away for a minute.'

'Long enough,' said Dot, joggling the baby expertly.

'Thank you, Miss Williams. What do you want to know?'

'Tell me about how your wife passed on.'

'Not much to tell. She was always nervy. Ever since Tommy was born. Then she got better for a while, and then after Elsie she got worse again. Of course, her parents cut her off, so we had a bad start.'

'Oh? Why?' Dot burped the baby and nursed it in her lap as Mr Green talked.

'For marrying me,' said Mr Green with a wry twist to his mouth.

'What was their objection?' asked Dot.

'I'm one-eighth Aboriginal,' he said bitterly. 'They said it would come out in the babies. It hasn't, has it?'

'No,' said Dot. 'Wouldn't matter if it did,' she added. 'Perfectly sweet,' she said to the baby in her lap. It gooed and pawed at her face.

'But the Hewlands said that if she married a

man with a touch of the tar brush they'd cut her off and never speak of her again, turn her picture to the wall, all that melodramatic rubbish, and they did it. Not a word, not a Christmas card. Things she sent to them came back "refused by addressee". It upset her, though she said it didn't.'

'That's terrible,' murmured Dot.

'But she was all right until the babies came. She kept finding some trace of blackness in them, the palms of their hands were too pale, their eye colour changing from blue to brown.'

'All babies do that,' Dot told him.

'She wrote to that bitch Artemis from some women's magazine and she believed the answers when she wouldn't believe anyone else. Artemis kept telling her that it was nothing, just a passing mood.'

'Did she keep the letters?'

'I burned them,' said Mr Green savagely. 'Artemis told her to ignore the doctor who told her to go and talk to a psychiatrist because she had post-natal depression. So she refused to go. When I took her to see the man the doctor recommended she screamed at me that I was trying to lock her up in the madhouse.'

'How did you feel about that?' asked Dot.

'I was angry. I lost my temper. I told her that if she didn't do something to help herself I would send her to the hospital. I shouldn't have said that. But the house was always dirty, there was never anything to eat, I couldn't bring anyone home. The children were always grubby and crying. Some days she didn't even get out of bed and I'd come home to the babies screaming and nothing to give them. And then she wouldn't let me help. She'd drag herself out of bed in her old nightie and haul herself around the house dropping things and crying. Almost as though she was doing it for revenge. Almost as though she hated me.'

'She didn't hate you,' said Dot.

'Then one day I came home and the babies were crying and the house was filthy and I stormed up the stairs to yell at her and she was dead. And cold. She'd taken an overdose of chloral. The doctor said she must have taken it as soon as I left for work in the morning. I called the police and they took her away.'

'And left you with two babies and no idea of how to cope.'

'Yes.'

'Did you know who Artemis was?'

'No, but once I get a housekeeper settled in and the house running again, I'm going to hunt the bitch down and kill her. If she hadn't interfered, I might still have a wife and the children might still have a mother.'

'Too late,' said Dot. 'Someone already has. She's dead. Murdered.'

'Oh,' said Mr Green, blankly. Tommy, who had spread his biscuit all over his face and his father's shirt front, wriggled off his lap and headed for the fire irons. Dot fended him expertly and sent him back towards his father. 'Is that what you are investigating?'

'Yes. Grab Tommy, Mr Green, and send him back this way. That brass pot is none too stable.'

'Back to the lady, son,' said Mr Green, who was

getting the idea. 'Well, if someone killed that woman, she had only herself to blame.'

'Perhaps,' said Dot. 'Tell me, have the Hewlands been told of their daughter's passing?'

'I sent them a letter,' said Mr Green, catching Tommy and directing him towards the window. 'They live in a fancy boarding house in Toorak.'

'Tintern Avenue?' asked Dot.

'Yes, that's the place. But I've not heard a word. I'm sure they won't come to the funeral either. Not that I want to see them.'

A key turned in the lock and a large, dark-haired, robust-looking woman came in, laden with bags. She set them down in time to catch Tommy as he made a spirited attempt to fall out the window.

'I can't imagine how anyone survives being two,' she exclaimed. 'Up you come, my lad. Hello, Bob, I've got the supplies. A couple of women are coming tomorrow to start the cleaning and I can stay until you find a housekeeper. Cheer up, old chap.'

Tommy grabbed at her hair and secured a long lock.

'This is Miss Williams,' said Mr Green. 'This is my sister Joan. Miss Williams came to ask me about Artemis. It seems that she's dead.'

'Good,' said Joan. 'Now you can stop thinking about her.'

'Baby's asleep,' said Dot, handing her over. Miss Green took her with an offhand gentleness which boded well for the Green children. She looked Dot up and down and approved of what she saw.

'Thanks for coming,' she said. 'It's a weight off

his mind and he's got enough to worry about, poor chap.'

'Not at all,' said Dot, and saw herself out of the house.

'How did you go?' asked Mr Butler, easing the big car away from the kerb.

'Dead end,' said Dot, and was shocked at her callousness.

CHAPTER FIFTEEN

The third line, divided, shows the subject straitened before a frowning rock. He lays hold of thorns. He enters his palace and does not see his wife. There will be evil.

Hexagram 47: Khwan
The I Ching Book of Changes

Dot was driven back to the city. She was glad of the silver-mounted thermos to which Mr Butler directed her attention. Really, that Artemis had made a hash of things! Although Dot's sympathy lay with the bereaved father and, if pressed, she also might have told Mrs Green to get up and at least feed the children and wash the floor, she did see that in some cases this was not useful advice. Vapours were one thing, real mental illness another, and who could hope to tell the difference from a letter? Artemis had been either very daring or very stupid, and neither sounded like Miss

235

Lavender, despite her fascination with fairies.

Women's Choice was largely occupied with watching Mrs McAlpin take a photograph of Miss Herbert in a very old-fashioned dress. In order to take advantage of the big theatrical floodlights, Miss Herbert was standing insecurely on a chair in her high heels, bustle and train, and Mrs McAlpin was paying no attention to anything at all except the placing and focusing of her camera.

Dot sidled in. Phryne drew her to stand by the door.

'Is she going to fall off that chair?' asked Dot. 'And what a horrible old dress!'

'I hope not, and it's a Worth model and I won't hear a word against it,' said Phryne. 'You wait and see what Madame Fleuri can do to it.'

'Oh, if it's Madame,' said Dot. 'She can do anything. She could make an elegant ensemble out of two sugar sacks and a hay bag for a hat. Miss, I met Mr Green. Poor man. His wife killed herself and left him with two small children. It was all Artemis's fault. He said he'd hunt her down and kill her when he got his house settled.'

'But he hasn't got his house settled yet?'

'No, Miss.'

'And therefore he hasn't started hunting?'

'No, Miss.'

'That will be a relief to Miss Prout. Much as she might enjoy being hunted down by a good-looking man,' said Phryne venomously.

'Miss Prout wrote the letters? I thought they were wrong for Miss Lavender.'

'You thought right. And I have some other things to try. Miss Prout voluble but useless.

What a distressingly stupid young woman! And yet I suspect she is right about what women want. Scandal broth, with envy and malice *en crouton*. Oh, well,' said Phryne, dismissing the future of women's magazines with a wave of her cigarette holder. 'Some will survive to hand out book reviews, recipes and gardening hints, with a few sly bits of information on man-management and divorce. For, Dot, have you ever thought what will happen when the present generation of little boys grow up? They'll want the world back, and we'll probably be fools enough to give it to them.'

'Maybe,' said Dot.

Miss Herbert wobbled perilously but did not fall. Mrs McAlpin finally said, 'Stay just like that,' and vanished under her black hood. A shutter clicked. Mrs McAlpin emerged.

'That might be quite passable,' she said. 'Could someone help Miss Herbert down? And we can switch off the floods now. They do make the room so hot.'

She took her precious plate and disappeared down the stairs to the darkroom.

'Well, Madame,' said Phryne, helping Miss Herbert onto terra firma and dusting her a little, 'what do you think?'

Madame Fleuri was a small woman, clad in deepest black. Her figure was that of a cottage loaf, stuck about the bosom with pins and threaded needles. Scissors hung at her belt on a piece of tape. Her hair was drawn straight back into a chignon. She was brisk, intelligent and an acknowledged priestess of the mode, which she

237

served with grim devotion.

She had been head forewoman in the *ateliers* of Poitou when she had fallen in love with an Australian soldier as he rode through the Champs Élysées with feathers in his hat. She had followed him to Melbourne. Such, as she liked to say, was the power of *l'amour,* for she still missed Paris badly, especially in the autumn.

The aged Frenchwoman clicked her tongue. 'The muslin is *inutile* and must go. Then we unpick a little – such stitching! It seems an offence! – and then we relay the fabric over your model. We can use the beaded front panels, yes, they will do.'

'I'll leave you to it,' said Phryne.

'You see, 'ere,' said Madame Fleuri. 'The fabric 'as been discoloured by sunlight. It 'as made a *charmant* effect, turning the red towards blue. We shall use it.'

Something chimed in Phryne's head. There had been something out of place in Miss Lavender's Wee Nooke. What had it been? Among a sea of pink, something of another colour?

The connection refused to be made. Phryne watched Dot sit down with Madame and begin to undo the side seams. Swathes of heavy satin spread themselves over half the room. Mrs Charlesworth had retreated to her office. Miss Nelson, much comforted by having come through her ordeal with her honour intact, sat peacefully unpicking the hem. Phryne threaded her way through the rampant dressmaking and arrived at Miss Grigg's desk. She and Mr Bell were sorting through the remaining bulbs and packing them in a smaller box.

'What's wrong with the other ones?' asked Phryne.

'Small flaws,' said Mr Bell. 'Too immature, worm-eaten or frostbitten. I plant them in the nature strip, so they're not wasted.'

'How difficult is it to grow primroses in an Australian climate?' asked Phryne. He raised his head quickly and looked her in the eyes. He had been good-looking before the burns had disfigured and distorted his face. Now it was hard to guess his expression.

'You can't grow them except in places where there is a reasonable snowfall,' he replied. 'One might keep the seed-tray in the bottom of the icebox, of course. The rest of the household mightn't like it, though. Why do you ask?'

'Just curious. What sort of bulbs are these?'

'Daffodils,' said Miss Grigg. 'Doubles. I always put the bulbs in when the tomatoes come out.'

'This year I thought we might try some of the smaller, more delicate flowers under the elm tree,' observed Mr Bell. His hands on the bulbs were tanned and coarse, gardener's hands. 'Sparaxis, bluebells, ixia, maybe cyclamen. You remember them in the Toscana, drifts of purple points in the coarse grass?'

'My word I do,' said Miss Grigg.

'When were you last in Italy?' asked Phryne. 'I was there in twenty-four. In spring.'

'Lucky,' said Miss Grigg. 'That's when I left. Couldn't stand that bounder Mussolini. Me and Gally packed up the house and home we came, like swallows to Capistrano.'

'Boomerangs,' chuckled Mr Bell. 'That's what they say. Australian girls are boomerangs. They always come home. And before you ask, Miss Fisher, I returned to these shores in twenty-six, when my father died.'

'Was your father in the antiques business, too?' asked Phryne, selecting a bulb and turning it in her fingers. Amazing. Packed into this onion-shaped little package was force enough to hammer a shoot through a cobbled street and beauty enough to adorn a palace and scent a whole room. Mr Bell took the bulb, politely but firmly.

'If you wouldn't mind not handling them while you are smoking? Tobacco contains little germs which don't do plants any good. Mosaic leaf, for instance. Yes, my father was in the antiques business. Not in a major way. I've managed to improve trade with a bit more import and export.'

'I see. What do you make of Miss Prout's actions?

'Silly bi–' Mr Bell caught himself in time. 'Sorry, ladies. Foolish young woman. She might have known that someone would find out. And she hasn't the brain God gave to geese.'

'Amen,' said Miss Grigg. 'Well, that's your bulbs, John. I'm not a lot of use in sewing, so I'd better be getting back to my wiring. I don't think this new amplifier is going to work, you know. But I'm not making any judgments in advance.'

'I can't sew either,' said Phryne. 'So I might just go and watch. Like the idle rich.' She smiled and clambered back over what seemed to be acres of plum-coloured satin, faded by sunlight into an attractive bluish sheen.

An idea had taken root and was growing like one of Mr Bell's bulbs. But premature action would ruin all. She needed the information from the Companies Register in Sydney. In the meantime, she would go and talk to the Hewlands about their dead daughter. Could they really be as unconcerned as Mr Green supposed?

Mrs McAlpin came back with a wet proof sheet, which she held by the corners.

'Not bad,' she said, allowing Phryne to see it.

'You have this remarkable talent for revealing the soul of the model,' exclaimed Phryne, peering over her shoulder. 'There's Miss Herbert, a little frightened, a little unsteady, but terribly pleased with herself and rather innocent.'

'Thank you. Shall I pencil you in? I should like to photograph you,' said Mrs McAlpin.

'I don't know if I want to be revealed,' said Phryne frankly. 'You might show me something about myself which I don't want to see. Like that portrait of Miss Lavender. And I would have said that you liked her, if anyone did.'

'That is true,' said Mrs McAlpin. 'I did. But the camera sees things differently. And in your case, Miss Fisher, it won't show you anything you didn't know was there. I fancy it might have come as a surprise to Miss Lavender, though.'

'Yet she kept the picture,' wondered Phryne.

'It was a good picture,' said Mrs McAlpin.

Miss Herbert, invited to inspect her likeness, gave a squeal of delight. Mrs McAlpin plastered the picture against a bundle of advertising spills to dry.

'I've read Miss Lavender's will,' said Phryne.

'Did you know she left half of her estate to your church?'

'Her church as well. Did she so? That is interesting. Poor Marcella. Trying to buy her way into heaven. Not that others haven't had the same idea.'

Phryne collected the letter book, retrieved Mr Butler from downstairs, and had herself driven to Toorak.

Mr and Mrs Hewland were sitting in their absolutely clean, absolutely neat front parlour when Phryne came calling. Both pairs of calm eyes turned on her as she was shown in by Mercy Porter.

'I have come to offer condolences on the death of your daughter,' said Phryne.

'We have no daughter,' stated Mr Hewland.

'Yes, you have. Well, you had. I'm talking about Alexandra, the one who married Mr Green and gave you two fine grandchildren,' said Phryne.

'Bastard slips shall take no root,' said Mr Hewland. His face was as responsive as a terracotta Etruscan warrior. Beside him, his wife nodded agreement.

'Unless there's something you're not telling me, she wasn't a bastard. She was your legitimate daughter. She developed post-natal depression and drank chloral to cure it, which it has. You must remember,' Phryne urged.

'No,' said Mr Hewland, with a curious, martyr's smile beginning to dawn on his stony face. 'We have no daughter. A young woman who was related to us married against our wishes to a man from an inferior race. Thus she demon-

242

strated that she was not of our blood and we cut off all contact with her and her debased brood. "Thou art cast out of thy grave like an abominable branch",' he added, for emphasis.

'Well, in that case,' said Phryne, on whom scripture lessons had not been wasted, 'all I can say is "Though I speak in the tongues of men and angels and have not charity, I am become as sounding brass or a tinkling cymbal", 1 Corinthians 13:1, and I will bid you good day.'

'I will see you out,' said Mrs Hewland.

Once she was out of sight of her husband, Mrs Hewland grasped Phryne's arm.

'How did she die? Was it suicide?'

'More like accident,' said Phryne. 'She was so depressed that she wouldn't have remembered how many swigs she had taken from the chloral bottle. Her husband is coping. But the children – who, by the way, are as white as I am, no shame to them if they were not – could do with a grandmother.'

Mrs Hewland dragged in a deep breath. 'She sent me a photograph. I steamed open the letter before I sent it back.'

'Why didn't you keep it?'

'Mr Hewland would not allow it. If he felt that I was carrying on a clandestine correspondence he would be very angry. And the doctor says that he'll die if he bursts an aneurysm. I can't let him upset himself. Perhaps, after...'

Phryne knew what was being inferred. After Mr Hewland had gone to his own narrow and unpleasant version of heaven, Mrs Hewland might dare see her grandchildren as she had not dared

243

see her daughter.

'Why do you stay?' she asked, not expecting an answer but anxious to be out of this suffocating air of piety, which meant retrieving her arm which Mrs Hewland still gripped tightly.

'"The wife should be in subjection to her husband",' quoted Mrs Hewland with St Paul, who was also low down on Phryne's list of favourite people.

She walked back to the car murmuring Hilaire Belloc's 'Epitaph on a Puritan': '"He served his God so faithfully and well, That now he sees him, face to face, in Hell."'

'What was that, Miss Fisher?' asked Mr Butler.

'Nothing at all, Mr B,' said Phryne. 'Drive on.'

At four o'clock Phryne received a message from Bert and made an appointment. At four-fifteen she telephoned Li Pen and gave her password. At four-thirty she gave orders for an early dinner and refilled her flask with old brandy.

Bert and Pirates had found the SS *Gold Mountain*.

'I knew as soon as I heard its new name,' she told Li Pen when they met on the dock.

'Which is?'

'SS *Apu*,' said Phryne.

'Ah,' said Li Pen. 'The famous pirate. That was unwise of them. I have heard of an offer of silk of very good quality at a very low price. The merchant's name is not given. The auction is tomorrow.'

'Then we had better do something about SS

244

Apu tonight.'

Li Pen inclined his head.

It was nine o'clock.

Bert whistled. Phryne and Li Pen crept along the wet black tarmac of the dock. Slab-sided ships rose and fell gently on the ebbing tide. Rain scattered, making a rattle like small shot. Phryne tightened the scarf over her head. She was dressed in the loose black pyjamas worn by Chinese sailors and her hair was plastered flat by a broad bandanna. She could not hear Li Pen's feet on the asphalt, but that was to be expected.

'She's the same,' said Bert quietly. 'Had it from Pirates himself. She's been painted green and yellow and her superstructure's been gussied up a bit, but it's her and Pirates'll swear off the grog if it ain't. What're you goin' to do now, Miss?'

'Can you find out if her crew are still aboard?'

'Most of 'em'll be in the fleshpots by now,' said Bert. 'Bar a nighwatchman and an officer.'

'I want you to distract them,' said Phryne. 'Cec can wait in the taxi and keep the engine running. We might want to get away quite fast.'

'How?' asked Bert, spreading his arms wide in a gesture of entreaty.

'Ask for passage, ask for a job, complain about the rats, pretend you are drunk. Try not to annoy them so much that they throw you in the river. But if they do I'll pay you double. That's the *Gold Mountain* and if Lin Chung is aboard, I am going to find him.'

Bert, who was about to call upon his maker to deliver him from unconscionable demands from stroppy sheilas, decided not to on receipt of a

245

fifty megawatt glare from those strange green eyes. He felt a moment of gentle Christian pity for whoever tried to stop Miss Fisher from retrieving her Chink, and began staggering along the dock, singing, 'Roll me over, roll me over, even though you've never done before...'

'Roll me over,' whispered Phryne, 'in the clover, and you'll never be a maiden any more.' She had sung it to Lin Chung, and been surprised when he joined in the chorus.

'Miss?' asked Li Pen. 'Are you ready?'

'Let's go. How do we get onto the ship?'

'Hawser,' he grinned. 'If the rats can do it, so can we.'

'Squeak,' agreed Phryne.

The hawser was as thick as her waist. She crawled along, grateful for the soft shoes which allowed her feet to flex. The hawser swung a little and the ship moved, adjusting herself to this extra weight. Bert was bellowing 'Roll me over!' at the top of his voice and two people were demanding in fluent Cantonese what in the devil's name he thought he was doing, waking respectable seamen at this hour with his drunken roundeye bawling.

This didn't mean a lot to Bert, who kept singing, mounting the gangplank so clumsily that it creaked and swayed. Phryne reached the gunnel, arched and caught the side, then went over in one fluid leap and crouched, out of sight of the gangway, a black puddle in the night. Li Pen dropped beside her. He touched her shoulder and she followed him as he slid to the open companionway and went down, turning sharply to the right and into a 'tween deck.

246

The ship was crammed with cargo. There were corded boxes and bales of silk. Li Pen glided through the darkness. Phryne found that if she shut her eyes some sixth sense prevented her from colliding with anything as long as she moved with the same gentle self-assurance as warm air. She began to feel invulnerable, invisible, as the argument went on overhead and nothing moved in the bowels of the ship but Li Pen and Phryne and a few rats.

Working lights were on in the companionways, giving a dim unreliable light. Li Pen opened doors gently, scanned the contents and closed them again. Crew's quarters, squalid and depressing. More boxes and bundles, strings of partially dried fish, bundles of herbs which stank so foully that their only use could be in a witch's brew of henbane and mandragora. Nothing moving, nothing breathing. And overhead Bert must have been running out of arguments by now.

She touched Li Pen. 'Split up?' she mouthed. He thought about it, then nodded. He pointed to Phryne and then the floor, to himself and the smoke-raddled ceiling. Very well. Phryne would go down and Li Pen up – presumably to cope with the argument above.

Li Pen vanished like a mosquito who has provided an appetiser for a carp. Phryne searched for a way to go down.

To find the ladder, she had to creep back across the 'tween deck and up the other side. The air was thick with stenches, man-made and machine-made. Twice she halted and grabbed her upper lip to stop a sneeze.

Then she found the engine room. A drunken engineer was asleep on the floor, flat on his back, snoring like a whole orchestra. Phryne slipped past him, looking for another way out.

There was none. If the *Gold Mountain/Apu* went down and the crew couldn't leave by that one ladder, then they would drown along with the rats. The ship was alive with rats.

The slumbering man gave a cough and a grunt; Phryne froze. She stood so still that a questing rat paused in its passage across her foot, whiffling its whiskers, wondering if the engineer was dead enough to provide a late-night snack.

Loathing washed over Phryne so strongly she was afraid that she would retch. The clammy tail was across her bare ankle. It was cold. It was one of the vilest things she had ever felt in her whole life and if it had gone on for another second she might have flinched.

But the engineer turned over in his rancid couch and the rat moved on to seek for more comatose prey. On impulse, without any reason, Phryne followed it.

The rat heard a footfall behind it and speeded up to a fast walk. It was clearly unafraid of whatever its next target might do. Phryne hung back, not wanting to frighten the creature. She had searched through all that she could see of the *Gold Mountain/Apu*, and this might be as good a guide as any.

The rat trailed its revolting tail around a machine and then scrabbled up over a watertight sill through a small door which she had not noticed. Seated in front of an indistinct bundle on the filthy floor was a guard with a pistol.

He was so sleepy that he did not rouse at once. He saw the rat and kicked at it half-heartedly. Then he saw Phryne and leapt to his feet.

At the same time the bundle swore and tried to sit up.

Phryne knew that voice. She had a knife in her belt but she did not bother to draw it. She tripped the guard. Just as he was getting up he found that he was actually getting down. He shouted something, and then Phryne was on him. She dropped on his chest with both knees and vengefully banged his head on the floor, once to knock him out and twice because it made her feel better.

'Quick,' she said to Lin Chung. 'It's me. Get up! Can you walk?'

'Not with all these ropes,' he said quietly. She drew the knife and hacked at the knots and the ropes fell away. Then she extended both hands and dragged him up and into her arms at last.

Lin Chung indeed, not crippled, not nailed to anything, and apart from some surface grime and the blood-blotched wound on the side of his head, in one piece. He staggered as he tried to move. Phryne held him strongly for a moment. He smelt like he had stolen his garments from a previous owner who had been dead at least a week.

'Come,' she said. 'Li Pen and I have come for you.'

'I knew you would,' murmured Lin Chung. 'Where are we?'

'Melbourne,' she said. 'Talk later. The engineer's asleep outside–'

'No,' said Lin Chung dreamily. 'I think you'll find that actually he's awake and in here.'

Phryne ducked a swung club, grabbed a sinewy arm, and helped the engineer on his journey into the bulkhead. He hit it with a satisfying clang, rebounded, and dropped the club. He dived for her throat, both arms outstretched and huge hands clutching. Phryne kicked him hard in the groin and he went down screaming.

'Grab that pistol,' she snapped. 'That idiot will rouse the whole waterfront! Shut up, you fool!' she snarled at the engineer. Lin Chung obliged with a translation and the injured man, comforting the offended parts with both hands, clamped his mouth shut with a click.

'What did you say?' asked Phryne, interested, shoving Lin Chung rung by rung up the ladder.

'I told him that if he was quiet you'd go away, but if he kept yelling you'd bite them off. And eat them.'

'Nice,' approved Phryne. 'Shows a realistic appraisal of my mood.'

They emerged through the hold into the main part of the ship. Lin was walking with more confidence, as though his feet had been recalled to their duty. Even in the dim glow of the working lights he was blinking.

'Where now?'

Phryne listened. There was no sound overhead. What had they done with poor Bert? Where was Li Pen?

She shrugged. 'Is that gun loaded?'

Lin showed her the gun. It was rusty, but the action was oiled and it had six bullets. She rotated the chamber and clicked it back together.

'Up?' asked Lin Chung. He still felt that he was

in a dream, but it was an engrossing and delightful dream and he was interested to see what
would happen next.

'Might as well,' said Phryne.

She pulled down his head, very gently, and
kissed him on the mouth. He stank like the long
deceased and he tasted of starvation and fear, but
he was Lin Chung and she did not mean to lose
him again.

The kiss awakened Lin Chung. He had never
managed a kiss like that in a dream. Dream kisses
tasted of flowers and wine, not old brandy and
excitement. Perhaps he was actually free and
awake, as unlikely as that might seem to a logical
mind.

The companionway was deserted. They climbed
up and up and saw no one. There was no sound
but a murmur of conversation overhead, quiet
and in Cantonese. Phryne wondered who was
talking.

They clambered up the last flight to the deck.
Lin Chung went first. Phryne was close behind
him.

Perhaps his long captivity had made him clumsy.
As he stepped over the sill, he stumbled a little and
the man at the gangway turned around and saw
him. Phryne, flinging herself sideways along the
deck, saw him open his mouth in a perfect ellipse.

But no sound ever emerged. Two hands reached
from behind the watchman and closed around his
throat. He gave a small sigh and slipped out of the
action. Li Pen lowered the body gently.

He smiled at Lin Chung.

'So, she found you,' he said softly. 'I thought

she would.'

'I saw what they did to you,' said Lin Chung.

Li Pen made a dismissive gesture. He reached out a hand to help Lin Chung towards the gangway. Phryne got up and brushed herself.

'Stop,' said a voice. There was a flapping of discarded tarpaulin and a grating screech as something metal was dragged across metal.

'It's a good gun,' said a smooth voice, in English. 'We got it off an English ship. It's a Hotchkiss and at this range there will be little left of you or that Shao Lin to cremate.'

CHAPTER SIXTEEN

The third line, divided, shows the subject bringing himself round to whatever may give pleasure. There will be evil.

Hexagram 58: Tui
The I Ching Book of Change

This is it, thought Phryne, staring down the barrel. Now we will all die. What a pity. I haven't done half the wicked things I wanted to do, and the ones I have done I haven't done anything like enough.

'The noise might create rather a stir,' said Lin quietly. 'Melbourne is not used to gunfire by night.'

'You need to give that warning to someone who

cares,' said the smooth voice. 'I, as it happens, do not.'

'And would not our dissolution into mangled fragments rather destroy your scheme?' asked Lin, leaning on the rail.

'Scheme?' asked Phryne. 'What scheme is this? Who is this person, Lin, dear?'

She slid under Lin Chung's arm, supporting him and masking the disappearance of Li Pen behind the deckhouse. The unseen maniac had his finger on the trigger. Her gun was of no immediate use.

'Oh, haven't we been introduced? My apologies. My name is Lin, also, Miss Fisher. Might I say how fetching you look in that sailor's garb? Lin Tai, at your service.'

'My cousin,' explained Lin Chung. 'And heir, if Grandmother disinherits me, to the Lin family lands.'

'And despite your shameful behaviour with that roundeye harlot, she shows no signs of doing that. So, when the pirates freed you, I intercepted the cargo. I had every intention of delivering you once the handover of the Lin family lands was completed with my agent in Bias Bay,' he added. 'But now that you've managed to free yourself–'

'I was rescued,' Lin pointed out.

'–and forced me into declaring myself, I have to kill you. I assume that this threat will be sufficient to make you and the interfering Miss Fisher tie each other up and jump overboard. They say that drowning is an easy death, once you stop trying to breathe. No, I really would advise you not to move. And tell that monk to stay where he is. I really don't want to shoot you, Chung, though I have always hated you. And you, Miss Fisher. My agents have shown disgraceful lack of initiative. I thought that they would have killed you by now. I knew you would try to retrieve Chung.'

Phryne had been guiding Lin Chung towards the voice. Lin Tai came into view. There was a family resemblance, Phryne thought. He had the delicate bone structure of the Lin family, though he was heavier and his eyes were red-rimmed. Secret opium smoker? Or had he looked on the gin when it was cheap? He did not stop them moving forward because they were directly in the path of his gun. Now they had their backs against the rail and the river behind them.

She had never contemplated a Hotchkiss gun before, though she had read about them in Edgar Wallace. It had a range of two hundred yards and was as accurately sighted as a rifle. And it appeared to have the bore of a cannon when you were staring down the barrel. Edgar Wallace's *Sanders* had described it. 'The little gun which says ha ha' the Africans called it.

The situation, as far as Phryne could see, had no humour in it at all. At her side, Lin Chung was shaking. Tears ran down his cheeks as the bright dock lights stung his eyes.

'So you took me,' he said to Lin Tai. 'You blindfolded me and roped me like a beast and you've been extorting ransom from Grandmother. And your agents mutilated Li Pen.'

'The work of but a few weeks,' agreed Lin Tai. 'Of course, I had a good teacher.'

'Who?

'Lai Choi San,' he said. 'Don't move, Miss Fisher. I, at least, will now never underestimate the power of women.'

'A moral improvement,' said Phryne. 'And probably about time,' she added tartly.

'Strip,' said Lin Tai.

'Why?' asked Phryne, raising an eyebrow.

'I don't want you identified by your clothes,' said Lin Tai, though Phryne saw him lick his lips. She must give Li Pen time and Lin Tai's lechery might provide her with some sort of chance.

'These clothes are a disgrace anyway,' she said, peeling Lin Chung out of his revolting garments and allowing them to sulk to the deck. Then she slipped off her shoes, pulled off her blouse and trousers and stepped slowly out of her underwear. The thin silk whispered down her flanks. Lin Chung blinked. She was unashamed, perfectly white in the lights, utterly distracting. She was an ivory carving made by a master. She posed, one hand on hip, one hand cupping a small breast.

'Is this what you wanted to see?' she cooed, thrusting a hip forward.

Lin Tai moved, just a fraction. Li Pen struck. The Hotchkiss swung and began to fire and Phryne collected Lin Chung and threw them both into the river.

Rain speckled the surface as Phryne groped around for Lin's hair, found a handful, and swam strongly up. At least there was no doubt as to the direction in water. One always knew which way was up. The water was cold and filthy and she hoped that in his weakened condition, Lin Chung's heart had not stopped. Their heads broke the surface and she was amazed to find him keeping himself afloat and laughing.

'Not a dream,' he said, giggling. 'Not a dream.'

He embraced her in the water, twining his legs around hers and almost pulling her under.

'Real,' she said firmly. 'Perfectly real. And perfectly cold and disagreeably wet.'

'I dreamed about cold water,' he said. 'All through the tropics. I stank and the cargo stank and the ship stank and I thought, how many times have I woken up too lazy to go and swim in a clear, bright pool, or walk down by the sea, or even drunk tea rather than turning on a tap and drinking clean, cold water? Such a lot of chances wasted. And who would have thought it of Tai? It's too much,' he said, sinking so that Phryne had to grab him and arrange him into a float.

The gunfire had ceased. There seemed to be a lot of shouting on board SS *Gold Mountain*, also known as SS *Apu*. Phryne heard a police siren. This would be, if nothing else, a scandal of monumental proportions. The rain stung her face. She was about to see if she had remembered anything at all of the lifesaving lessons which she had taken in what Lin would call a clean, bright pool, and to find out how applicable they were to a dirty cold river, when she heard a rhythmic sound and a creaking of oarlocks.

Bert drew up beside her in a providential rowboat.

'Fancy a ride, Miss?' he asked, without expression.

'Bert, dear, you're a saint. Can you get us out of this without attracting attention and bullets?'

Bert responded with Cec's invariable reply to any question. 'Too right,' he said. Then his eyes widened. He observed Phryne's naked shoulders emerging from the scum and added, 'Need to get you a shirt, but.'

Lin was dimly aware of water. He appeared to have been in a boat of some kind. He had heard someone swearing, continually and with remarkable fluency, in the Cantonese of his childhood, the Mandarin of his education and the English of recent teaching. He had been lifted and carried, laid on something hard, wrapped in something warm.

Then he was rocking. Not the movement of a ship but of a car. He was cushioned from the jolts by a pair of cool wet thighs. He slipped out of the world again.

When he woke he was being carried into a house which smelt of potpourri and cooking. It must be midnight but bacon was frying somewhere. He was laid down again on a soft surface and someone raised his head and gave him cold water to drink, exactly the taste he craved. He croaked for more and the cup came back.

Then a sharp pain shot through his head and his eyes snapped open. Li Pen held his shoulders as he struggled.

'It's all right,' soothed Phryne. 'Well, Doctor?'

'His ear has been severed some time ago by a sharp blade. It's healed well enough.' A Scots voice, female and trustworthy. She was bathing the side of his head with great delicacy; soaking off old caked blood and revealing clean scars underneath. 'Doesn't even need a bandage. Let's have a look at the rest of you, my lad.'

She shone a light into his eyes, examined his ears and mouth, clicked her tongue over his fine collection of scrapes, welts and bruises and tested each finger and toe, wiping the stinging medicinal fluid over the red rings around his ankles and wrists.

'Good enough,' she said. 'Shamefully misused but not permanently damaged apart from the ear. Nought I can do about that. Give him a good scrub with carbolic soap and then a nice hot bath and a lot of fluids. I'm leaving some sulphur for any infection. Have you had a fever, young man? Dysentery?'

'No,' said Lin Chung.

'Then I'll chance a little morphia for the pain of the next operation.' Lin Chung did not feel the needle go in. 'Watch for blood in the urine. He has been dehydrated and his kidneys must have been overstressed.'

Lin made a great effort, put out his hand, remembered his English and said, 'Thank you, Doctor.'

Doctor Macmillan shook his hand and said gruffly, 'Well, young man, you've been rescued now, so there's no need to worry about anything for the present. Drink lots of water and I'm sure that Phryne here will arrange suitable accommodation. Now, I'm off to my eggs and bacon. I'm on night shift.'

Lin was aware of being carried again. He seemed to have no strength in his limbs. He lay back in Li Pen's grasp, as secure as a baby. Lin saw Phryne's maid Dot's worried face through the steam. Steam? He heard Phryne's voice.

'This might be a bit unpleasant, Lin, dear, but you've got lice. And fleas. And God knows what else. So, in you go.'

He was lowered into very hot water and bit back a scream as all of his scrapes shrieked at once. The medicinal smell was very strong, obliterating a dreadful reek of long-dead flesh which Lin realised with shame must have been coming from him. Dot seized one hand and Li Pen his feet and Phryne began to wash his face and soap his hair.

This was the strangest dream. It was comforting, in an odd way. There were none of the beautiful maidens of his visions in the pirate jail, who had wafted through the wall to seduce him with their soft hands. These hands were relentless, extinguishing his face occasionally in drafts of fresh, hot water, scrubbing and rinsing. Li Pen, scars glowing on his bare chest, was applying the same concentrated effort to removing the patina of adventure from Lin Chung as he had given to learning the Five Forbiddens. He opened Lin's mouth and scrubbed his teeth with salt and soda, even scraping the hard brush across his tongue and polishing his gums to a hot glow. His mouth was rinsed with something antiseptic which tasted strange. Phryne, her hair still plastered to her head by river water, was cleaning his nails with a sharp instrument, which stung. Dot was scrubbing his arms and chest with the vigour she had given to floors when she had been a housemaid.

It went on and on. They lifted him, drained the bath, refilled it, and lowered him again. More

259

suds rose before his eyes. Weight seemed to have fallen off him. His muscles relaxed. The water ceased to sting and began to feel luxurious. He smiled, even though his skin felt ready to split, and splashed with his feet. Li Pen laughed.

Lin Chung had seldom seen Li Pen laugh.

Then his sense of scent began to return. He smelt the river on Phryne and Li Pen – so that part had been true – and floor soap from Dot. He smelt the ebbing sting of carbolic from the first bath and the increasing smell of pine salts, aromatic, fresh, delightful. Dot put down her flannel and fetched a cup of water as Lin was allowed to wallow in the bath, sipping water as cold as ice.

'Thank you, Dot, dear, you've been a great help,' Phryne told her.

'He'll be all right, Miss? What did the Doctor say?'

'Just in need of a good wash and a rest.'

'It's a shame about his poor ear,' Lin heard Dot say in a compassionate tone. Since he was now in the elevated state of the extremely exhausted, he only lifted a hand and felt the side of his head. No ear. But the rest of him seemed to be present and accounted for. His new scrubbed hands were fizzing with returned circulation. He felt down his body. Floating in water and morphia, he did not feel pain as he counted scars, scratches, hot spots which were bruises. Both hands, yes, his hands travelled downwards. Genitalia all present, thighs, knees, feet. An ear was a small price to pay.

He knew that there was something else, some terrible betrayal, which he ought to be remembering, but it slipped away. He was dreadfully sleepy, but he was unwilling to close his eyes in case this bliss proved to be a dream after all.

'I will stay with you,' said Li Pen, guessing what was going through Lin's mind. 'I will not leave you.'

'Nor I,' said Phryne. 'Now, we had better get you out of this bath and dried and into a nice clean bed. Mine, for preference. You are going to sleep away the day and night, my dear, and Li Pen will be with you, and you do not need to worry about anything for the present. Does he?' she asked Li Pen, and the Shao Lin bowed. Phryne grinned widely.

'How?' she asked.

'Regrettably,' said Li Pen, 'I fear that an accident with an unlawful weapon may have been the cause of the demise of a member of the illustrious Lin family.'

'Oh dear,' said Phryne. 'What a shame. *Tant pis.* Tut, tut, what a pity; how unsafe Melbourne has become, it used to be such a nice city; I think that's a sufficient number of clichés, what do you think?'

'The Silver Lady is, as always, meticulous.' Li Pen smiled at her. 'You have the courage of a lion, as I always said.'

'And so do you. How did you get behind him?'

'You were distracting him. And when the gun fired, you took my master into the river. Very wise, Silver Lady. My compliments.'

Phryne accepted the bow of a half-naked Shao Lin monk marked with characters which glowed red on his breast and gave him a deeper bow of

261

her own.

Lin was pleased that his rescuers were pleased, and thought no more as he was lifted out, dried, combed, scented, dressed in silk pyjamas and tucked into an unimaginably soft bed under warm woolly blankets. Dot manifested herself by his side and offered him a cup of thin, hot, beef bouillon. He drank it in careful mouthfuls, feeling something in his body sitting up and crowing at the taste.

Then Morpheus, father of sleep, gathered him into a close embrace.

Phryne stripped unaffectedly as the bath filled again. Li Pen sat down on the edge as she bathed.

'I am probably in defiance of my vows,' he informed her. 'I am not supposed to be in the presence of a naked woman.'

'I'm not a woman,' said Phryne, challenging the evidence of Li Pen's own eyes. 'I'm a fellow warrior.'

'True,' said Li Pen. 'Though I doubt that my abbot would see it that way.'

'Would you like my bath, fellow warrior?' she asked. Phryne emerged from the water. Li Pen handed her a towel, took off his own clothes and stepped into her bath. 'So, fellow monk,' he said, sloshing hot water over his face, 'What should we tell Madame Lin?'

'When Lin Chung is quite recovered, we shall go and see Madame Lin. But I will send a message that Lin is well and with me and that she should not pay the ransom. Who is – sorry, *was* – this Tai?'

'Madame Lin's favourite after Chung. He was

262

always obedient, always polite, always the perfect grandson. But he was not in the direct line and he had to find another way to use Chung to get the property. Therefore he bought him from the pirates and brought him home. Why he kept him alive I do not know.'

'Perhaps he thought he might need another ear,' said Phryne grimly.

'Possibly. Tai was there, I now realise, when they cut these characters into my chest. He manufactured his own destruction,' said Li Pen quietly, scrubbing at his hands.

That sounded like a good epitaph. The scandal had been averted, Lin Chung was home, alive if not entirely unmarked, and he was asleep right now in Phryne's bed.

And Phryne was worn out. She donned a nightdress, found her bed, climbed into it, and fell asleep.

She woke to the sound of household business being conducted. It was seven am. Mr Butler was using the new vacuum machine. Bottles were clattering. Lin Chung was sleeping beside her with a faint smile on his face. She got up and almost stubbed her toe on Li Pen, sleeping across the doorway.

Of course, it is impossible to actually trip over Li Pen, Phryne thought, because he would not be there by the time the trip was complete.

'I'm going to get some food,' she said wolvishly. 'Back soon. What shall I send you?'

'Porridge, bread and Vegemite,' said Li Pen. 'And a pot of Chinese tea, if you have some.'

'Certainly, we have Chinese tea,' said Phryne haughtily. Then, replaying the last sentence, she asked, 'How on earth did you get a taste for Vegemite?'

'It's vegetarian, unlike Bonox,' said Li Pen. 'Salty and interesting. I lived for a whole summer in Tibet and ate tsampa, uncooked barley bread. What it really needed was Vegemite.'

'Bread and Vegemite it is,' said Phryne bemusedly.

She ate a large meal of toast, eggs, bacon, sausages, grilled tomatoes and coffee. Bert and Cec had gone, after eating a gargantuan breakfast and telling the story to the assembled staff. Pirates had gone with them. The girls had gone reluctantly to visit a friend. Mr Butler, having delivered a meal of tea, bread and Vegemite to a man sitting cross-legged on the floor, was restoring his spirits with a little glass of port and the word puzzle.

Dot delivered the afternoon newspaper. Interesting. 'Outrage at the docks!' it screamed. 'Last night shots were heard and a Hotchkiss gun was fired on board the Macao vessel SS *Apu*. Police and dock security attended immediately and found that a passenger onboard the ship had been tampering with the gun – used against pirates and supposed to be struck down into the hold – when it fired, killing him. The master of the vessel will be fined for allowing a gun with live ammunition to remain mounted on his ship in port. The dead man has not yet been identified.'

'Then I'd better send a note to Madame Lin, telling her that also,' said Phryne to Dot. 'He needs to be identified.'

264

She wrote the note and sealed it with the chop which Lin had given her, a fanciful calligraphy which said Silver Lady.

'Get someone to take this to Madame Lin in Little Bourke Street,' said Phryne. 'Now, I am going back to bed.'

'Will there be any answer, Miss?' asked Dot.

'I will be very surprised if there is,' said Phryne.

'Detective Inspector Robinson,' announced Mr Butler.

Phryne suppressed a curse, but greeted the policeman politely.

'Well, well, Miss Fisher, had a strenuous night?' he asked.

'An interesting one,' she told him. 'Remind me not to frolic with the younger set, they play much too rough.'

'So you weren't out on the waterfront last night?'

'Why should I have been?' Phryne did not like lying to policemen, much less this one she was fond of, but had no intention of telling him about the Lin family's little domestic problems. Which, in any case, were now solved.

'Well, no one reported a fashionably dressed woman strolling down to Five North,' said Robinson jovially, 'so I suppose we'll have to cross you off our list.'

'Oh, good. Is that what brings you here so early?'

'No. I've got the Companies Register stuff from Sydney.'

Phryne read the extract. Despite her weariness, she felt a throb of excitement.

'My, my,' she commented. 'Well, I've almost got your solution, Jack, dear. I only need to know two more things.'

'And they are?'

'The first, what is in Mr Bell's warehouse. The second,' she yawned. Jack Robinson waited, pencil poised. 'The second is, what colour was Miss Lavender's little bird.'

'And that's all?'

'Yes, that's all. I'll see you tomorrow at Tintern Avenue. Now I really must get back to bed, Jack, dear, my head's not what it should be.'

'Too many cocktails,' said Robinson unsympathetically. 'Next time, stick to beer.'

He took his leave. Phryne yawned, stretched, and climbed the stairs.

Lin was still asleep. Li Pen was sitting straight and meditating on a spot of light on the wall. It had been a tiring few days. Phryne snuggled up next to Lin and went back to sleep.

It was black dark when she woke with a hand over her mouth.

'Quick,' said Lin. 'We have to get away.'

She freed her mouth, leaned over and clicked on the small bedside lamp. Pink light bloomed over the green walls and the embroidered hangings. Li Pen woke and leapt to his feet. With a certain amount of difficulty, Lin Chung sat up in bed with his back against the padded headboard. His mouth was open in astonishment. Li Pen brought him water and he drank it.

'Phryne?' He touched her breast. The narrow shoulder strap had fallen down. The touch seemed to reassure him. That was a real breast. Nothing else felt like that. 'And Li Pen? So it wasn't a dream.'

'No. I'm real and so is he,' said Phryne shortly. 'This is my bed and this is the middle of the night. How do you feel?'

'Clean,' said Lin Chung ecstatically. 'As clean as though I had been scoured like a floor – no, wait, don't tell me. I have been, haven't I? That was you and your maid Dot and Li Pen who nearly drowned me in suds. Sit down, Li Pen, please. Phryne, tell me what happened.'

'First you must visit the ablutions,' said Li Pen. 'Can you stand? And I will fetch you whatever you want to eat or drink.'

'I want cocoa,' said Lin Chung. 'No, it's too warm for cocoa. I want a brandy and soda and a caraway biscuit.'

Phryne fetched the brandy bottle, the soda siphon, and the tin of caraway biscuits. When she returned, Lin was sitting up with two pillows behind him. In the soft light, he seemed to radiate joy. She hoped that nothing would happen to squelch him. He was definitely too thin and the scar under the clean, glossy hair was far too visible. She mixed him a very weak brandy and soda, made a strong one for herself, gave a nice glass of neat soda to Li Pen and offered Lin Chung the tin of biscuits.

He bit solemnly into one, reminding Phryne of Wendy Opie and her ice cream. Phryne was suddenly touched and turned away to hide her stinging eyes. There he was, clean and safe and rescued, eating caraway biscuits and drinking a b and s, and she was very proud of him.

'All right,' he said. 'What happened?'

Phryne allowed Li Pen to describe how they

had discovered that the *Apu* was actually the *Gold Mountain*, the assault on the ship, the discovery of Lin Chung, the attack by Lin Tai and his unfortunate death.

'So he is dead?'

'Regrettably,' said Li Pen, without expression.

'He must have hated me for years. I never knew. Grandmother always held him up as an example of Confucian virtue. Married the girl found by his parents. Never wanted an education. Never strayed from the path of rectitude.'

'He strayed so far off the path of rectitude as to buy you from the pirates who freed you,' said Phryne. 'He wanted everything you have, including me. Though he didn't get me,' she added with satisfaction. 'Or anything else.'

'And Grandmother persuaded the others to cede the Lin possessions in China?'

'She is a formidable adversary,' said Li Pen. 'So is your Silver Lady. She found you when I could not.'

'Actually it was the rat,' said Phryne. 'I was standing in that filthy engine room and this rat walked right over my foot and then it decided the engineer wasn't dead enough to nibble on and went in search of you, so I followed it.'

'How did you know it was searching for me?' asked Lin Chung, wincing a little as he recalled the rats which had waited, bright-eyed, for him to sleep.

'I didn't,' said Phryne. Li Pen laughed again.

'Truly blessed, as I have always said,' he told Lin Chung, who joined the laughter.

Phryne felt that she had missed the joke.

'Why?' she asked.

'Because both you and he, Silver Lady, are born in the year of the rat,' said Li Pen. 'The rat is his totem animal, as it is yours. It is not surprising that a rat was able to reveal to you where those murdering beasts had stowed my master.'

'Oh,' said Phryne, wondering if it was some sort of sin to hate your totem animal. 'And you, Lin, what happened to you?'

'I can't separate out the days,' he said. 'I got to Macao, bought the silk, and the bribes I had to pay were double the price of the silk and other things, but I got them, they should be aboard the *Apu* this moment.'

'Bert is seeing that they are unloaded and delivered,' soothed Phryne. 'Then?'

'Then I was on the ship and it was seized by pirates. They had hidden among the passengers. They took the crew by surprise, threw them to the sharks, and found me by the label in my jacket. They had special orders about me. The rest of the passengers they divided into two lots. Those who had relatives who would ransom them, they kept. The others they killed or sold as slaves to the Japanese.' He drank some brandy and Phryne refilled his glass. 'I was kept in a grass hut by the shore. They had me tied closely. Li Pen was beside me. Then he suddenly wasn't.'

'I stayed free in their encampment, just to make sure that nothing went wrong,' said Li Pen. 'There were too many to fight for the moment. I knew that Madame would pay the ransom.'

'I didn't see anyone except some children, who came to throw things at me. I wasn't tortured.

269

They call such people *p'iao* – tickets. I was in Bias Bay. Finally they came and untied me, told me that the ransom was paid and that I could go. I was walking down to the shore to see if I could find a ship when I saw the old *Gold Mountain*, newly painted, and I was seized again. I think I lost hope then. They took me to Lai Choi San and she said that I was captive, despite the ransom. Then by threatening to kill me they called Li Pen and cut characters into his chest. I will never forget how they cast sea water over the cuts and laughed. They would have laughed more but he gave no sign of pain.'

'They sent me as a messenger,' said Li Pen, evenly. 'I did not fail to deliver the message.'

'Then they said I could write a letter, so I wrote to you, Phryne. I thought I might have no other chance of a farewell. I wrote in English on the envelope so the letter would be delivered. Then they said they had to enclose something convincing, held me down and–' he stopped.

'I got the letter,' said Phryne. 'With its enclosure. It was that, rather than the scars on Li Pen's admirable chest, that caused Madame to call a family council.'

'Then they stowed me aboard that filthy ship and finally after what seemed like years, you rescued me. Thank you. But it was Tai, wasn't it?'

'Yes,' said Li Pen.

'Grandmother will be very...' his voice trailed away. Phryne took the glass as he slumped down into sleep again.

'He will recover his nerve,' she said.

'He never lost it,' said Li Pen, proudly.

CHAPTER SEVENTEEN

The first line, undivided, shows the pleasure of harmony. There will be good fortune.

Hexagram 58: Tui
The I Ching Book of Changes

A cold touch woke Lin Chung. He managed to stifle a cry. A rat! No. He had been rescued. He was in a soft bed, in a house on dry land. The rocking he felt was not the ocean but the arrival of Miss Fisher's black cat Ember, who had clearly ascended the foothills of Li Pen and scaled the north face of Phryne in order to stick an inquisitive nose into his undamaged ear.

Bright green eyes surveyed him coolly in the pale light. It was dawn. He stroked the thick sable fur, from ears to tail, and Ember settled down to purr.

Phryne half woke as something near her face gave forth a soothing sound. Ember must have eluded the vigilant Li Pen and dropped in for a little conference about the timing of breakfast and night starvation in the feline species. She pushed the furry body aside and found Lin Chung watching her.

'Silver Lady,' he said, turning to her and sliding one arm under her neck, drawing her close. 'How can I thank you?

'You'll think of something,' purred Phryne, as roughened hands slid down her body, cupping her breasts.

They moved slowly, tranced and bleached by the cold early light. Phryne caressed the scarred back, the damaged skin, lingering over bruises as though her touch could heal them. Lin moved under her handling easily, as though he was weightless in hot water again. His fingers had not lost their skill, drawing shimmering trails down her sides, her back, her breasts, the inner skin of her thighs.

'I looked at the moon,' said Phryne. 'But I could not see you there.'

'I dreamed of you,' said Lin Chung. 'But when I woke you were never there.'

'I'm here now,' she replied.

'You are still a dream,' he said.

They kissed slowly, lingeringly, as though they knew that there was all the time in the world. Lin tasted of sleep and brandy. His skin was scented with pine. Phryne sucked at his lips, tasting nectar, feeling the orgasm beginning to build, slowly, sweetly. His fingers found the pearl. Her senses tingled and then stung. He lay as still as he could while she examined and lazily stroked his belly, his testicles and his phallus growing in her hands. Familiar and delightful, a body she knew well. One she had missed all the time he had been gone. One she had almost lost.

Then they grew urgent, as though there was no time at all. They scrambled and gripped. Phryne locked her legs around him, driving bones together so hard that they might have cracked.

She reached a climax which was like being struck by lightning. Every tendon went into rigour and shook and she heard herself scream.

Lin Chung made no sound, but collapsed into her embrace as though he had been shot with a Hotchkiss gun.

In seconds they were both asleep as they lay, and Ember came back to the pillow, from whence he had removed himself when the humans began to play their kittenish games, beneath the notice of a decent, sober, mature animal.

Li Pen threw the coverings over them and looked down with an expression remarkably similar, in human form, to Ember's.

Phryne woke when she heard the door bell.

'Drat,' she swore. 'I'll bet that's Jack Robinson, bringing me the last pieces of my jigsaw puzzle, and I'll have to get up and do something about it.'

'Which puzzle is this?'

'"Who killed Miss Lavender? or Who poisoned the poison pen?" Everyone's playing it,' said Phryne. 'All I've been doing for a week is gathering evidence of who didn't do it.'

'So you must arrive eventually at who did,' said Lin, scrubbing a hand through his hair and wincing as he touched the scar. 'Must you leave me, Silver Lady?'

'Not if I can help it.'

She pulled the bell rope and presently Dot's voice said, 'Miss?'

'Good morning, Dot, dear. Who was at the door?'

273

'Detective Inspector Robinson. Off to look at Mr Bell's warehouse, wants to know if you want to come along.'

'Has he got an appraiser with him?'

'No, Miss, just a couple of cops in dustcoats.'

'Ask him about the Gallery's man, Dot, and bring some coffee. I need another week's sleep, but it doesn't look as if I am going to get it. Lin, I have to get up. Damn it. Promise me you'll be here when I get back,' said Phryne with sudden vehemence, embracing him fiercely. 'I'm not going to lose you again.'

'I promise,' said Lin.

He was already drowsing back into sleep when she completed a hasty wash and brush-up and donned warehouse-going clothes. She was damned if she was going to risk a good pair of stockings on Mr Bell's warehouse.

Dot and the coffee arrived at the dining room table as Phryne came down. She gulped the inky Hellenic beverage, a lethal dose of caffeine in every cup, munched a piece of toast and put on her hat. Robinson was impressed. Only a quick change artist, a co-respondent or a midwife could dress as fast as Miss Fisher.

'Off we go,' said Phryne. 'Have we got the appraiser?'

'Meeting us there,' said Jack. 'I had a bit of trouble getting this warrant, Miss Fisher. I hope you know what you're doing.'

'Me too,' said Phryne.

'You'll be interested to know,' said the policeman, 'that we can't find a service record for Mr Bell at all, at least not under that name. In fact,

274

there's no record of a John Bell born in Australia who answers to his description.'

'Really?' asked Phryne, getting into the police car. 'How singular.'

'Why do I get the impression that you know this already?' asked the Detective Inspector. Acid etched the edge of the sentence.

'Mmm? Sorry, Jack, I'm still a little hungover. Mr Bell is not who he seems, Jack, dear. Well, none of us are, perhaps. But we shall know in a moment. Where is this warehouse?'

'Richmond. Not far. I also know the answer to your other question. Miss Lavender's bird was blue. That's why she called it Bluebird.' Robinson informed Phryne with heavy irony. 'Why did you want to know? When we buried the poor little thing, it was pink.'

'Like the Worth,' said Phryne incomprehensibly. 'Something changed its colour.'

'And you'll explain this in your own time?'

'I'll have to show you, Jack, or you'll never believe me. We'll need to go to Tintern Avenue after this. Then I can demonstrate. Really, I'm not doing an Agatha Christie on you. I won't know who did this until I can set up a trap.'

'Oh, very well.' Detective Inspector Robinson obliged Miss Fisher with a light to her cigarette, lit his own pipe, and subsided. Like the Lord, Phryne moved in mysterious ways. The road rushed past.

Phryne sank into reminiscences of Lin Chung, and was quite surprised when the car stopped in front of a flat, red-brick warehouse in a street of red-brick warehouses. This one had a painted sign indicating its owner. Marshall and Co.

A man in a dustcoat – were they everywhere, and she just hadn't noticed them until now? – sidled up to the Detective Inspector and said, 'No one inside, sir. Door's been opened. Caretaker had a key.'

'Good. Is Mr Jones here?'

'Yes, sir.'

A man in a business suit, complete with bowler hat and rolled umbrella, gave the Detective Inspector a small bow, and then a deeper one, removing his hat, as Phryne clambered out of the car. Her stockingless legs seemed to affect him profoundly.

'Shall we?' asked Robinson, and pushed open the door.

The space was crammed with crates. A light coating of dust showed that they had not been disturbed recently. A policeman with a jemmy began on the first crate, extracting two canvases, made fast to stretchers, padded and wrapped very carefully. Mr Jones carried them to the light and sneered.

'A copy of a Raphael madonna. A copy of another Raphael madonna. Not very good copies, either,' said the man from the Gallery.

'Keep unpacking,' said Phryne. 'Mr Jones, can you have a look at the canvas? Is it new?'

'No,' said Mr Jones, his interest piqued. 'No, it's old. In fact it appears to be very old. And this is a wooden plaque ... olive wood, and antique. What's your suggestion, Miss?'

'Can you remove a little paint from a corner?' asked Phryne. 'We can always pay for the damage. What's the value of the copy?

'About two and six,' said the Gallery man. He laid the painting of the smirking woman and overweight child down, opened his square leather case, removed some swabs and cleaning fluid, and began to rub carefully at one corner of the painting.

'There's something underneath,' he said without much excitement. 'That's not uncommon in Italy. They're always painting over old paintings. Cheaper than buying new canvas.'

Phryne, losing patience, took the swab and swept it over the surface, making a broad swathe through the new paint. Underneath, a saint's face sprang out of the garish new colour. Aged, haggard, compelling, even under the crackle of dark varnish.

'Dear God,' said the Gallery's man prayerfully. 'Give me that.' He grabbed the swab and refreshed it with cleaning fluid. 'I think...' he dropped swabs as he cleaned. Phryne watched. Mr Jones might be a pompous ass, but he loved paintings and he was treating this one with such a loving touch that if it had been a cat it would have purred.

Policemen wrenched opened more crates and piled more terrible copies of Raphael madonnas into heaps as the appraiser laved the surface of the painting with linseed oil, applied with his own perfectly clean, perfectly folded linen handkerchief to stop the solvent from eating into the original paint.

'There's the signature,' he said, wiping his brow with Phryne's handkerchief. 'Giotto. My God. Stolen from Florence three years ago. I beg your pardon, Miss. I thought this was just some sort of joke. I mean, why would someone take the risk of sending stolen art work to Australia? There isn't the market. The dealers for this sort of thing are in Paris or London or New York.'

'Import/export,' said Phryne. 'A consignment from Italy to London might attract notice. A consignment of Raphael copies from Melbourne wouldn't rate a glance. I don't expect that these are all disguised Old Masters,' she added. 'Can you find the mark for me which would allow the receiver to identify this one?'

'I'll need to go through them all,' he said, 'but this appears to be just a new painting. And this,' he took a tiny portion of paint off the corner of another couple of Raphaels. 'Yes, see? There's a stamp on the back. A flower.'

'A primrose,' said Phryne.

'What about the boxes?' asked a policeman. 'Do we open them as well?'

'Of course,' said Phryne.

There was a shrieking of nails as they reluctantly left their homes. Phryne peered into a box and gently lifted out a vase from its bed of wood shavings.

'Terracotta,' grunted Jack. 'With a rude scene on it. Cheap tourist souvenir.'

'Cheap Ancient Roman tourist souvenir,' said Phryne. 'That's why the consignment came from Napoli,' she said, putting the vase back with some regret. Was that satyr ever going to catch that nymph? She didn't seem to be running very fast, looking back over her shoulder like that and clutching at draperies which were definitely coming adrift.

'Pompeii,' commented the man from the Gallery, sweeping the cleaning fluid across another painting. 'Lots of stuff going astray from there at the moment. They say that a few thousand lire in bribe money and you can walk into the excavation with a large sack.'

'Well,' said Phryne. 'That's rather conclusive, isn't it?'

'We've certainly got Mr Bell on large-scale art theft,' said Robinson. 'But what about Miss Lavender?'

'In due course, Jack, dear. Don't press your luck. What do you have there, Mr Jones?'

'A real Raphael,' said Mr Jones in an awed whisper.

Among the flock of puddingy females, the real Raphael madonna shone with a dewy innocence which radiated from the canvas. The copied child, obese and soap-skinned, was entirely eclipsed by the original, a soft, plump, rosy cherub clearly too good for the world, raising gentle hands to bless the viewer.

'Jesus,' said Detective Inspector Robinson. Phryne chose to believe that this was an ejaculatory prayer. She herself, unbreakfasted and cross in a dusty warehouse with a beautiful man left alone in her bed, was feeling elevated, which was both the intention and the genius of the artist.

'I can't do any more under these circumstances,' said Mr Jones. 'We need to get them back to our laboratory and clean them properly. I'm not going to run the risk of injuring any of them. What a find! Detective Inspector, I congratulate you! This will be the crown of your

279

career, the crown! These paintings have been stolen from churches all over Italy. Even if there are only these two, it is a great coup. You will have them brought to the Art Gallery? This afternoon? I will go and prepare.'

Mr Jones was babbling with excitement. Robinson detained him with a hand on his black serge arm.

'They'll be brought by unmarked van,' he said. 'And they'll be guarded the whole time by two of my men. There's a chain of evidence to maintain, you understand. And not a word, Mr Jones, to anyone outside your organisation. Not one word. I don't want to miss the thief because you've been unable to contain your excitement.'

'No. Of course not,' said Mr Jones, reassuming his city personality with his bowler hat and his umbrella. 'Not a word. Will you inform my employer?'

'I will. If you wouldn't mind staying and making an inventory, we can sign them all out to the Gallery. Call the station and get four more men,' said Robinson to an underling. 'Get a van. They don't move until they're all listed and a copy is on my desk, understood? And no one is to leave anything unguarded. And in case anyone is thinking that one little vase won't be missed, which I'm sure no man of mine would ever dream of thinking, I'm leaving Mr Jones here. Anyone turns up and asks what's going on, arrest him as a material witness. Clear?'

'Clear, sir,' said the underling. 'Should be able to get 'em all crated and on their way by noon.'

'Carry on,' said Robinson. Phryne, who had

thought that perhaps one little satyr vase wouldn't be missed, sighed in the face of this massed honesty and followed him out to the car.

'Well, Miss Fisher, you've done me a bit of good,' said Robinson. 'How can I thank you?'

'Breakfast at the Windsor would be a good start,' said Phryne. 'Pity you wouldn't let me take that cross little harpy pot, or the satyr lecythus, I really fancied them and no one is going to miss them ... oh, all right, don't look at me like that. Then we'll go to Tintern Avenue and see who passes my little test.'

'You know, sometimes you almost frighten me,' said Robinson. 'The Windsor, driver.'

Breakfasted, Phryne was more centred and less cross. She had returned home and dressed for the day while Robinson made phone calls to his chief, his subordinates and the Art Gallery, all of whom showered compliments upon him.

Tintern Avenue was quiet. This being a Saturday, the inhabitants were all home, occupying their leisure as suited themselves. Phryne gathered them as she walked, Mr and Mrs Opie, Mrs Gould, a hungover Mr Carroll, Professor Keith and his niece, Mrs Needham, Mercy Porter, Miss Gallagher and Miss Grigg, both Hewlands and Mr Bell, who had been planting bulbs in the herbaceous border.

'What is all this about?' he demanded as the whole party wedged themselves into the main room of Wee Nooke.

'A little experiment,' said Phryne grimly.

'Are you going to let this person experiment on

us?' asked Mr Bell. 'She hasn't any official standing, has she?'

'Quite enough official standing for me,' said Robinson. Phryne began.

'When I was brought here for the first time I was told that Miss Lavender's bird had died,' said Phryne. 'It was blue, but when it was buried, it was pink. I wondered about that. Then I kept trying to recall why something in this room struck me as wrong.'

They all looked around. The stultifying pinkness of the room was still overwhelming. Only one thing was the wrong colour. Phryne wound up the clockwork of the music box with a bright red fairy on top which had been on Miss Lavender's desk when she was found dead.

Again, someone in the room was holding their breath. Phryne could taste the tension. She looked around, holding the key of the music box. The Hewlands kept their dead-fish impassivity. Miss Gallagher looked puzzled, Miss Grigg worried. Mrs Opie hung onto Wendy, Mr Opie looked irritated, Mr Carroll sleepy, Professor Keith interested, Mercy Porter and Margery Keith agog, Mrs Needham concerned.

'Miss Lavender knew a lot about you all,' said Phryne. 'But it was mostly unimportant. She knew about Margery's outings, Mr Carroll's drinking and the Hewland's daughter. She knew about–'

'Yes,' screamed Mrs Opie, clutching a surprised Wendy to her bosom. 'She knew about my fiancé. She had one of my letters to him when he was away. I never stopped loving him. She knew I never did.'

282

'And what did she want from you?' asked Phryne.

'She wanted me to be her friend,' sobbed Mrs Opie into Wendy's hair. 'She wanted me to speak well of her. So I did. So now you know,' she said to her husband. 'I told you when I married you that I loved another man. It was true.'

'Helen...' Mr Opie was astounded.

'All that time you groused and complained about me and Wendy and lack of sleep you thought I was a devoted wife. Well, I wasn't. I made a bargain and I kept it. It was hard to keep,' she added, 'after he came here, but I kept it.'

'He's here?' asked Mr Opie. 'Your wog lover? Giovanni Campana?'

'John Bell,' said Phryne. 'A straight translation. He told me he was a flyer, but it wasn't in our air force, was it? It was in Mussolini's.'

'Mussolini's?' exclaimed Miss Grigg. 'You dog, you criminal.' She shook her fist at Mr Bell. 'And I liked you! I even made things for you! There's one of my creations on the table. I made a damn good fairy music box for Miss Lavender because you wanted to suck up to her. Damned if I know why it's red, though,' said Miss Grigg. 'I made her a blue fairy, like the Blue Fairy Book she was so fond of.'

'I'll show you,' said Phryne, and let go the key.

Jack Robinson caught Mr Bell as he dived for the door. He struggled as the large policeman brought him round to face the group, both arms behind his back. The music box tinkled 'Fairy Bells' into the astounded silence.

'The mechanism is exhausted,' said Phryne. 'I

283

wound it up and played it the first time I came here and got nothing worse than a rendition of "Fairy Bells". The remains of the cyanide crystals, however, will be quite enough to hang you. Why was this music box jumping up and down and yelling at me, "Hello! I'm a clue!"? Because it was red. Miss Lavender had a mania for pink but not red, there's no red in the whole house. You said you sat in the garden after a long night of recovering from quinine overdose. You had to admit that someone came to Miss Lavender's door and delivered a package. You had to admit that because Miss Grigg heard the messenger as well, though she didn't see him. It was you, Mr Bell. Alone and unassisted. "For me?" Miss Lavender said. A nice lethal present. You altered Miss Grigg's music box so that when the clockwork turned, a pill of cyanide dropped into a lemon juice solution and – puff! Cyanide gas. It killed her in an instant. That's why Mercy Porter fainted. She got a good whiff of the stuff when she opened the door. Cyanide is metabolised quickly in the body and is hard to identify except by its effects. But it has one peculiar feature. It turns blue things red. It changed the colour of the blue fairy. It altered the feathers of the poor bluebird.'

'She was squeezing me dry,' he said. 'I couldn't keep paying her fees. And she was threatening Helen. I understood why Helen married while I was away. But she never stopped loving me and she loved me even disfigured as I am. We were going to go away together but she wouldn't leave Wendy.'

'Don't like you,' said Wendy coldly to Mr Bell.

'And Miss Lavender knew about the art treasures which come into Melbourne disguised as bad copies of Raphael madonnas, and the pots from Pompeii,' said Phryne.

'They owed it to me,' Mr Bell ground his teeth. 'I was nearly burned to death in a training exercise, trying to get those bloody I-ties into some sort of shape. Did they offer me any compensation? Did Il Duce condescend to visit? No. Nothing but a notice of dismissal as I could no longer fly. They owed me more than that. Then Mussolini declared that no ancient treasures should leave Italy and I thought, want to bet? So I set up the network. There are so many churches in Italy and no one even looks at their pictures. The peasants are just as happy with a new copy in bright colours. And the Pompeii site is being looted by anyone with the money. I just joined the throng.'

'And every time a shipment came in, it was announced by a letter to *Women's Choice* asking how to grow primroses. Which was passed on to you. I checked the letter book against the bills of lading. The dates match the measurements of the putative garden beds. Miss Lavender must have known that, too.'

'You asked about primroses yesterday,' said Mr Bell. 'That's how I knew you were onto me, Miss Fisher. That's why I'm not going to stay to face a trial. Goodbye, Helen. Grigg, don't forget the ixias. Goodbye, Phryne.'

He grinned at her, a grotesque parody of a young man. His jaw moved in a sideways crunch. There was a strong smell of bitter almonds.

Before Robinson could bear him up, he was dead.

'*Arrivederci,* Giovanni,' said Phryne.

The inhabitants of Tintern Avenue gathered at an impromptu tea party in Mr Bell's Italian garden. The body of Mr Bell had been taken away in an ambulance. Wendy was clinging to her mother and glaring at her father, who was visibly weakening under the assault. Miss Gallagher was sobbing on Miss Grigg's shoulder.

'Oh, Grigg, I thought it must have been you!' she confessed.

'Whatever for, old girl?' asked Miss Grigg gently.

'You got the majolica from John Bell,' said Miss Gallagher. 'You were friends with him. I knew he was smuggling. He said as much when I was talking about import duty on our china and he laughed and said there wasn't any. That's what I told Miss Lavender when she was being so sympathetic. I've been flirting shamelessly with everyone because I was so angry with you. I'm so sorry,' wept Miss Gallagher. Miss Grigg patted her on the shoulder and murmured, 'There, there. Don't take it to heart, old dear.' She looked up at Phryne. 'It's just her way,' she mumbled.

The Hewlands had withdrawn for a session of private prayer. Mrs Needham was cheering up. The murder was solved, the murderer had had the decency to kill himself and save them all from a terrible scandal. Her household was her own again, she could get rid of all those policemen and that interfering Miss Fisher, and re-let Wee Nooke. She fed a fish-paste sandwich to Ping, who so far forgot himself as to wag his tail.

Professor Keith was disdaining tea in favour of a whisky and soda, which Mercy brought from his own apartment. He smiled at Margery and offered her a drink. She blushed and accepted. So did Mr Carroll, who was several yards behind events.

'I told you I never fainted,' said Mercy Porter to Miss Fisher. 'I was worried that there was something wrong with me. I've been that worried all week.'

'We can all stop worrying. Anything else which Miss Lavender had on anyone is now obliterated. Jack can make his report and close his file, eh, Jack?'

'Not to mention telling the Italian Ambassador that we've recovered a lot of his treasures,' said Robinson. 'Did you know he'd break, Miss Fisher?'

'I thought he might. I did wonder about Miss Grigg,' confessed Phryne. 'Ever since I found that bit of blue net wrapped around an oil bottle I thought that you had made the music box.'

'So I did,' Miss Grigg agreed. 'But I never turned it into an infernal device.'

'And it was your own letter you were looking for in my box,' Phryne said to Mrs Opie. 'I made a serious error there. Miss Lavender had put it in the safety deposit box. You were feeling for the seal, weren't you?'

'Giovanni gave it to me,' sobbed Mrs Opie. 'It was a Roman one, the winged victory Nike driving a chariot. A carved chalcedony seal. I never knew it was stolen. Oh, what am I to do?'

'Dry your face,' said Phryne. 'Take Wendy down

287

the shop for an ice cream. And I think you'll find your husband amenable, if you give him time. It was a hopeless affair,' she added, the voice of experience.

'Ice cream,' said Wendy, flashing a conspiratorial glance at Phryne. 'Ice cream!' she added, as her mother seemed to waver.

'All right, Wendy, I'll just put my hat on,' mumbled Mrs Opie.

Phryne turned back to the gathering. Professor Keith was following his line of thought.

'And one must never underestimate how badly people are twisted by being deformed,' said Professor Keith, musingly, into his whisky and soda. 'A limp, say, or a missing hand. Bell's whole spirit was mutilated, not just his face. Saw a lot of it in the war. Some chaps with two missing legs bounced back like a rubber ball, cracked jokes, managed the pain and humiliation as though it had happened to someone else. Some of the others were wounded to the heart and pined to death, like Aborigines when someone has pointed the bone at them. The scars weren't just on their bodies, but went all the way to the soul. Bell felt a burning sense of injustice. It's not surprising that he rewarded himself when Italy failed to reward him.'

'No, that part makes perfect sense,' said Robinson. Phryne was struck with horror. How would Lin Chung bear his mutilation? Would his spirit be twisted as well, like John Bell's?

'Glad it has worked out well,' she said. 'Now, Jack, I really have to go home.'

CHAPTER EIGHTEEN

The topmost line, divided, shows the pleasure of the subject in leading and attracting others.

Hexagram 58: Tui
The I Ching Book of Changes

Phryne stayed in bed with Lin Chung for the better part of two days. A message came from Madame Lin that the transfer of land had been cancelled and that the remains of Lin Tai had been claimed, identified as far as possible, and were to be cremated in a suitable ceremony which Lin was not expected to attend.

Phryne was vindicated, exalted, floating in a sea of sensuality. She presided over large meals which Lin began to be able to eat, watched him gain weight, presence, and confidence. She was there when he requested a mirror and pushed back the overlong shiny hair to survey the extent of his mutilation.

He turned his face this way and that. The ear had been neatly removed almost flush with his head. His face was put out of perspective by its absence.

'I'm fortunate,' she heard him murmur.

'In what way?' she asked.

'That it wasn't a nose or a finger. Cousin Lin Choi can make me a passable rubber ear which will balance out my appearance and improve my hearing. A nose would be harder to fake. People have false teeth,' he said with a small laugh. 'Will you still love me with a false ear?'

'You know that I will,' she responded.

'I'm doubly fortunate, then.'

'You're a very brave man,' said Phryne.

'Not particularly,' said Lin with some surprise. 'I was dreading this sight, but it's not too bad.'

Phryne told him about John Bell.

'There's one difference,' said Lin. 'He retained his sense of grievance. Whereas I, Silver Lady, was amply revenged. Stop worrying, Phryne. I'm not going to forget about this. I will still have bad dreams, and I doubt I shall ever forgive Lin Tai, though I shall try, of course. But I am still my-self,' said Lin Chung, laying down the mirror and drawing Phryne into an embrace. 'I am still Lin Chung.'

'More than ever,' Phryne agreed, and gasped as his lips touched her breast.

'I will have to go home,' he said that night as they lay down again. 'Li Pen has brought a message from Grandmother. She would have been most upset by Lin Tai's betrayal. She has asked to see you, in the most polite and formal terms. "If the Honourable Miss Fisher would deign to shed the light of her countenance on my unworthy hovel" sort of polite. A tone, I have to add, which Grand-mother has never been known to use. Also my silk has been unpacked and I have a few little things which I bought for you in Macao.'

'Very well,' said Phryne. 'If you think you can

cope with being stared at.'

'Let them stare,' said Lin Chung, stretching out his arms. 'They may well stare. Am I not returned from the dead?'

He laughed. Phryne felt comforted. She knew she couldn't keep him with her. But she knew that now their bond was so profound that it could not be severed.

'Tomorrow,' she said, and snuggled into his shoulder.

The Hispano-Suiza edged down Little Bourke Street and stopped outside the Lin family house, blocking the road. Lin Chung was returning in style. Phryne, wearing a very plain black suit and hat, as befitted a woman going into a house of mourning, accompanied the heir of the Lin fortune up the steps, through the warehouse door, and into the garden, accompanied by Li Pen.

It was crammed with flowers in all shades of red. A red banner hung from the gable, displaying 'welcome' in broad calligraphy. Cousins and retainers lined the way and small girls in red jackets threw camellias and rose petals. Men in blue jackets pounded drums and banged gongs. Fireworks crackled. The noise was joyous and deafening.

Through the hail of sweet scented petals Lin Chung led Phryne up the steps into the house, followed by Li Pen. Madame Lin was waiting in the porch, attended by a couple of granddaughters, all arrayed in bright red. When she saw Lin, she bowed. She bowed to Li Pen.

When she saw Phryne, she bowed again.

The whole household held its breath. Phryne thought about it. It was this woman's preference for the cousin Lin Tai which had encouraged him to hope for better status, and had thus endangered Phryne's life on several occasions and nearly killed Lin Chung.

However, an *amende honorable* was an *amende honorable* and an olive branch was an olive branch. And Lin Tai was not Madame Lin's fault, but his own. Phryne clasped her hands and bowed to precisely the same depth, her black hair swinging forward to hide her face. With her eyes hidden, she might have been a dutiful Chinese daughter greeting her own matriarch.

The household exhaled. The drums and gongs broke out again with relieved pleasure. Li, Lin and Phryne were ushered into the house, seated on low chairs, and Madame Lin took her place on the blackwood throne.

Suddenly human, she took Lin's hand in her own and stroked it.

'I am very glad that you have returned,' she said in her off-key voice. 'My dear grandson. The traitor has been disposed of suitably. His family will be cared for. Choi has something for you if you will go with him.'

Lin smiled at his cousin and accompanied him out of the room.

'Miss Fisher,' said Madame Lin as soon as he was safely gone. 'You have done us a great service.'

'Li Pen did you the greatest service,' Phryne pointed out. 'I just helped.'

'Li Pen has retrieved his honour,' she conceded. 'But you are too modest. You found the ship. You rescued Chung. You recovered the cargo. What would you ask of the Lin family?'

'When Lin is required to marry,' said Phryne deliberately, 'he will still associate with me. We are too close now to be separated. You will need to choose a wife who understands this.'

Madame Lin inclined her beautiful head.

'I have thought of this,' she replied. 'And such a woman shall be found, and the bargain, Miss Fisher, is made. I will soon step down from my position. The family has lost some confidence in me, because I allowed my grandson to be kidnapped and made an error of judgment in relation to Lin Tai. Chung will take over. He will marry. And he will still associate with you,' she said. 'This much we certainly owe you, Miss Fisher.'

Phryne nodded. She did not want to marry Lin Chung. But she could not bear to lose him. Now she would no longer be haunted by the imminent severance of relations. It was worth a few bumps and scrapes and the loss of a set of embroidered camiknickers.

She had a sudden thought. Lin Tai had made her strip. Her knickers, carefully marked 'Fisher' in indelible pencil, must still be on board the SS *Apu*. And Jack Robinson would have found them. He had known all along. And he hadn't taken any action. The sly old police dog.

She dragged her mind back to the matter at hand.

Lin Chung returned. He seemed to have come back into focus. In place of the scar was a perfectly believable rubber ear, exactly tinted to match his skin. Cousin Choi was grinning with delight. So was Lin Chung.

'I said I was fortunate, did I not?' he asked Phryne, seeking her approval first.

'Very nice,' she responded. Madame Lin nodded, as though she had had an opinion confirmed.

'The banquet is being prepared,' she said. 'Perhaps you would like to inspect your cargo, Chung? It has cost you a great deal.'

'It has gained me more than I hoped,' he rejoined. 'Therefore, our family's profit increases. Will you come and see, Phryne? The war has interrupted trade, but I have brought back some very fine cloth.'

Phryne took his hand.

The main hall was filled with silk. Bolts of cloth from gauze to double damask lay side by side from one wall to the other. The thick oilcloth, the underlying blue cotton and under that the inferior silk which had been sewn around them to protect them from weather had been removed. Bright as jewels, coloured like a rainbow. Phryne marvelled that anything so beautiful could have come out of the noisome holds of that well-known phantom, SS *Apu/Gold Mountain*.

'The silk is well enough,' said Lin Chung dismissively. 'But these are the most valuable treasures. I stored them in the centre of the bolts.'

'Incense burners?' asked Phryne. They were overelaborate and fussy, made of greenish metal. Twelve of them were set out on a long table. They needed a polish, whatever they were.

'One of them, sold in New York, will pay back the money borrowed for my ransom three times over,' said Lin Chung. 'The peasants have looted many former Imperial palaces. I bought these from some charcoal burners who were using them to cook their lunch. They are Shang bronzes,' said Lin, a little disappointed by Phryne's response. 'But I bought this for you.'

It was a statue made of the most precious jade, mutton-fat. A lady danced in a swirl of draperies and flowers, perfectly poised, almost translucent. Every petal was present. Her face was averted, but she was smiling.

'She's gorgeous,' said Phryne. 'Perfectly beautiful! Where did she come from?'

Lin shrugged. 'The Winter Palace, I believe. I paid a reasonable price for her; the merchants in Macao know the meaning of profit. But I couldn't leave her there, Phryne. She reminded me of you.'

'I've never been paid such a compliment,' said Phryne. 'Who is she?'

'A Taoist divinity,' said Lin Chung. 'A translation might be the Flower Fairy.'

'I don't seem to be able to get away from fairies,' said Phryne. Lin Chung laughed and kissed her.

Phryne bought Dot a drink at the Adventuresses Club. Phryne had a negroni, a fragrant mixture of gin, Cointreau and Campari. Dot, who did not usually drink during the day, had a sherry cobbler, a decoction of sherry, mint and lemonade. The bartender, a small, wizened old woman called Nell, mixed a wonderful drink. She had been badly embittered by her failure to become a recognised drinks mixer and was delighted that the Adventuresses appreciated her skill.

'I made some serious mistakes in investigating Miss Lavender's murder, Dot,' said Phryne.

'Your mind wasn't on it,' soothed Dot. 'Anyway, you found Mr Bell.'

'In the end. I should have been onto him as soon as I heard that evasion about being a flyer. And he was looking for something in Miss Lavender's letters, too. I should, also, have thought about Mrs Opie. She was looking for that letter from "Devoted" with its fine linen weave and its flashy seal, not the embossed one. The letter she was looking for was in the safety deposit box.' Phryne toyed with the orange zest from her drink. 'And all's well that ends well, as you would say, but there are still some question marks above certain people. Did Miss Grigg really not wonder about the purpose of her music box? Miss Gallagher – was she really flirting with me because she was worried that Miss Grigg was involved with Mr Bell in some smuggling racket? Is Wendy Mr Opie's child, or that of the long lost Giovanni? Was Mrs Charlesworth unaware that the letter book contained a letter about primroses every few months? Did it matter that a poisonous person like Miss Lavender got killed? Was Mr Bell actually doing anything wrong by removing pictures from places where they weren't appreciated and selling them to people who would love and cherish them?'

'Murder is wrong,' said Dot, who was firm on this point.

'True,' said Phryne, and drank her drink. Nell brought her a sour, refreshing cocktail of her own devising, known as a 'Phryne' in her honour.

'Don't worry about it,' counselled Dot. 'As you

say I always say, all's well that ends well. By the way, a man in a uniform delivered this for you.'

'Another parcel?' asked Phryne. It was a square box, large enough to contain a big dictionary but not nearly heavy enough. She opened it with Nell's seal-cutting knife.

'Lots of shavings,' said Phryne. 'Dear God, I hope it isn't...' She put both hands into the box, not without trepidation.

And lifted out a Roman pot. It was of red terracotta and figured on it in black was a fat, cross little harpy. She had pendulous breasts and her beak gaped with displeasure. Phryne loved her instantly.

'With the grateful thanks of the Italian nation,' read Dot from an embossed card. 'And you are to visit the embassy to be awarded the Order of St Michael.'

'Remind me to write them a really nice thank-you letter,' said Phryne.

'Will you accept the award?' asked Dot.

'Not even from Il Duce's own hand,' said Phryne.

Three days later she attended Miss Lavender's funeral. She had thought that she might be the only mourner, but the Presbyterian church had summoned the congregation and both Hewlands were there, separated by enough space to preserve their purity from a mob from *Women's Choice*. Phryne was glad to see them again.

'Miss Fisher,' Mrs McAlpin greeted her. 'How nice. I trust that you will return to see what that remarkable French woman has done with the

Worth? I am taking the photograph tomorrow.'

'I'll be there,' said Phryne. 'Hello, Mrs Charlesworth. I'm sorry about Mr Bell.'

'Not your fault,' said Mrs Charlesworth graciously. 'Our new Agricola is a nice reliable old lady with an interest in botany and the most beautiful garden. And Professor Keith has agreed to answer the gardening questions for the next issue. Miss Herbert is going to take over the fashion pages. I have promoted Miss Nelson and I'm sure that she will replace Miss Prout, though not too enthusiastically, I trust.'

'Indeed,' agreed Phryne. It was a nice day for a funeral. The service had been restrained, delivered by a pastor who had known Miss Lavender and forgiven her her trespasses. The sun shone brightly on the uncut green grass and twinkled off mourning angels and broken columns.

Miss Prout was standing on the other side of the congregation, in black, pointedly ignored by all. Phryne decided that she hadn't seen her.

'She was a strange woman,' commented Mrs Charlesworth. 'Mrs Opie says that she was being blackmailed just to be her friend.'

'How is Mrs Opie?'

'Better, I think, now that it is all out in the open. Her husband has received a salutary shock. Of course, we knew about this early lost lover, poor Mrs Opie talked about her Giovanni a lot. But never in my life would I have expected him to be John Bell! He never spoke to her, never reacted to her – in fact he was very seldom in the same room with her. Of course, Wendy disliked him. I assumed that was why he made tracks

298

whenever Mrs Opie came into the office.'

'Wendy's instincts were sound,' commented Phryne.

'Small children, like dogs, are hard to deceive,' agreed Mrs Charlesworth.

'I suppose so,' said Phryne.

The cortège moved towards the grave. Birds sang. There was a smell of crushed grass. Six stalwart coffin bearers sweated under the weight of an elaborate casket with brass handles.

The solemn ritual continued. The pastor gave his final blessing. The coffin was lowered into the grave and earth cast on it; the most final sound in the world, Phryne thought, clods thudding hollowly on the lid.

'We've ordered a gravestone; there it is,' said Mrs Charlesworth. The others clustered around, waiting for Phryne's judgment, waiting also for some release from the pall of death and mourning. A final word needed to be spoken.

The gravestone was propped up against another tomb, waiting for the earth to settle on Miss Lavender's resting place. It was of pink granite, Miss Lavender's favourite colour. On it was carved the usual information surmounted by a fairy, dancing. Phryne recognised Miss Lavender's own drawing, from the border of 'Hilda and the Flower Fairies' which she had proofread some aeons ago.

'Poor Miss Lavender,' said Phryne, speaking the epilogue. 'She was a strange, unhappy, unpleasant woman who did some questionable things and to some extent ensured her own destruction. But she wasn't entirely responsible. She was always, and now she is eternally, away with the fairies.'

The Hewlands, sour-faced, withdrew in extreme dudgeon as one by one the whole congregation began to laugh.

BIBLIOGRAPHY

Adams, WH Davenport, *Stories of the Lives of Noble Women*, Thomas Nelson and Sons, London, 1913

Allen, Charles (ed.), *Tales from the South China Seas*, Futura, London, 1983

Australian Woman's Mirror, 1928

Barrow, Andrew, *Gossip: A History of High Society from 1920–1970*, Hamish Hamilton, London, 1978

Cleary, Thomas, *The Taoist I Ching*, Shamballa Press, Boston, 1986

Cordinger, David and John Falconer, *Pirates in Fact and Fiction*, Collins Brown, London, 1992

Grump, Mrs Thelma and Miss Helen Potter, *100 Tested Recipes*, Colonial Gas Association, Melbourne, 1935

Department of Public Instruction, *Cookery*, 30 cards, Victorian Government Printer, 1903

Gaute, JHH and Robin Odell, *Murder 'Whatdunit'*, Pan Books, Sydney, 1982

Gibbs, May, *The Complete Adventures of Snugglepot and Cuddlepie*, Cornstalk, Melbourne, 1991

Giles, HA, *Early Civilization in China*, Henry Holt and Co., New York, 1911

Glaister, John, *The Power of Poison*, Christopher

Johnson, London, 1921

Hepburn, James, *The Black Flag,* Headline, London, 1995

Holliday, RW, *A Group of Small Crafts,* Pitman, London, 1932

Joyce, Christopher and Eric Stover, *Witnesses from the Grave,* Grafton, London, 1993

Kingston, B, *My Wife, My Daughter and Poor Mary Ann,* Nelson, Melbourne, 1975

Kwan, Choi Wah, *The Right Word in Cantonese,* Commercial Press, Hong Kong, 1989

Legge, James (trans.), *The I Ching Book of Changes,* Dover, New York, 1963

Lilius, Aleko E, *I Sailed with Chinese Pirates,* privately printed, London, 1930

Methodist Hymn Book, Wesleyan Conference Office, London, 1904

Moriarty, Florence (ed.), *True Confessions: Sixty Years of Sin, Suffering and Sorrow,* Fireside, New York, 1979

Punch or the London Chiaviari, bound volume for 1928–29, London

Rohmer, Sax, *The Bride of Fu Manchu,* Allan Wingate, London, 1977

—*The Shadow of Fu Manchu,* Allan Wingate, London, 1978

—*Dope,* Allan Wingate, London, 1979

Tullett, Tom, *Clues to Murder,* Grafton, London, 1987

Wall, Dorothy, *The Complete Adventures of Blinky Bill,* Angus & Robertson, Melbourne, 1975

Watson, William, *Early Civilization in China,* Thames and Hudson, London, 1966

West, Rebecca, *The Thinking Reed,* Virago

Modern Classics, London, 1983
—*The Harsh Voice,* Virago Modern Classics,
London, 1984
Woman's World magazine 1928–29
Yutang, Lin, *My Country and My People,*
Heinemann, London, 1936

We do hope that you have enjoyed reading this large print book.

Did you know that all of our titles are available for purchase?

We publish a wide range of high quality large print books including:
**Romances, Mysteries, Classics
General Fiction
Non Fiction and Westerns**

Special interest titles available in large print are:
**The Little Oxford Dictionary
Music Book
Song Book
Hymn Book
Service Book**

Also available from us courtesy of Oxford University Press:
**Young Readers' Dictionary
(large print edition)
Young Readers' Thesaurus
(large print edition)**

For further information or a free brochure, please contact us at:
**Ulverscroft Large Print Books Ltd.,
The Green, Bradgate Road, Anstey,
Leicester, LE7 7FU, England.
Tel:** (00 44) 0116 236 4325
Fax: (00 44) 0116 234 0205

Other titles published by Ulverscroft:

THE CASTLEMAINE MURDERS

Kerry Greenwood

Phryne Fisher, her sister, Beth, and her faithful maid, Dot, decide to go to Luna Park for an afternoon of fun and excitement with Phryne's two daughters, Ruth and Jane. But in the Ghost Train, amidst the squeals of horror and delight, a mummified, bullet-studded corpse falls to the ground in front of them. Digging to the bottom of this longstanding mystery takes Phryne to Castlemaine where it soon becomes obvious that someone is trying to muzzle her investigations. Meanwhile, Phryne's lover, Lin Chung, has his own mystery to solve involving feuding families and lost gold, when he learns that Phryne herself has become a missing treasure.

MURDER IN MONTPARNASSE

Kerry Greenwood

Seven Australian soldiers, carousing in Paris in 1918, unknowingly witness a murder and their presence has devastating consequences. Ten years later, two are dead — under very suspicious circumstances. Phryne's wharfie mates, Bert and Cec, appeal to her for help. They were part of this group of soldiers in 1918 and they fear for their lives and for those of the other three men. It's only as Phryne delves into the investigation that she, too, remembers being in Montparnasse on that very same day. Meanwhile, her lover, Lin Chung, is about to be married . . .

DEATH BY WATER

Kerry Greenwood

A succession of jewellery thefts from first class passengers aboard P&O cruises looks like the work of a passenger. Phryne Fisher, with her Lulu bob, green eyes, Cupid's bow lips and Chanel travelling suits, is exactly the sort of elegant sleuth to take on a ring of jewellery thieves aboard the high seas — or at least, aboard the SS *Hinemoa* on a luxury cruise to New Zealand. With the Maharani — the Great Queen of Sapphires — as the bait, Phryne rises magnificently to the challenge.

QUEEN OF THE FLOWERS

Kerry Greenwood

In 1928 St Kilda's streets hang with fairy lights. Magic shows, marionettes, tea dances, tango competitions, lifesaving demonstrations, lantern shows, and picnics on the beach are all part of the Flower Parade. And who else should be chosen to be Queen of the Flowers but the gorgeous, charming and terribly fashionable Hon. Phryne Fisher? Phryne needs a new dress and a swimming costume but she also needs a lot of courage to confront her problems: a missing daughter, the return of an old lover, and a young woman found drowned at the beach at Elwood.